THE UNSUITABLE

THE
UNSUITABLE

a novel

MOLLY POHLIG

Henry Holt and Company
New York

Henry Holt and Company
Publishers since 1866
120 Broadway
New York, NY 10271

www.henryholt.com

Henry Holt® and 🛡® are registered trademarks of
Macmillan Publishing Group, LLC.

Distributed in Canada by Raincoast Book Distribution Limited

Library of Congress Cataloging-in-Publication Data

Names: Pohlig, Molly, author.
Title: The unsuitable : a novel / Molly Pohlig.
Description: First edition. | New York : Henry Holt and Company,
    2020.
Identifiers: LCCN 2019019769 | ISBN 9781250246288 (hardcover)
Classification: LCC PS3616.O45 U57 2020 | DDC 813/.6—dc23
LC record available at https://lccn.loc.gov/2019019769

Our books may be purchased in bulk for promotional, educational, or
business use. Please contact your local bookseller or the Macmillan
Corporate and Premium Sales Department at (800) 221-7945, extension
5442, or by email at MacmillanSpecialMarkets@macmillan.com.

First Edition 2020

Designed by Devan Norman

Printed in the United States of America

1 3 5 7 9 10 8 6 4 2

This is a work of fiction. All of the characters, organizations,
and events portrayed in this novel either are products of the author's
imagination or are used fictitiously.

For mom, and for Wendy, and for Finn.

And I could kill you with my bare hands if I was free.

PHOSPHORESCENT, "SONG FOR ZULA"

THE UNSUITABLE

1.

you killed me, remember that.

yes, i remember. i remember.

you don't remember me.

i may not remember you, but i cannot forget you. i poke my finger a little further underneath the scab and the pain radiates like the heel of your palm pressed against your closed eyelid, all starbursts and twinkles. i am dead i am dying i am dying you are dead. it throbs and pulses and my arm twitches three times and then falls still.

The way Iseult moved, it was like she was defusing a bomb all day long. If you are defusing a bomb or, say, building a house of cards that for some reason your life depends upon, you will move slowly and carefully. Every move measured. She moved to make herself seen, but only because a disaster could be imminent, and everyone needs to be accounted for in a disaster. The skin on her forehead was so paper thin that you could see the messages her brain sent to her body: *Take a step with your right leg. Now the left. And the right again. Brush that lock of hair off your cheek. Smile. Stop smiling.*

It was the way she moved that caught your eye, in the beginning. Each foot lifted too high and set down too precisely, and you would be forgiven for looking above her head to see whether she had strings, or peeking around her back expecting a rotating handle. The next thing you would notice would be the folds of black crepe that constituted her mourning dress, so voluminous that you wondered how many people had died to inspire such a display of lamentation. Had a fire turned her extended family to ash? Had they been poisoned by a vengeful maid? You were not to know that her clothing was merely the work of an overzealous aunt and her slavish seamstress, who drowned the poor girl's frame in enough yards of dyed muslin to clothe the inmates of a small orphanage. And as for deaths, there was only one, years ago. One. And it resulted in all of this. The clothes, and everything that came before, and after. Just the one.

The clothes held her secrets close. She could fold her bitter hands, fingers flapping like hummingbird wings, underneath the mountain of fabric. Her sole request as far as style went had been pockets, and her aunt had noted, pleased, that when they were filled they produced the illusion of a feminine silhouette. She did not like to be touched, and lived in fear that her pocket collections would be discovered. But she lived in fear anyway. If you listened closely, you would hear a mild disturbance, the slightest jangle, as she passed by, but it was so muffled by the fabric that you reasoned you were hearing things.

The lace collar crawled to the top of her throat, and the fierce edges worked hard to press their way through the pale flesh of her pointed jaw. She strained to push her head above it, her too-tight sleeves pushed past her wrists, making her arms seem even longer than they were as her hands tried to escape the lace cuffs.

She has walked through the park all day, and if anyone had

asked what she had seen she would have responded as though her tongue had been recently cut out, and she hadn't yet figured out how to communicate this new change. But no one asked. She mounted the wide slippery stairs of her front steps as usual: One foot, two feet. One foot, two feet. One foot, two. Every movement programmed to undo the hex a little more. But the hex always came back, so it was less of an undoing and more a holding back of the tide. She lifted the brass door knocker, oiled into smug silence, and let it drop. That's how they would know it was her, by a bang followed by its echo, smaller and smaller.

get us out of the wind, iseult. we are likely to be blown away.

we won't blow away, mother, we would need much more wind for a thing such as that to happen wish as we might.

but your skirts iseult we could use them as a sail. you can be the ship and i will be the captain and we will sail away to where we are wanted where we make sense.

and where is that, mother?

There is no answer.

Even now she forgets her mother does not like questions. Or answers.

"Oh, there you are, dear, and bless me if you aren't chilled to the very bone." Mrs. Pennington always answered the door to Iseult in precisely the same way; it was a routine that was comforting to both of them. Naturally the phrasing depended on the season— "chilled to the bone / damp as a rag / wilted like a flower"—but the sentiment never varied. You poor poor lamb, poor dear poor darling. Poor motherless nobody, poor changeling with no one to look after you.

Not that Mrs. Pennington didn't look after Iseult Wince as best she could, but Mrs. Pennington, after all, was someone else's mother. She did the best she could.

As Iseult was coming in, her aunt Catherine was coming out. She kissed Iseult's cheek, her face powder wafting its familiar cloying scent through the air. "Hello, dear girl, don't you look well!"

Aunt Catherine shot Mrs. Pennington a very obvious and meaningful look and said, "You'll remember what we discussed?"

Iseult's heart shriveled, because she knew where those conversations led. Mrs. Pennington nodded brightly as Aunt Catherine made her way out the door. Iseult got another smothering perfumed kiss and the tiny storm was over.

Mrs. Pennington gave the heavy door a good slam, which she hoped Iseult's father could hear from wherever he was in the house, and recognize it as a sign of her contempt for letting his daughter wander the city unchaperoned. She had been slamming the front door thus for nearly twenty years, and had never been gratified with the slightest hint that Mr. Wince took any notice.

"Now now now," Mrs. Pennington said as she drew a woolen blanket—one of many such blankets kept in a cupboard under the stairs—around Iseult's icy shoulders. When Iseult was younger and Mrs. Pennington let her in from her ramblings, she would shut herself into the small cupboard with the blankets and Mrs. Pennington would bring her a mug of hot milk and sugar. But it had been years since Iseult's body could be folded into the cramped space, and these days she took her hot milk and sugar in her room. Mrs. Pennington kept up a steady hum of chatter as they slowly climbed the stairs. Iseult looked through the large window on the landing at the gray outside.

i wonder if that would be high enough.

high enough for what?

you know i know you know what.

you can tell me iseult please i don't know.

to fall and not get up again. to see myself on the ground there outside the window, broken with you gone.

i will never leave you iseult, my little girl, never never. you can't kill yourself and get away from me. i am tied to you in you around you you you you.

i know mother. i was just wondering if it might be high enough. i think now maybe it isn't.

"Come on, my love, there's no need to drag those dainty little feet!" Mrs. Pennington was a great believer in the contagion of jollity, and Iseult knew it was pointless to resist. Her eyes remained flat, but as she was hustled upstairs, Iseult pasted a very good impression of a smile on her lips. She didn't feel like talking, she never felt like talking, but she knew how it pleased Mrs. Pennington when she put forth a little effort.

"And what are we having for supper?" Iseult said as Mrs. Pennington fussed her into the pale blue chair by the window. Mrs. Pennington's eyes were as round and shiny as what would certainly be solid, dependable brown buttons.

"Pheasant, dear. Now, now," she said before Iseult could interrupt, "I know it's not your favorite but you're going to be a good girl and eat it tonight because your father has invited that family, remember? Those . . . that family. That he wanted you to meet." Mrs. Pennington, running up against what was known in the Wince household as "a subject," quickly changed tack and began to fret at the armchair. "I keep saying we ought to move this beautiful thing out of the sunlight, the color has simply spoiled, and your mother loved it so."

Mrs. Pennington was famous for dodging one subject only to run headlong into another. "We shall leave it where it is," Iseult said mechanically. "It is where it needs to be, Mother says."

"Yes of course, my dear." Mrs. Pennington moved her fretting over to the tea tray on the desk and fretted it right over to the low table next to the chair. Iseult at once regretted mentioning her mother, as the tray was as carefully arranged as ever, with the steaming mug of milk, the silver bowl of crumbly sugar cubes, the spoon polished to a high shine, the lace-edged napkin that Iseult never touched, and the porcelain vase, delicate as a baby's fingernail, with the tiniest spray of flowers. Mrs. Pennington's customary reaction to Iseult's bad behavior was to love her even more. Iseult attempted to wind her way back in time.

"Who did you say was coming, Mrs. Pennington? Who is so important that I will be required to eat pheasant?" Her voice was calm and sweet, but her hand was creeping up to her shoulder, a quiet spider, stealthy but slow.

"The Finches, my dear," Mrs. Pennington said brightly, while firmly taking Iseult's hand and wrapping it around the mug of milk instead. The contrast between the two women's hands was marked, and confusing. Mrs. Pennington had the plump soft hands of an idler with never a chore more pressing than turning the pages of her light poetry, while Iseult's wouldn't have looked out of place on the lowest scullery maid, chafed and cracked with blood waiting just below the surface if required. "You recall your father speaking of them, I'm sure. Distant, very distant cousins, I believe. Down from Manchester."

Iseult gripped the mug, her nibbled fingernails turning white in their red beds. "Yes, I recall. The ones with the son."

Mrs. Pennington tried to smooth Iseult's hair as the girl stiffened, then held herself in very close, shrinking from the mothering hand. Mrs. Pennington straightened as much as a woman of her diminutive height reasonably could, and exhaled all sorts of frustration through her nose. "Surely you've noticed by now, Iseult. They've *all* got sons!"

She rustled out of the room in a huff, calling over her stout shoulder, "I'll be back in one hour, Miss Iseult, and I expect no talk of mothers, or sons, or pheasants, and keep your hands off that neck of yours for pity's sake!"

Iseult moved her hand off her neck and back to her mug.

it's an insult she can't talk to you as if you were a little girl with you a grown woman of twenty-eight why by the time i was twenty-eight i'd been dead and buried six years iseult.

she wants to help me she's all i have.

—

all i have besides you i mean mother i mean.
what about your father you know he loves you
he doesn't believe me. he doesn't believe i have you.
he will he will be patient he'll believe he'll know he'll know once you get me out.

Iseult looked to make sure that Mrs. Pennington had closed the door behind her. When she was particularly worried about Iseult she left it open. Today it was closed. Iseult placed the mug down on the tray without a sound and rose from her chair like a somnambulist. As she made her way to the vanity table in the corner, one hand unbuttoned the neck of her dress and the other slipped into her pocket. She perched on a worn black velvet stool in front of the table, a sparrow in a cage built for a peacock. She was drab and faded, but the table and its mirror were immense and elegant, clearly intended for someone else.

A large, creeping spot on the patinated mirror hovered in front of Iseult's left eye, giving her the appearance of a forlorn pirate. Her right hand slid down the left side of her neck, the stiff black fabric falling away from skin that got paler as more of her neck was revealed. She flicked a finger against the fabric. The dress fell from her shoulder, revealing a gnarl of fierce red and pink, so jarring that it scarcely seemed to be skin, even to Iseult, who knew that it must be.

Her fingers began to patter lovingly on the scar that had been left when her collarbone broke through her skin on the day that she was born and killed her mother, Beatrice. Her fingers knew each rise and dip and twist, each nook and every cranny. She took a hatpin from her pocket. Slowly, with dreadful calm, Iseult traced the scar with the point of the pin.

But a rustle in the hallway heralded the approach of Mrs. Pennington, and, quicker than one would think she could move, the pin was back in Iseult's pocket and she was reaching for a jar of ointment.

"Is it hurting you, dear?"

Iseult felt a pinprick of regret every time she elicited Mrs. Pennington's pity under false pretenses. Iseult was covered in pinpricks, some real, some not. She had a beautiful tiny pincushion that she treated with the utmost care, feeling such empathy for it. But she didn't feel enough pinpricks to be completely honest.

"A little bit. Would you mind?" She kept her gray eyes downcast under her sparse lashes and held out the ointment.

Mrs. Pennington took the jar happily. "Of course not, love; you know that."

And so began the only time of reliably companionable silence in Iseult and Mrs. Pennington's day. She scooped up a dab of salve, not so much as to be oily, not so little as to leave Iseult's scars dry. She kneaded the stiff, shiny skin as if it were to become a delicate pastry, to be served to someone important.

i know what you're thinking iseult you stop it immediately.

i'm just thinking that it feels nice. am i never to be allowed something as simple as a sensation that feels nice? only pain?

is that all i am to you? pain?

no mother no no no mother no.

2.

She couldn't remember a time when she had been unaware. Beatrice, her voice, her feeling, were so much a part of Iseult's being that for a long time she thought everyone had someone like that, someone dead inside them. When she was small it was the nicest. She always had a friend. And since she was already always talking to someone, the other children kept their distance. By the time she reached an age of self-awareness, where friends you could see and touch and walk arm in arm with were more important than the invisible one you carried with you, it was too late. She did not know how to keep Beatrice in a pocket somewhere and so interact with the world by herself.

A classmate, Eleanor Frigate, was deaf as a post, and thereby the happiest girl Iseult knew. The schoolmistress would pose the simplest of questions, and Eleanor's only response was to rest her chin, quaking like an unset pudding, on her fat fists and blush furiously. Which everyone thought was very charming. When Iseult couldn't answer a question (which she never could), she pinched her mouth into a thin line, approximating deep thought. The schoolmistress often threatened to throw a book at her head, and once, indeed, she did. Luckily her aim was poor.

Iseult studied Eleanor, and decided the reason she couldn't hear was because she was so enormously fat. Iseult came to the conclusion that there was so much fat that it simply filled up her ears. Maybe the way to make her mother stop haranguing her, and pushing the other children to where Iseult did not know how to reach them, was to fill up her ears. With fat.

So Iseult began to eat. One evening at dinner she asked for a second helping, and a third, and a fourth. The fourth came back up, so she learned to temper herself. She set herself to a regimented diet to increase her weight. Any time she could, she sneaked food from the larder. It wasn't as if doing so was difficult. Mrs. Pennington tended to avoid the kitchen as much as possible due to her own . . . proclivities, and the cook whose tenure loomed over Iseult's childhood was a ruddy-cheeked slattern with far more self-confidence than was justified; she spent most of her time attempting to wheedle her way into the affections of a young man who was said to be on the rise through the ranks of the navy, not hanging about the kitchen to see Iseult stuffing her face with great handfuls of baking flour. (The cook was herself butchered by this young naval prospect several years after her employment with the Wince family had come to an amicable end. No one went so far as to suggest that she got what she deserved, but . . . there was a lot of talk at the time.)

Iseult ate and she ate. And the more she heard her mother telling her to stop, the more she ate. She ate as much as fat little Eleanor, and then she ate more. Mrs. Pennington was driven frantic running back and forth to the dressmaker's, always pleading for a larger seam allowance, just in case. It got to the point where even her father raised his permanently furrowed brow, and queried the housekeeper as to whether there wasn't something wrong with the child, as she was beginning to be noticeably ungainly and unattractive. Edward Wince did not care a good deal about whether his daughter was clever or kind, but he had enough sense to balk at the idea of an unattractive daughter. He didn't hope she would be a great beauty; that would have been unseemly. Just as long as she didn't besmirch the Wince name.

But around the time that Iseult reached her zenith, she realized something curious. Her mother wasn't getting quieter; if anything, she was growing louder. Everything was growing louder. The whispers and jeers of classmates; Mrs. Pennington's scoldings; even the geese in the park were more likely to honk, and to chase her as she clumsily tried to run away.

So she gave up.

"Iseult."

"Mm."

"Are you listening?"

"Yes."

"You know how important it is for your father that you—"

"—make a good impression this evening, yes, Mrs. Pennington. I won't remark upon the pheasant, or Father's nasty little smile, or the Finch son's pimples, which he is sure to have."

". . . or?"

"Or what?"

"Listen to me, miss, you know exactly what—"

"Yes, I know. And no, I won't. I won't speak of her tonight."

"Do you promise? Last time was—"

"I know. I apologized for last time. It won't happen again. I shall behave. I shall be good. I won't let Mother . . . I won't let her . . ."

"Please. No scenes tonight, my dear. Do what your father asks."

"Yes, Mrs. Pennington. I will. Not like last time."

Iseult's was a world of stark opposites. If black didn't work, try white. If fat didn't drown out her constant companion, then she would take it away, and more. On Iseult's tenth birthday, she enjoyed a polite tea party with the daughters of her father's acquaintances who agreed to be roped into the business. She opened the gifts in which she had no interest; when they played blindman's buff she flailed her hands uselessly until they agreed her turn should be over; and she ate a gratuitous share of cake. From midnight onward, she resolved to drastically cut her food intake. And she did.

At first it wasn't as easy as she'd supposed it would be. Hunger clawed from the inside of her stomach in the same way that Beatrice clawed from underneath the skin of her neck. Sometimes she was tempted to eat more than she knew she should. But when she heard her mother say, *there there my dear love you eat what you want why do you punish yourself please i only want your happiness your happiness and mine ours both please eat you need our strength,* she found the resolve to put the fork down next to the plate.

At first, Mrs. Pennington was overcome with pleasure at the onset of Iseult's fast, which returned to her within a matter of months the reasonably sized child she'd been charged with bringing up. The seamstress was visited again, but this time to hide the allowances rather than constantly uncovering yet another fold. But it was only a couple of additional months after that before the sight of Iseult in her bath was enough to make Mrs. Pennington shudder, as bones she didn't know a human child possessed threatened to poke right through Iseult's skin.

This time, though, Iseult was right. As her flesh shrank, voices got quieter. Mrs. Pennington's no longer had the ability to move her to pity, and she no longer felt compelled to seek forgiveness when she was naughty. Her father's stern voice no longer sent a thrill of nervous electricity through her body. The schoolmistress's voice, the voices of the girls who now jeered at a body that was the opposite of what they jeered at before—they all faded. It was as if she had pillows over her ears. So much so that she once tried tying a pillow over each ear with twine, and then tried to see if she could still hear her own voice. She wore the pillows all day, until Mrs. Pennington wept in frustration. It was a pleasant sensation, she tried to tell the housekeeper, like when you're in the bath and you let the water into your ears. Muffled. Numb. Like you are still aware of everything going on in your usual world but you find that you are not at all bothered by the things that used to bother you.

Except.

Except that Beatrice's voice was still coming through loud and clear. Iseult couldn't credit it.

please my darling eat a little something for mother today.

no. i shan't. stop bothering me.

i will iseult i will bother you until the day you die.

then i will go on until i die and then we'll see where things stand.

Even then, it was not lost on Iseult that Beatrice was dead and yet not, and she wondered whether that was how it would be for everyone. Did we all die only to move into someone else's ears? Did a soul need a body, no matter whose?

"Mrs. Pennington?"

"Yes, my love?"

Do you remember? Iseult thought. *Do you remember the first time that you knew? No. She still doesn't know. She still thinks she doesn't know.* Iseult said quietly, "Do you remember the first time I said it?"

"What's that, dear?" The plump hands stilled momentarily, just a hiccup, but Iseult knew what it meant. *Don't bring it up. It never goes well. They get angry and sad and talk about sending you away.* Until she was twelve Iseult thought there was a town called Away. Sometimes she was afraid of it, sometimes she couldn't wait to go. The seaside town of Away, where she and Beatrice would live in a stone cottage. And maybe when they were finally alone like that, her mother would become visible, more tangible than the dour wedding portrait in the hall, not so stiflingly close as the tangle of scars that Mrs. Pennington was attempting to soothe.

No. Better not.

"I'm wondering what dress I should wear this evening." Nothing cheered Mrs. Pennington more than Iseult taking an interest, however slight or feigned, in social activities. She didn't even answer Iseult, just rushed off to the armoire with a look of joy on her face, wiping her salved hands on her apron.

"I promise you, Iseult, this is the year we get your father to relinquish the mourning!" She called through a clatter of wooden hangers and the violent swish of too much fabric. "That's why we haven't seen you married yet: What young man wants to think of a pretty young wife all in black?"

If only that were the only problem, Iseult thought, grabbing up her heap of skirts and making her way to the armoire.

"What young man wants a wife who loathes him, and whom he loathes in return?" Iseult passed a rough hand over the rows of black, each dress as pointless as the next if you were hoping to make a favorable impression. Mrs. Pennington paused in her frenzy to hand Iseult a sharp look, and found what she was looking for.

"See here now, this one is so light as to be almost a . . . dark gray, don't you think?" She waited for no answer before whisking the dress out of the armoire and thoughtfully arranging it on the bed, flicking off bits of lint invisible to the human eye. Iseult stood by, somber, arms folded. Mrs. Pennington continued to smooth the tiniest wrinkle, but she said softly, "Say you will keep an open mind, Iseult, please?"

Iseult's arm jerked, and she tried to cover the ensuing small shudders by turning back to her dressing table and rummaging in a drawer. "What if I said I'd even wear a ribbon in my hair?"

Iseult didn't even have to turn around to know she'd said the right thing.

you bait that poor woman iseult. you shouldn't. i didn't raise you to—

you didn't raise me. she did. i shall treat her as i please.

—

i do as i please. i am my own girl. my own . . . woman. i can make decisions too. maybe i will marry this one.

you haven't even seen him you can't you can't you don't want to marry i assure you, my girl.

my own woman, i said! maybe i will marry this bird, this finch, and i will have a child and she will kill me and i can go and live with her and you can stay here in iseult's sad little body.

you won't i promise you you won't.

Predictably, Mrs. Pennington was in high spirits as she readied Iseult for dinner. She laced the corset so tight that each breath made the bodice of Iseult's dark gray dress ripple, and it must be said that she overdid the hair. Too many curls over the ribbon. Privately Iseult thought she looked like a sheep at a fair, but she held her tongue, determined to be good for Mrs. Pennington. Or was it bad for Beatrice? Was there a difference? They so often amounted to the same thing. They both claimed to want the best for Iseult, but one was black to the other's white. It depended on the day, whom Iseult wanted to please and whom she wanted to harm. She could never please or harm both at the same time. Someone always had to suffer. Iseult always suffered.

Mrs. Pennington was completing the final details of Iseult's ovine coiffure when Mr. Wince knocked on the bedroom door. Both women jumped, which was both surprising and not. Surprising because he was the only person who would be knocking on the bedroom door, but not surprising because he was the sort of man who caused people to jump, the sort of man who reveled in their jumping.

Mrs. Pennington pinned a final curl into its frivolous place and hastened to open the door. She stepped outside and closed the door behind her. Before Beatrice's untimely passing, this had been her bedroom. Mr. Wince had not stepped inside the room since, even though it was the only bedroom Iseult had ever had.

Iseult could hear murmurs of conversation through the door, sounds that seemed to float up from beneath the surface of the ocean. Many of Iseult's dealings with her father occurred from this distance. She sat at her mirror avoiding her own eyes, watching the fabric over her diaphragm shimmer with each breath and quiver with each heartbeat. The door chime rang, and the voices drifted away down the stairs, and it was time for dinner.

3.

To spoil the surprise: the dinner was not a success. It began well enough, with polite though stilted questions and answers, with pleasantries that had been uttered so many times by so many people that they were utterly meaningless. The Finches were predictably dry and colorless, which Iseult had learned from experience was the best that she could reasonably hope for. And she had been right about the son. Pimples. Swarms of them. The kind that you can't stop staring at.

"And business continues to go well, Edward?" Mr. Finch's knife scraped through the poor pheasant and shrieked against the china. Iseult did her best to force down the spasm threatening to shake her arm.

"I think you can tell that by the beautifully appointed house, my dear," Mrs. Finch said, delicately poking at her dinner, "unless it is perhaps attributable to Iseult's talents in terms of thriftiness?"

Mr. Wince spoke before Iseult could open her mouth to deny this. "I do believe that it is both, Mrs. Finch. I cannot complain of the Wince Steelworks' success, and Iseult manages the house every bit as well as her dear mother did."

Iseult's arm jerked and she nearly upset her water glass. Mr.

Wince flinched, and the Finches could feel the evening slipping from their grasp for reasons beyond their understanding.

"Miss Wince, I am told that you are very fond of walking." Alexander Finch's voice was as unpleasant as the scrape of his father's knife against the plate. It might settle in time; he was only nineteen, after all. Iseult clenched her napkin in her fist below the table.

"Yes, indeed I am."

These were the first words that Iseult had ventured to speak, and all had leaned forward in anticipation. Sadly, she was not inclined to continue.

"And . . . where do you prefer to walk? In the park? Along the streets? Looking into the shop windows? Or do you plunge forth into the countryside?" Alexander was hoping that someone would stop him; otherwise he would have no choice but to keep going.

"Good healthy exercise for a young woman, better than being shut up inside all day." Mr. Finch scraped again, then crashed his teeth into his wineglass. His wife simpered at him. Alexander scratched at a pimple, which burst. All eyes were on Iseult again, and she thought of the lecture she was going to receive if she got this answer wrong. But then she considered the possibility of a future inextricable from these most disagreeable dinner partners. And not only at mealtimes. All the time. Forever. No.

"I walk everywhere, anywhere, Mr. Finch. I walk until I am so tired I can barely stand. And then I go to the churchyard and visit my mother's grave. She likes it there." In the ensuing silence, Iseult swore she could hear her father's mustache bristle. The Finches exchanged uneasy glances.

"We-e-ell, I have not yet had the pleasure of seeing your churchyard, but I have been told that there are excellent views of the town. I'm sure it is a most pleasant . . . place to . . . rest . . . for you . . . and your mother." Iseult glanced up. Alexander's face had gone red in his efforts to finish the sentence.

"What Iseult means to say is that exactly. She has a singular turn of phrase, does she not?" Mr. Wince was well accustomed to cleaning up after Iseult's conversation, and that hadn't been an insurmountable disaster.

"Actually, Father, what I meant was that Mother and I like to go there together." Iseult turned from her father's face, which was turning to stone, back to the quizzical Finches. "She is with me, you see. Inside me, as it were."

Iseult derived a real satisfaction from causing a true, panicky silence. And then she worked to prolong it. "So you see, it wouldn't just be me you marry, Mr. Finch. My mother comes too."

The elder Mr. Finch choked on a large swallow of wine, and Mrs. Finch's ample bosom heaved erratically. Iseult noted with interest that once the color drained from Alexander's face, the pimples were much less noticeable. Mr. Wince rang the bell sharply for the maid, who must have been pressing her ear toward the door, she appeared so quickly. Her heels cracked the silence against the shining wooden floor, and Iseult smiled warmly at her as she cleared her plate.

"Thank you, Sarah," she said happily. Sarah's saucer eyes widened further, and after taking Mrs. Finch's plate as well she quickened her pace back to the kitchen, no doubt to tell Mrs. Pennington that some form of disaster had struck. Iseult never smiled like that when things were going well.

Iseult spent the rest of dinner smoothing her skirts and not touching her neck. Everyone else spent the rest of dinner speaking of the steelworks and trying to pretend that she wasn't there. Everyone else drank a large quantity of wine. Predictably, the Finches flew away early. The Winces saw the Finches to the door, and all exchanged lovely hopes that they would see each other soon, which of course they wouldn't, preferably ever if it could be arranged. Mr. Wince closed the heavy front door and fixed his gaze somewhere above his errant daughter's head. Many people had noted the marked similarity that Iseult's frighteningly large eyes had to her late mother's, and because of that resemblance Mr. Wince rarely had the temerity to meet them. His own eyes were hard, nasty little pebbles. He could not recognize the hardness in her eyes that echoed his.

"Iseult." This was how it began. Iseult bided her time and shuddered, a chill spreading through her collarbone before dissipating somewhere past her shoulders. "Iseult, you may not continue to behave like this."

tell him dear tell him now tell him it's not necessary for him to continue parading this poor show of bachelors through the front hall.

he doesn't won't doesn't listen to me mother. you tell him. he will only say i am a belligerent girl who deserves to be married off to the first decent man who passes.

nonsense. he loves you still. still. i believe.

"You are a disgrace to your mother's memory. You behave like an insolent child. I am tempted to marry you off to the first man who passes in the street."

see?

well you've been baiting him stop baiting him.

if i stop baiting him i will have to marry one of them. and you don't seem to want me to marry. so what am i to do mother, what to do? something is about to break. i am afraid. i am afraid. i am afraid it will be me again.

"Have you nothing to say in your own defense?" The only sounds were the relentless tick of the hideous clock on the mantelpiece

and the flutter of Mr. Wince's mustache hairs. Iseult stared at
them, wondering as always how they could make a sound, those
tidy little reddish hairs with gray interlopers. In her pockets, her
fingers began to move of their own accord, cracking the knuckles.
Right: crack. Left: crack. Right: crack. Left: crack. And so on. So
lost in the simple pleasure of each hollow crack, she was startled
to find her father's face discomfitingly close to her own.

"Iseult, dear darling daughter," he jeered, the sour smell of
wine seeping between his clenched teeth, "I have reached what
I believe is the end of my rope where you are concerned. I am
very liberal in terms of women being allowed to make their own
decisions, and you know that I abhor violence unless absolutely
necessary, but at this point, any man offering a fair price could
carry you out that door"—here he pointed helpfully at the front
door, an angry tremor shaking his finger—"and beat you into
something resembling sanity and I would rejoice!"

say something, say you're sorry! he doesn't deserve this you love
him i love i love him.

but there is nothing to say. i am caught between you and
nothing that i say will placate either of you. i want to be left
alone. i should wish that he would die as well, but then i'd have
an angel on one shoulder and a devil on the other and never be
sure which was which. no. mother. i will hold my tongue.

brat. ungrateful wretch. tell him you love him and will
obey him.

so you can tell me to defy him again the next time he hauls
home another pockmarked prospect? no thank you, madam. you
may have stunted my growth thus far, but i know my own mind.
i will not marry because he tells me to, nor abstain because of
your wishes. i shall make my own choice, if he ever comes along.

if not i will remain alone. as alone as it is possible to be in this madhouse of my mind.

Mr. Wince straightened, reeling back slightly on drunken heels. "You shall marry, Iseult. Your mother has left me saddled with you long enough. If I am not to have her, I'll be damned if I'll be forced to look at your pinched face another year."

He crashed off to his study, receding into the bowels of the house until everything quieted again. Iseult's fingers flinched into motion. Right: crack. Left: crack. Right: crack . . .

Mrs. Pennington was too galled to appear at bedtime, and she sent Sarah to help Iseult out of her clothes. Silent Sarah, who was petrified of Iseult and could get her into her nightgown in five minutes flat. Iseult had only to smile at Sarah to send her rushing from the room, and she locked the door behind the fleeing maid.

She pulled a battered black book from underneath her mattress and sat with it at her desk, scribbling down the particulars of the odious Mr. Finch. She blew out the candle and returned the book to its hiding place.

Only a sickly stream of moonlight spattered the room now, but it was enough. Iseult stood in a pool of yellow light, working her nine toes into the plush carpet. She looked down at them. Poor little middle toe. No matter, it wasn't coming back. She plunged her hand into the pocket of the dress that Sarah had so carelessly discarded over the chair and pulled out the first thing she touched, which happened to be a needle for leatherwork, ever so sharp. Be very careful. Don't touch the end. Sharp as a bee's sting, that.

Her too-long nightdress swished against the edge of the rug and she seated herself at her dressing table. A shrug of her left shoulder freed the scar, a nest of sleeping snakes in the dimness.

Iseult held her breath, held the needle, and jabbed: once, twice, three times. Three bubbles of blood grew until they merged and became a stream. The stress of the evening flowed out with the trickle, down over her breast, little ups and little downs over each rib. A stain bloomed on the cotton of her nightdress, and she would be scolded in the morning, but she was so routinely scolded that it made little difference. Mrs. Pennington would make a show of rounding up all of the sharp objects she could find, but she never found all of them, and Iseult always procured more. Poor Mrs. Pennington. She was sweet, but that wasn't good enough.

Iseult sat, relieved, breathing again at last, as the warm trickle turned cold. This respite would last her through a night's sleep, at least. These . . . diversions bought her less and less peace these days.

4.

When had she first taken something sharp to her skin in the perverse hope of healing? She hated that initial scar, the living reminder that she had killed someone. No one of import had ever said that to her in so many words, but she had known for as long as she could remember that the scar and the death were intertwined, like the serpents of the caduceus that hung outside the pharmacy a few streets away. She knew that she had been born broken, and that her brokenness had something to do with why her mother never appeared. For a long time she thought that Beatrice had died of disappointment. There was no great revelation, no moment when the clouds parted and she knew exactly what had happened, no servant girl with loose lips trying to teach young Iseult a lesson. But somewhere over the course of the yearly visits to her mother's grave (with Mrs. Pennington, of course; Mr. Wince was said to prefer solitary visits, which is to say that he had not once visited his wife's grave after the funeral) she gradually learned the facts. Beatrice had been too small and delicate for the rigors of childbirth, and Iseult had gotten firmly stuck, her slick squirming body and legs dangling over the ground while her arms and head remained firmly wedged inside. The Winces had been doubly stuck, with a weepy, inexperienced midwife, whose one bright idea when faced with the prospect of both a mother and an infant in dire distress was to brace one panicky hand against poor Mrs. Wince's hip and then yank on Iseult's feet for all she was worth. Mrs. Wince had long since fainted from the pain, and Iseult's head was still snugly in the womb, so the only one who heard the sickening crack of baby bones the second before Iseult burst forth into the world was the oafish midwife. It was a miracle she managed to catch Iseult before she hit the floor. She was so preoccupied with trying to arrange the squalling infant in a position in which the bone shard protruding from her skin wasn't quite so noticeable that only when the doctor finally arrived (he'd had opera tickets) did anyone notice that Mrs. Wince had bled to death. The midwife was disgraced; the doctor lost a good many well-heeled patients and his practice never fully recovered; and as for the Winces, who had begun the day as two with every expectation of becoming three—well, they ended the day as still only two.

The wound did not heal easily. Iseult endured a number of procedures in her childhood that were intended to improve matters, at least cosmetically. She was often in a good deal of pain, but she got the impression that it would be gauche to mention that. It was not her father who was behind these procedures. It was his sister, Iseult's aunt Catherine, who largely controlled what happened to her. She would make proclamations as to the child's dress, music lessons, and so forth, and Mrs. Pennington would faithfully carry them out, even if she might have grumbled about it now and then.

The last surgery was performed when Iseult was fourteen. It did have the benefit of loosening the muscles so her father could at last stop telling her fruitlessly to stop slouching. It also increased the pain that Iseult was so loath to mention, and the scar, previously a pale jumble of lumps, was now a persistently inflamed knot, a throbbing weight that was never relieved. When Iseult's father was told of the aesthetic results of this operation, he swore they were finished with doctors. Mrs. Pennington was the only one who guessed at the pain; she did what she could with massages and hot baths, which wasn't much.

It was a happy accident in Iseult's eighteenth year that led to her own peculiar brand of relief. It was summer, and sickly hot outside. Her walk had pulled her to a small lake with the merest hint of a breeze coming off the water, and she fell asleep in the shade of a flowering pear tree. By the time she woke up, her neck felt twisted and raw, and she knew that she would be late for dinner, an unforgivable sin in the Wince household. Hastening home put a stitch in her side, and she just had time to throw herself in front of her mirror to try and tidy up. Mrs. Pennington made sure her hair would pass muster, and as she hurried downstairs she called over her shoulder, "And there's a dreadful thread coming out the top of that dress. You'd best see to it before you come down!"

Still out of breath, Iseult fumbled in her drawer for a pair of embroidery scissors, which were difficult enough to manage when one had all of one's faculties about one. The offending thread sprang from the fabric of the neck, and would surely have caused Mr. Wince great distress. Wielding the scissors more like a knife, Iseult jabbed at the thread while pulling it with her other hand. This proved to be an exercise in futility, and in her frustration, she stabbed the open scissors through the fabric and into her scarred skin.

Her mouth in the mirror made a perfect O as she waited for the pain to strike. But instead there was a peaceful numbness.

oh iseult what what what have you done?

   i'm not sure mother. are you hurt? have i hurt myself? it doesn't hurt why doesn't it hurt?

That was when Mrs. Pennington came back into the room and shrieked at the sight of a pair of scissors sticking out of Iseult's neck. The shrieks brought Mr. Wince to the threshold when it became apparent that dinner would be delayed. He stormed off to eat his meal in peace, which was what he preferred anyway.

Mrs. Pennington performed the delicate operation of removal herself, as the maid at the time was deathly afraid of blood. Iseult sat still and white-faced while Mrs. Pennington examined the dilemma from every angle, finding that the scissors had sunk at least an inch into the flesh. She did send the maid running for a glass of red wine, which she made Iseult down in one go. She apologized profusely in advance, warning Iseult that she would try her best not to hurt her further, but that meant she would have to go slowly, and that might require some wiggling. Iseult shook her head sharply. Mrs. Pennington took that as a sign that the pain was too great for her to speak.

"Best get it over with, dear. Close your eyes," she said grimly.

Iseult's eyes remained wide. Mrs. Pennington placed one fat hand on Iseult's shoulder, and with the other she gingerly grasped the handles.

As Mrs. Pennington wiggled, the scissors snipped as scissors are meant to. Every bit of blood that escaped caused her to pause and gasp and lose her grip on the handles, which made things a good deal messier as she had to begin all over again. Once the scissors were finally out, though, order was restored and Mrs. Pennington deftly cut the ruined fabric, now heavy with blood, away from the wound. Iseult meekly apologized for making such a mess.

Once she had been cleaned and bandaged and tucked up into bed, fed and fussed over, Iseult at last lay alone in the dark. Wobbly from the sight of so much of her own blood, she had done a very good impression of someone not registering great pain due to shock. But she wasn't in shock. And she didn't feel any pain. Well, not exactly. She felt it, but it felt . . . good. She hesitated to actually think so, but it felt good. When the blood had rushed out with the removal of the scissors, all of her usual anxiety had whooshed out of her with it.

Moreover, her mother, whose voice she had heard whispering away while she wrestled with the errant thread, had whooshed away as well.

Iseult lay in an unhappy patch of jaundiced moonlight and gingerly patted the bandage covering her wounded scar. She did not know it at the time, but it would become her favorite sound in years to come, that *pat pat pit-a-pat* of her fingers on her neck, as she gently, sweetly, soothingly coerced a new wound to sink into the scar. To sink into its place. It was so quiet it was almost not a sound, and Iseult alone could hear it, Iseult and Beatrice, buried deep within the scar.

It wasn't an unfamiliar sound that first night, either. Iseult had always loved the peculiar silence of falling snow, and would slip out of bed whenever snow fell, bundle herself in blankets and curl up on the cold window seat to listen to the almost-sound of it falling onto the sill. If you listened hard enough, if you watched it hard enough, you heard it. She would fall asleep watching the snowflakes disappear into themselves, listening to her mother say

pat pat pit-a-pat

And trying to watch each snowflake for as long as possible, trying to keep them separate instead of letting them merge when they landed in the white. She loved the dusky pink of the sky and the smell of burning leaves that came with it, and the quality of the air like a muffler was wrapped around her face. It had the same effect as her childhood pillow headdress, except that instead of putting her at a remove from the world, it seemed to put everyone at the same distance, at the same disadvantage, for once.

After the fateful Night of the Scissors, things were different. Or, things were the same, but Iseult could make them different if she needed to. She lived quietly, with her mother as her constant companion, a generally tolerable presence. She didn't tell other people that her mother lived inside the scar on her neck. She found that this unsettled them, and they would refuse to believe her.

When she became anxious or agitated, it was much the same as before. She felt a heat in her torso, like she was a little furnace, with her mother shoveling the coal. Her mother would get louder as the heat grew, and Iseult's head would hurt. The things Beatrice said sounded so much like the words of everyone else that Iseult would respond to them out loud. And then, when she was asked whom she was speaking to, she found she couldn't help herself. She would tell the truth. She was a great one for honesty. Lying never gets you anywhere.

But after the Night of the Scissors, it was a new world. Iseult now had control. Anxiety loomed on the horizon: a social engagement, a lecture from her father, and her mother's voice would rise as sure as the tide. Iseult would reach into her sewing reticule (when she was still allowed to keep such a thing), pull out a needle, and jab at the scar until her mother's voice and the nausea receded.

For many months it worked beautifully. A few smart stabs and all was blessed quiet for weeks. Mrs. Pennington grew suspicious when the scissor wound refused to heal, and there was a scene, but she resolved not to tell Mr. Wince. She did so only when the bloodstains kept cropping up. There was another scene, and there was much talk of doctors being consulted, but if a doctor was consulted—well then, someone would have to be told. Oh, no. That wouldn't do. Instead, Iseult was inspected whenever she left the house, and whenever she returned.

Beatrice regained control.

Iseult knew the ways in which she and Beatrice were and weren't alike. Were: Thin; hair the color of dust; sparse eyelashes fringing gray eyes like pavement after a downpour, hard and watery. Long fingers and toes. A certain reserve. Weren't: Beatrice had had a dainty nose that could have been sculpted painstakingly with a fine chisel. Iseult's was strong and Roman, possibly completed in haste. Beatrice had been elegant and graceful; Iseult had a propensity to fidget, as if she were plugged into electric current. Beatrice was said to have had a serene smile. Iseult's looked like something she'd had to study in a book, and never gotten the hang of.

But Iseult knew the mother who lived inside her as well as she knew herself, as well as anyone can know themselves. She was noisy and nagging and over-opinionated. She was cruel and compassionate and bitter and sweet and vengeful and sad. She was a living creature inside Iseult's body, as real as a sea creature hidden inside a shell. Just because you can't see it doesn't mean you can't hear it rustling.

why do you wish me away my dear aren't i haven't i been amn't i the only one who loves who understands who knows you? if i am gone then so are you i think i fear.

but why can't you help me rather than hurt? you always win and i want to win. i want what i want you to be quiet and with me i know you won't go i'll tug i'll shove i'll heave and toss but you won't go so if you're here i need you quieter please to let me be let me have a choice in what i say and what i do and who i become. please. please?

but i am your mother iseult. if i don't know what's best who does i'll tell you no one. no one is closer than we two. isn't that wonderful?

Iseult was nineteen when they took everything sharp out of her grasp, and then she went seventeen months without so much as a *pit-a-pat* on her neck. Beatrice's voice was a constant drone, and it grew so loud that she barely held a conversation with anyone during that period. It is hard to converse with someone when another person inside your own ears is drowning them out. It's difficult to look interested when something inside you is trying to get to the other side of your skin. It's not easy to stay calm when you're worried that your lungs might have caught on fire. But just as a drowning man's flailing is often mistaken for waving, Iseult was merely considered introspective.

Mr. Wince had decided that after those many months of good behavior, after being checked for blood and sharp things and talk of Beatrice on a daily basis, Iseult was ready to be reintroduced to the outside world. At least, to his carefully curated version of the outside world. He decided to host a small dinner for the members of the steelworks' board. Dignified, reasonable men and their exquisitely polite, reticent wives. One or two demure daughters, one or two awkward, blushing sons. Perhaps Iseult would even make a positive impression on one of these daughters, or better yet, a son. She was almost not unpleasant to be around. Quiet, but that was better than being disruptive. Mr. Wince felt a vague positivity as he headed into the evening.

Iseult, having been warned weeks in advance about her fate, felt the engine in her stomach churn, and Beatrice had to shout to be heard over the whirring. Every day Iseult walked longer and farther, higher and harder and faster, trying to outrun the future, ending every day so exhausted she fell asleep over her dinner. Her father assumed that she was excited. Her dreams were plagued with wretched visions, herself, in a wedding dress, chained to a faceless man, her mother sprung out fully formed on her shoulder while Iseult struggled vainly to keep a ladylike posture.

She woke every morning feverish and wobbly, but what else could she do? Iseult had long ago learned that the more you wobble, the faster you have to keep moving. That way, if you fall it's easier to understand than if you were simply standing still.

She was subjected one blindingly sunny day to a walk with Aunt Catherine, Mrs. Pennington trailing behind at a respectful distance but ready to jump in should an opinion be required. Walks with Aunt Catherine were the antithesis of Iseult's solitary rambles. Whereas Iseult charged recklessly, almost blindly, enjoying the places she ended up if she let fate determine her route, taking a turn simply because she never had before, Aunt Catherine followed a regimented path. They turned at the Anglican church, and again just past the hospital, and they entered the park not by the main entrance, but by the one just past. Aunt Catherine found the main entrance common and ostentatious. And she walked slowly. By the end of a walk with her aunt, Iseult's nerves were frayed and jumbling, and she often had to take another walk alone to calm herself.

"My dear Iseult," Catherine said grandly, sounding very rehearsed, "since the unfortunate passing of your poor mother I have taken it upon myself to be as much of a replacement as I could."

bitch that bitch she never cared for me always looked down her stubby nose didn't care for me nor you

"So I thought it only proper that we have this little, shall we say, mother-daughter chat before the upcoming occasion," Catherine said, nodding at a gentleman who was strolling in the opposite direction, and Iseult realized the conversation had been not only rehearsed, but staged. She would not have been surprised if her aunt had even arranged for the too-bright sunshine.

Beatrice became a twinge in Iseult's neck at the phrase "mother-daughter," and Iseult stumbled slightly on a tree root. Her aunt shot her a glance, peeved that she could not orchestrate every detail of the scene. Iseult felt that she was expected to offer an apology at this juncture, but she wasn't sure of the etiquette of apologizing for a future unknown sin, and she waited for her aunt to enlighten her.

"Your father has suffered such bad luck," her aunt said daintily, "with your mother's untimely passing, and having to raise you alone, and of course he is all at sea when it comes to delicate discussions with his daughter!"

Beatrice's presence softened at the mention of Mr. Wince, while Iseult's hardened.

and what about me and my suffering, having a father who never even tried? must i hear a lecture advocating that he be pitied for it?
sweetheart hush and listen perhaps she will have some guidance

Iseult resolutely crossed her arms tightly over her chest, a pose she knew her aunt loathed, and Catherine's posture bristled in response. This conversation was becoming more like a battle, and the change in the air was sensed by Mrs. Pennington, who drew closer, like a reinforcement battalion.

"All I mean, Iseult, is to remind you of your duties toward the man who has raised you, in terms of decorum. If your mother were here, surely she would do the same," Catherine said icily. Iseult's neck grew warm, but was it placation or a warning?

Catherine stopped suddenly, grabbing Iseult's elbow, and Mrs. Pennington, following too close behind, bumped into them. The three (*four*) women stood in an uneasy huddle. Catherine gripped Iseult's forearms, which were still crossed like armor across her body. She had a queer, searching look that Iseult had not seen before. "I am not saying that you have to be happy about it, I am not saying you have to agree with him, but I am promising you, child, you will only make it worse for yourself if you continue to go against him."

Mrs. Pennington wrapped an arm around Iseult's waist and said gently, "She's right. You know she's right."

Usually Aunt Catherine discouraged the closeness between Iseult and the housekeeper, but even Iseult could see her aunt soften visibly, touched perhaps by an affection that she herself only pretended to feel for her niece.

you know they don't care for you don't love you as i do they are being kind to you now but how long do you think that will last it only suits them right now to be kind iseult don't forget

Standing in silence on this beautiful sunny day, Iseult looked between the faces of the two women, and, more than anything, despite good intentions, misguided or otherwise, love or something like it, she felt her toes gripping the edge of a ship's plank, and she was about to be pushed off, and she would fall alone.

The morning before the dinner, she had an appointment with the dressmaker. Mr. Wince was not to be budged from the black (he had never felt that Iseult had truly suffered enough from Beatrice's death, certainly not as much as he himself had; he did not see how her peculiarities and indecencies and bad manners counted as suffering) but after some heavy pressure from Mrs. Pennington, he admitted that perhaps a small amount of adornment might go toward making Iseult look brighter. She had been sallow of late. Nerves, surely? He made sure that the cook provided a good deal of red meat in her diet, as rare as she could make her eat it. (Mr. Wince was unimaginative enough to never have even suspected the presence of a wide ledge underneath the dining room table. Iseult was an expert at secreting near entire meals on the ledge, and then removing all evidence before it was noticed.)

Mrs. Pennington always accompanied Iseult to the dressmaker to oversee alterations, but some problem arose with the vol-au-vents. Everyone had begun to trust Iseult more and more over the past months, and thus she was sent on her way alone, only to discover Aunt Catherine there waiting for her. Iseult's heart, which had buoyed slightly on the short escape, plunged downward again.

Iseult assumed her usual meek position on the dais while Aunt Catherine and the dressmaker lamented her figure, her complexion, her hair (although Iseult didn't see what that had to do with anything).

"Can't the shaping here"—Aunt Catherine gestured vaguely to Iseult's midsection as she spoke—"be made more flattering?"

The dressmaker frowned, pulling the fabric this way and that. There was precious little that could be done, so a heaping basket of jet and obsidian beads was thunked on the floor next to the dressmaker's podium. One by one, gaudy trinkets were sewn on, and Iseult twitched each time the needle approached.

"Now, don't you worry, Miss Wince, I'm sure I've not pricked anyone with my needle in years!" Iseult didn't bother to explain that the twitches were more an ecstasy of hope that she might. It wasn't too long before the ordeal was at an end, and Iseult was undressed and redressed and left alone in the waiting room to attend to her vanity. She stood idly before the full-length mirror and contemplated her disappointing figure, swamped in her skirts. She was aware of her mother's voice.

iseult you mustn't go tonight mustn't mustn't. mustn't go.

and how do you propose i escape? i've been told already i mayn't play sick, and would be propped up at the table with the ragingest of fevers. i'm afraid i must go and i'm afraid i must behave.

but you can't you can't i know you. when you're like you are you are like to be unlike yourself. if you could only find a way to calm. if you could only find a way.

i know a way, mother, but i don't know a how. i've no access to what i need. they may trust me but i am still watched hawk-like and they turn out my pockets when i come in the house.

. . . just the pockets?

Beatrice fell silent. The day was hot and still and Iseult was aware of her face moving through the air as she turned her head to look around the dressing room. There was the usual array of ladies' niceties: brushes and ribbons and pins and powder puffs. And pins. A pink satin pincushion all stuck with pins. She knew that she had to leave directly or she would be missed, and that she would have to think of a hiding place fast, but the thought was there and not to be denied.

There was a soft knock on the door, and Aunt Catherine asking if everything was all right, and so there was nothing to do but follow the instructions.

"I shall be ready in a moment." Iseult put on her best confident voice, which could be convincing, especially when she was engaged in the pursuit of relief. She hoisted two armfuls of skirt up to her elbows and stuck her right foot on the armchair by the dressing table. The black boot was laced high and tight, so she had to be quick, and she couldn't be fussy. Her eye had first been caught by the lovely gold sheen of some immense safety pins, but she realized with regret that there would be no room. There were, however, a number of evil-looking hatpins. All with a bit of tarnish, none of them quite straight anymore. Iseult grabbed the lot, wormed a finger into the small gap between her right boot and her ankle, and shoved them in.

She made it out of the dressmaker's shop without a word, just nodding as her aunt answered the requisite questions. Yes, it's all fine, yes, someone would be along to pick up the dress later, yes, put it on Mr. Wince's account. Sometimes it is best to be known as strange, because then a little extra strangeness doesn't raise any eyebrows. After a hug and a kiss and an exhortation to be good, Aunt Catherine bustled off back to her own life, and Iseult managed to walk naturally, if mechanically, out of sight of the shop and into an empty mews, where she leaned against the brick wall and let out the breath that she had been holding.

She didn't dare peek. There was no time. She steeled herself for the short journey home, a course of shallow steps and shallower breaths, and off she went.

When Iseult arrived at home, the Catastrophe of the Vol-au-Vents was still in full swing, and Mrs. Pennington was standing in the doorframe giving what-for and plenty-of to the girl from the market. Iseult slipped through practically unnoticed. She gritted her teeth for the stairs, and before she closed her door, she called out to Mrs. Pennington that she would take a nap and preferred not to be disturbed. She locked the door.

Collapsing into her mother's chair, she gingerly lifted her skirt. The only sign that something was amiss was a tidy row of pinheads lined up along the boot's edge, and a bubble of blood. Iseult slowed her breathing and began to unlace, pausing for a little gasp now and then. After what could have been quite some time or mere moments, the lace was completely out (Mrs. Pennington would be furious, but no time to worry now). She eased the boot off with infinite care, keeping her foot as rigid as possible.

She looked. She reached out to touch her foot, then thought better of it. The stocking was a total loss. Each hatpin had ripped its own hole in the stocking, and the holes were destined to grow worse with their removal. She tore at the black silk so she could at least see better what she was working with. Four of the pins were stuck in right behind her ankle. The fifth had gone rogue and bitten into the slightly fleshier part in front of her ankle. Blood was trickling, but the deepening color of the surrounding skin showed that there was more in store once she stopped using her foot as a pincushion. Of course the thing now was to avoid a mess. She pulled two handkerchiefs from her pocket (she liked to be prepared, in case) and pressed both neat squares over the entry wounds. With a surgeon's steady hand, she approached the pins. With as little fuss as possible, she simply grabbed them and jerked them free.

After stanching the blood, Iseult peeked under her makeshift bandages. One handkerchief was soaked clean through, but the other was hardly wet. And only a syrupy trail oozed from the wounds themselves. She replaced the sodden fabric with the cleaner one, and from her pocket she fished a hair ribbon, which she secured round her ankle. She laid the offending stocking on her bed; she would tell Mrs. Pennington something about a tree branch in the lane, which would of course not be believed. She put on a fresh stocking and arduously relaced the boot.

It was murderous. It was torture.

It was wonderful.

5.

As much as they tried to stay positive in the lead-up, both Mr. Wince and Mrs. Pennington grew increasingly anxious, as Iseult seemed to shrink to something less than solid, although more than gaseous. But only just.

The day of the dinner, Iseult refused to let Mrs. Pennington into her room at all, saying over and over that she "required solitude." Panic seized the good housekeeper's heart, but Iseult's voice was free of the crackling quality it had when things were about to go irrevocably wrong, so she didn't push it. Mrs. Pennington busied herself with the preparations for the evening, but it was still with a sense of unease that she huffed her way up the staircase when it was time to get Iseult dressed.

She was about to knock when the door swung open. Iseult stood in the doorway in her dressing gown. Smiling. Iseult usually had to be coaxed into her dressing gown. She almost never smiled.

"Well come on, let's get me ready!" Iseult pulled Mrs. Pennington inside and rushed her off to the closet with such haste that the housekeeper was too delighted to detect the slightest hint of a limp.

Iseult was quickly laced and dressed in the newly enhanced

dress, and she didn't even complain, as they walked over to her dressing table, that the beads clacking together on her lackluster bosom would probably give her a headache by the first course. She didn't object when Mrs. Pennington forced the French wires with sapphires through her earlobes, even though they were heavy as sin. She didn't grimace when her hair was swept too far forward on her forehead, giving her what she considered a slightly simian appearance. Why make a fuss when she felt so very fine?

Distracted by what he perceived as a glaring ink stain on his shirt cuff, Mr. Wince was also not in a state of mind to notice Iseult's limp as she descended the stairs. He only noticed that she smiled, which on the one hand was exactly what he wanted. On the other:

"My dear," he said in a low tone, as if there was anyone else who could hear, "perhaps when you smile, you could temper your enthusiasm slightly. That right incisor will be considerably less noticeable with an expression less expansive."

dear he doesn't mean it he's being helpful do as he says you know that tooth has always driven you mad

you are the one who has driven me mad, mother. i cannot tell what you would have me do, shall i please them all and land us a husband? or repel them so we are locked in here forever?

Iseult's mother was silent only when Iseult was truly required to make a decision. When Iseult knew her own mind, she couldn't get Beatrice to shut up.

Iseult took her father's proffered arm and eased her smile down so her upper lip masked the offending tooth. The thought of knocking it out with a doorknob or a bookend flew across her mind like a bird skimming water, but it didn't settle, just kept flying. She stepped more firmly on her right foot to strengthen the clarity of her mind.

Truth be told, the evening was horribly dull. But the sort of dull that qualifies as a success. No one said the wrong thing. No one spilled anything. Nothing was broken. No voices were raised, and offense was neither given nor taken. Nor was there a single interesting observation or conversation. It was deadly, and afterward Mr. Wince asked Iseult to join him in the study.

Iseult was not fond of the study, it was strictly her father's purlieu and so she was only given access when she had behaved exceedingly badly, or exceedingly well. The room was dark and oppressive, and you could tell that Mr. Wince had been told that this was what a man's room ought to look like. He himself always looked uncomfortable in it—but he looked uncomfortable everywhere; even in his sleep he looked vaguely preoccupied.

But there they were, Iseult and her father, seated primly in the two armchairs before the fire. Although there was no natural way to sit in the hard, high-backed chairs, sitting there was preferable to being across from each other at the desk. They sat at the desk when Mr. Wince was displeased, and there Iseult could see the portrait of her mother looking at her sidelong. Beatrice couldn't have been more than seventeen. She wore a dress that bared her shoulders, and the sight of her creamy, unblemished neck always filled Iseult with rage, then remorse, then self-pity. No. It was not a nice place to sit.

Mr. Wince had gone to the trouble of securing for Iseult a glass of sherry, which she held by the stem as if it were on fire. Mr. Wince himself swirled around a ridiculously large snifter of brandy, as he had seen other men do.

(They were more alike than either one of them would have

been able to fathom. They had both suffered a great loss that haunted them daily, and neither knew how to come to terms with it. Neither of them felt at home with other people, preferring their own solitary company, although they both thought it might be nice to get rid of that as well. What an absolute dream. To be alone, but without oneself. But they could not speak of such things.)

"My dear"—in saying that, he always sounded like an actor who knows he won't get the part but must audition anyway— "you did your mother and me proud this evening. I must say that I had my doubts, but you were the perfect lady. I do believe a few of the gentlemen were . . . taken with you."

No one relishes hearing a parent voice a compliment about them that they do not themselves believe. But the night had gone so well, and Iseult wanted to end it without any bother, so, under cover of her sherry glass, she gave that pesky incisor a lick so her lip would slide right down. She turned to her father with a demure smile and said, "How kind of you to say so, Father. I do hope that you're right. They all seemed rather—"

wretched?

"—rather —"

unworthy?

"—rather, well, rather—"

moronic.

"Exactly."

"Hm?"

"Em, exactly the sort of gentlemen that I would want to be . . . taken with me."

Iseult's father had had a good deal of brandy. He patted her hand clumsily and, without looking at her, said, "Your mother would have been so pleased with your performance. Goodnight, my dear."

Iseult rose and placed the sherry glass on the mantel, suspecting that her father wasn't aware of how apt the word "performance" was. "Goodnight, Father. Sleep well." He was practically dozing already, so there was no need for the farcical exchange of goodnight kisses. Iseult limped from the study, and Mrs. Pennington met her at the door.

"Well, how did it go? I think it might have been a success!" Fresh as a daisy at any hour, she was.

"It was . . . Yes."

Mrs. Pennington could tell that Iseult had pulled down the shutters on the evening, and that she would have to wait until at least tomorrow to get anything out of her. So she prepared Iseult for bed in silence, except that Iseult said she could remove her own stockings, thank you very much. This was no more rude than Iseult usually was, so no notice was taken.

Iseult huddled in front of the window, where there was enough light but not too much. It was raining, and when the weak moonlight hit her mother's chair she could see the raindrops chasing each other spastically down the pane. She pulled off her stockings and stuck her bare legs out before her, pale as piano keys.

pat pat pit-a-pat pat pat

Her thrumming fingers began at her right knee and traveled down and down until they hit the white cloth tied around the wound. Dry-skinned fingers unpicked the knot and she began to unwind, around around around. The pasty skin was marked with lines like the ones you get on your face from the pillow. Wake up, little leg.

The end of the bandage was stuck fast with blood to the wound. Iseult gave two experimental tugs and then yanked hard, and a thrill ran through her. Pain, but not. She peered closely; the blood running down her foot was black in the moonlight.

She wadded the fabric under her foot so she didn't stain the rug, and thought about how she disliked the word "wad." She pressed a finger into the wound, squelching out more of the slow blackish liquid, so it looked like escaping slugs or leeches. She noted that the wound looked worse than it had yesterday, when she had sequestered herself in her room all day, picking and poking at the holes left by the hatpins until they were bigger holes.

but iseult iseult what is this going to accomplish

i don't know mother, shh, must all means have an end? can't they just be means? this makes me feel more myself.

it makes you distracted my dear

no no quite the opposite. if i scatter my brain i can focus more clearly. i need to do more at one time. just the one thing is never enough for me for you for calm for peace.

please stop—

shh. shh.

The skin surrounding the wound was a flat sickly gray—Iseult imagined it must be a dull aubergine in daylight—where the blood was pooling lazily under the surface, waiting to see if it was needed in some other capacity. The edges had begun to pucker and crust—to heal? Iseult was not interested in healing. She was interested in what was underneath, what was inside. If she could find out what was inside this wound, perhaps she would be able to see into other, deeper wounds. Find Beatrice. Get her out. Of course, she was not sure what would happen then. She didn't think that far.

She always liked to think of the future, to race to it, hoping to reach it before anyone else, to take its measure, to size it up, for once to be ahead of the game and in control of something. In the present, she controlled nothing.

She rubbed a fingertip back and forth over the crusted edge, and little black crumbs fell onto the white cloth. She bent her face closer to see what she could see. Wet and dark and impermeable. She nudged her finger inside and there was a slick noise that disgusted her. (You recall the family cook who ended up slaughtered by her seagoing sort-of paramour? Back in Iseult's heady days of gluttony, she was eating a great quantity of creamed corn in a kitchen cupboard [you must go wherever the solitude is available] when she heard the cook in a romantic clinch with . . . someone; she never saw his face. But she would always remember the inimitably human sounds, the wetness, the smacking. Even as a child, she had hated to be touched. Nothing about the prospect of adulthood was enticing.) But she held onto the sound for a moment and stayed in it, and supposed that if it was a sound you made all by yourself, then perhaps it was different. She pushed her finger further, and the tip of her fingernail disappeared into her skin.

Her lips curled into an approximation of a smile.

6.

After the hatpins, things were different. Iseult felt that she had a mission of sorts, or at least a calling. She was trying to please her father, for whatever that was worth, and a newfound sense of calm pervaded the house, rather than the usual uncomfortable chill she could feel, even in front of the fireplaces, when she knew her father was lurking.

What Iseult strove for was a careful balance, and it was not easy to achieve. Her father had to believe that she was good and sane and docile, that she wasn't going to derail everyone's future by saying shocking things about Beatrice, by sulking or raging, by generally presenting herself as an entirely unsuitable prospect for marriage. On the other hand, she couldn't appear to be *too* good and sane and docile, and thereby find herself affianced.

It wasn't easy, and Iseult was constantly on her guard. So many people to placate. Her mother, her father, Mrs. Pennington, the never-ending parade of dull men who marched through the house with their insipid parents. It would have driven a person of even the most placid disposition to tears.

The wounds kept her sane, although Iseult was aware that would sound quite mad to anyone else. She knew exactly what she was doing. If she wasn't feeling too terribly steady on the outside, it helped to see herself from the inside. Seen from the inside, Beatrice was quieter, kinder, more understanding. Why must pain be painful? Why couldn't it be soothing instead? Iseult had stumbled upon the solution, and she felt genuinely sorry for the rest of the world, which saw pain as pain.

It started with the scissors; it continued with the hatpins. Iseult realized that the actual madness would be to live by the rules of the rest of the world. She just had to be careful and quiet, and she could make herself like one of them.

At least enough to pass.

After that one successful dinner party, Mr. Wince was confident. Confident that his daughter was at last close enough to normal to be pawned off on someone vaguely appropriate. But no matter how many dinner parties he hosted and dragged her to, no matter how many unobjectionable men she was put in front of, it never worked. Everything would start off well, with banal pleasantries exchanged over the various courses. There was no denying that she was odd, that she was off, but Mr. Wince had seen many an odd, off young woman successfully married. Happily was another story, but happily was a lot to ask. Happiness came very far down on his list of hopes for Iseult's future. It certainly lagged far behind "financially provided for," "in a decent circle of society," "not a nuisance to anyone," and "in a house situated not too terribly close to her current residence."

Sometimes things fell flat during the dinner, which was to be expected; sometimes things progressed a little further, and the gentlemen were interested in continuing their acquaintance with the peculiar Miss Wince. But somewhere along the way, over tea with someone's mother, during a stroll in the park or an outing to a concert, things always went wrong.

Part of the problem was that Mr. Wince was rarely available (a less charitable observer might have said "willing") to accompany Iseult as a chaperone, so it was his sister who accompanied her. Aunt Catherine was not exactly an attentive chaperone, unless the topic somehow turned to her own children, in which case she could get very involved. In fact, several of Iseult's would-be suitors defected to her cousin Elspeth's long list of admirers.

When Iseult was twenty-one, there was a spark of interest (only on her side) for a "J" entry in her little black book of names and notes, a James. He was bright and friendly, with pleasing gold ripples of hair. He was somehow connected with Mr. Wince's banker, although it was never explained how, at least not to Iseult. They met on two occasions before it was arranged for Aunt Catherine to accompany them on a picnic. Her aunt mentioned Elspeth's artistic abilities (which were negligible, if Iseult had been asked), and James, with his bright friendliness, peppered her with questions until Iseult realized that she was no longer a part of the conversation at all. By the time the picnic basket was repacked and the trio had set off in the direction of Aunt Catherine's house in order to view Elspeth's watercolors, James was already besotted with the idea of her. And—what luck!—Elspeth happened to be home for him to meet.

It wasn't that Iseult believed that her aunt was so wicked as to plan this usurpation, but James did call on Elspeth several times after that, whereas the Winces never heard from him again. And when Aunt Catherine explained why his relations with Elspeth inevitably progressed no further, she said, "You know dear, his family was really not of the rank that we would like Elspeth to marry into," proving Iseult's suspicions that although her aunt purported to love them as equals, the standards that a gentleman was required to meet in order to court Elspeth were much higher than those required for courting Iseult.

Another part of the problem: it was all well and good to have trouble securing one's future before one turned twenty. (Admittedly, Iseult had had a late start, her father pushing the idea from his head, wondering if she would improve in some way if he waited.) And until she was twenty-five or so (to be exceedingly generous) her continued state of unattachment could be blamed on her motherlessness, perhaps even on a bohemian free-spiritedness (it would explain away all of that infernal *walking*, at least), but . . . Iseult was twenty-eight. She was firmly wedged in the land of the spinster.

Not that there weren't a few things still in her favor. Her father was relatively wealthy, and it was known around town that any groom would be handsomely rewarded for his trip down the aisle. And she didn't *look* twenty-eight.

There. She still had those weapons in her arsenal. They weren't much, but some were given less to work with than others.

Over the past few years, it was true, the quality of gentleman had seriously declined. Iseult had for many years maintained her little black book for the purposes of remembering who was who, in the event that she was called upon to do so. In her head she liked to call it "The Unsuitables."

It began with that first matchmaking dinner. She started writing in a fury, needing an outlet and having only a shabby, empty diary in which to write cutting, purposefully cruel observations of her hapless suitors, although in time it became more of a means of keeping track.

For instance, under "D" was the very first entry: "April 21, 1880. Donald Smythe. 23. Short. Ugly. Hair thinning. Employed as barrister, although presents as too timid for such an occupation."

Flipping through to "W": "September 1, 1884. Winthrop Cavini. 36. Dazzling white teeth. Father owns shipping company in Uruguay. Handsome to the point of unpleasantness, does not look me in the eye after introduction. Would be strictly business and I would remain living with Father. Is he already married? Is this the Uruguayan way? I shall never find out."

And then back to "M": "January 9, 1888. Malcolm Anderton. At least 65, likely older. Widowed with six grown children. Enormously fat. Hot vegetable breath."

The most recent entry was under "R": "July 16, 1889. Randall something. Old. Falls asleep."

On Wednesdays, when the linens were changed, she shoved her notebook down the front of her corset and kept it there all day. Mrs. Pennington never laced her very tight for everyday. On Wednesdays she felt impenetrable.

Beatrice was very helpful in making the entries, as the details slithered out of Iseult's mind as soon as they went in.

william . . . william . . .

william stockley.

he looked fifteen.

twenty-nine, dear.

he had a nasty little beard.

it was a nasty little mustache, dear. thin and uninspired much like the rest of him.

oh yes now i remember.

you do not my dear i know you you were deeply involved in a scrutiny of the china and didn't answer a single question which was more than adequate since it was his mother asking all the questions and your father had no choice but to take up the cause.

perhaps father should marry mrs. stockley.

It did not escape Iseult's attention that Beatrice was not keen on even the slightest hint of talk of Mr. Wince's remarriage. Iseult

did not know much about her parents' relationship, whether it
had been a happy one or not. She knew the barest details: they
had married when her mother was eighteen and her father twenty-
three, after an engagement that was notable for neither its length
nor its brevity. Mr. Wince had worked with Beatrice's father
for several years, rapidly moving up in the ranks. The marriage
seemed the natural next step, and when Beatrice's father died
(extremely unpleasantly, it must be said), in the year after the
wedding, it was considered extremely fortuitous that such steps
had been taken. Mr. Wince slid smoothly into the position of
head of the steelworks.

Iseult's father certainly never said anything very illuminating
about her mother, and her aunt cannily avoided the issue by saying it wasn't Christian to speak of the dead. Iseult got the bulk of
her information from Mrs. Pennington, and although she trusted
her honesty, Iseult was certain that she held back any details that
might have been unfavorable.

In the year when Iseult turned twenty-eight, she made fewer
and fewer entries in "The Unsuitables." The quality of suitor being
received at the Wince household dropped off sharply. Each had
more gray hairs than the last, with the exception of the very occa-
sional youthful visitor, who invariably had his own set of problems. Among the younger candidates there was a butcher with
one leg, a bank clerk who had very possibly been in jail, and a
nineteen-year-old whose hand shook so badly he finally gave up
on eating his peas. The more elderly (or as Mrs. Pennington said,
the more "experienced") among them included a number of widowers, one so fresh that he burst into tears twice during the meal.

Several of the widowers had children, which was of no concern to Mr. Wince, but of very great concern to Iseult. She had
held a baby once, her cousin Elspeth's. (Elspeth had ended up
marrying a man who wouldn't have deigned to be introduced to

Iseult, being in a much higher social stratum.) It had been after the christening, which Iseult and her father had been obliged to attend. Iseult was perched awkwardly in a corner, waiting for the afternoon to come to its natural conclusion, when Elspeth rushed by, wanting to show off some piece of furniture to a friend. She was trying to point out a particular feature but, finding her hands full, glanced around to see only Iseult.

"Iseult, be a darling, would you?" Elspeth didn't wait for an answer; she simply dropped the squirming bundle of lace and fat into Iseult's lap. There was nothing Iseult could do but catch it. She held her breath, waiting for Elspeth to swoop in and take it back. Since childhood, Elspeth had been a swooper, like an eagle with manicured talons, soaring down from her place on high to steal toys and companions and eligible bachelors. But as Iseult sat, rigid, Elspeth flitted from the room, arm in arm with her companion, to show off the simply adorable arrangement of end tables in the library. Adorable.

Iseult looked down at the bundle. It wasn't moving any longer, but its enormous blue eyes were staring at her as if they suspected her of a great crime. Iseult had heard that all babies were born with blue eyes, but she thought that surely this couldn't be so. It didn't sound right. But this one had clear blue eyes like . . . certain flowers. And Iseult felt a distinct discomfort with this warm lapful of cousin. It knew something distasteful about her. Something secret that even Iseult was not aware of.

whatever is the matter with you girl it's just a baby a sweet baby like you once were yourself, that i never got to hold i longed to hold you, you know that don't you?

i don't like it, i don't want it, i don't think it likes being with me it can tell that i don't trust it why does it look at me without blinking like i'm responsible for all of the wrongs of the world.

oh my sweet darling, hold that look hold those eyes keep them
for one hundred years.

Iseult felt an urge to stand abruptly and let the bundle tumble to
the floor. A shudder ran through her, top to bottom, as she resisted.
It was so hideously alive, so full of the in-and-out breaths that
would continue for another sixty or seventy years if it was (un)
lucky, and Iseult rolled her shoulders back, preventing her arms
from flying forth to the baby's neck, throttling it out of its ignorance. She could see only the squalling infant she must have been,
all angles and slings, and wish that her father or Mrs. Pennington
had had the good sense to end all this nonsense before it began.

Before she knew what she was doing, but while she knew what
she was doing perfectly well, Iseult's left hand cradled the christening cap, full of flaky baby acne and hair smelling of sour milk,
a smell that spoke of things that Elspeth now knew of but Iseult
did not, things dark and secretive and holy and shameful and vile;
and her right hand crept. Crept surely and steadily. It snaked and
crawled up through the lace to the fat neck with its sticky damp
folds and—

"Darling, thank you! You are an absolute angel and look how
he loves you, he's not even crying, he cries with absolutely everyone, it will drive Nurse frantic if I tell her how *calm* he is with
you!" Elspeth swooped again, so Baby was summarily saved from
whatever mischief Iseult might or mightn't have been about to
cause.

(The moment the baby was out of her hands, Iseult felt an
overwhelming combination of shame and nausea. How did such
thoughts get into her head? As much as she might think dreadful
things like that, she would not *do* them. She felt so ashamed that
she nearly sought out Elspeth to beg forgiveness, but realized that
to assuage her guilt in that way would likely be too complicated.)

But you can never tell until the end of a life, can you? Whether a quick, merciful twist of the neck in infancy mightn't have been preferable in the end to a *normal* life expectancy: an expectancy of hassle and heartbreak and dreams unfulfilled, loves unrequited and hopes dashed. It all depends on one's constitution. It seems, after all, a pity that such a thing can't be determined at birth, and that those unsuited for the travails ahead can't be sent blessedly along to a purgatorial way station to wait out their *natural* life. It might, after all, be kinder than condemnation to a rich, lengthy life spent hoping for something that never materializes.

But. The hapless child was rescued, and Iseult was left alone, forearms hollow and aching for she knew not what. But she knew it wasn't that. She wanted no part of that. Children unsettled her, no matter what age. They were an invitation to disaster. Either you killed them or they killed you.

Mr. Wince, of course, remained oblivious. He thought, in his dim, disconnected way, that a child (Iseult's own or a stepchild; he saw no difference between the two) might be exactly what Iseult needed to become what he considered a normal member of the human race.

Mr. Wince believed that his own child was the worst thing ever to have befallen him. What had she ever brought him but misery? She had killed his wife. It wasn't that theirs had been a great love affair; Mr. Wince was never capable of such a thing, and possibly neither was Beatrice. But she had been his wife, dammit. When he married Beatrice and took over the company, everything had slotted into its prescribed place. Iseult had been meant to be merely an addition to the previous successes.

With Beatrice suddenly gone, he had no one to rely on to see to the social side of business affairs, and after a brief, grim episode when Iseult was lodged with a wet nurse, every night he came home to the screams of an inconsolable infant. At great expense, an army of nurses traipsed in and out the door, each one more dismal at dealing with his daughter than the last. And things got worse as she grew. Not that it was so terrible to be unsettled by your own child. Mr. Wince's own father had been extremely distant with him and his siblings, and when they were children he often told them not to bother him: they could speak to him once they turned eighteen.

But Mr. Wince actively disliked Iseult, and was even perhaps a bit afraid of her. When she was a solemn, silent toddler, she would frighten him by suddenly appearing at his elbow as he worked in his study. She would stare at him with those fathomless gray eyes that were too large for her head. And he had no notion of whether she'd been standing there for a minute or an hour. He had a lock put on the door.

She was a nuisance, and he sometimes sat and pondered what exactly had gone wrong. He had colleagues and acquaintances whom he would run into around town with their daughters, and they looked contented; happy, even. He would overhear the men in his office or at his club bragging about their daughters—their beauty, or a good match they'd made. It was completely alien to him. If someone asked after Iseult, he said that she was fine, in a tone that put an end to the matter.

He had no idea what Iseult did when she was not in his presence, apart from the information in reports given to him weekly by Mrs. Pennington. Whenever difficulties arose, he charged her or his sister with sorting things out. Whenever a weighty decision had to be made, such as where her schooling was to take place, Mr. Wince was mightily put out, and his jaw would ache from the constant clenching of his teeth. He believed his agony came from being unsure that he was making the correct choice for Iseult's future, but it was always the correct choice for Mr. Wince's present that won the day. He chose her school because it was where colleagues of comparable social standing sent their daughters. He let his sister choose Iseult's clothing because he knew that her own daughter was considered well and respectably dressed.

And oh, the relief once a decision had been reached! He could put the wretched child out of his mind again, as he had put her out of his study when she was small.

7.

Mr. Wince wouldn't have known it, but the avoidance went both ways. Most of the week Iseult had the comfort of knowing that his schedule was rigid enough to set one's clock by, but on Saturday afternoons and Sundays one couldn't rely on it. Generally Iseult had Mrs. Pennington by her side, from the front door to the bedroom, to the dining room and back, and if her father was in the house, she knew where he was. But even with hypervigilance like Iseult's, it was possible to be caught unawares now and then.

Last Sunday, for instance, several days after the disastrous dinner with the Finches, Iseult had awoken past midnight, too thirsty to fall back asleep. She crept through the house in her fluttering nightie, like a ghost. Not a vengeful ghost, just a wayward spirit who got turned in the wrong direction. She flitted her way to the kitchen, where she stood at the sink drinking her water, gulping at first, breathless, then slowing. Searching through the window for the moon but having little luck despite a curious brightness, she slowly rose up on her toes and then down again, up and down.

back to bed you'll catch your death. if i were here i would tell you so. you would call to me from your room and i would bring you a glass of water and take it away again when you were through

but you are not and i must get it myself. i won't catch cold, i promise.

i would at least make sure that your slippers were always next to the bed. that woman will never be your mother she will never remember those simple things a mother would never forget.

i like the feel of the wood floor under my toes. it is soft somehow. i want to feel everything and remember everything, in case, in case,

"In case what?"

The glass crashed out of Iseult's hand and onto the white porcelain, shattering into a fine spray of shards that twinkled in a weak ray of moonlight. Before she turned around, before she thought the entirely natural thought *Why didn't he make his presence known when I entered the kitchen?* she thought: *He knew I would do that. That's why he said nothing. He wanted the glass to smash.*

Iseult swallowed a shudder, and turned to face her father. She had the advantage of the light on him, as her face was in shadow. His was displayed with every fault highlighted.

"You were talking to yourself again," he said with a sneer.

It was too late at night for a battle, and Iseult had no stomach for it. Another time she would have told him that she had been talking to her mother. But she did not need to see the crystal decanter on the table, its remaining liquid cloudy, to know that he was drunk. He only wandered away from his study when he was at a particularly cruel level of drunk. She could see his bitterness and anger as if they were another person in the room, and they always rose as the level of the liquid fell.

Sometimes she felt sorry for him. She knew he was jealous that she had her mother, and he did not. But she wasn't in the mood to humor him, to confirm every bad thing he thought about her.

"Yes, Father. I'm sorry. I was talking to myself. You should have said you were here."

"Would it have made any difference?" he said, getting to his unsteady feet. He picked up the decanter and glass, and raised his eyes to her. They bulged unpleasantly, pushed out of their sockets by the years of distaste that had collected in his head. "You will always talk to yourself, you will always talk to her. I should send you away. But who would have you?" A mixture of a laugh and a hiccup burst out of him. He wiped his mouth with the back of his hand, and Iseult saw with revulsion that a smear of saliva glistened at the corner of his mustache. "I've even asked at the convent!"

we are not even catholic

"If I had known that your Church of England membership made you completely ineligible I would have had you baptized a Catholic. I always thought the nuns would take any lost cause. Sadly I was mistaken." He spat the last words out and turned to go.

"You should have drowned me at birth."

Mr. Wince paused mid-step, then turned his head—enough so she could hear him, but not enough so that he had to look at her again. "Your words, Iseult, not mine."

He shuffled toward the hallway, all of the fight suddenly having left him. "Not mine," he said again, to no one in particular.

Iseult stood for a few moments, rising and lowering on the still-pleasant floor. Iseult liked to remember that no matter how bad things were, pleasures remained to be had.

darling girl you mustn't listen to him when he's like that he doesn't you know he doesn't mean those things

he does. he does and i understand why and it almost doesn't hurt. i understand him better than he thinks. i cannot be as angry as he can because i have the one thing that he wants and that is you. and he cannot have you.

i am afraid you will end up destroying each other.

we will, mother. there is no way around it. but there is no need to fear it. it is just what will happen. it's only a matter of who gets there first.

iseult i think you are bleeding.

Iseult looked down and saw that her left hand was covered in droplets of blood that were beginning to run together like raindrops chasing each other down a windowpane. It must have happened when the glass broke, she thought. Funny, she hadn't felt a thing.

8.

"Whatever happened between you and your father, love?" Mrs. Pennington burst in early the next morning, and for a moment Iseult, bed-warm and crusty-eyed, wondered with alarm whether the dream she'd had the night before had been real. She had thrust her arms in through a window, grabbed her father by the shoulders, and dragged him out through the glass. Woozy, she rubbed her eyes. Mrs. Pennington's button eyes grew several sizes. "What on earth have you done?"

Now truly alarmed, Iseult saw the blood smears still on her hand. She remembered the grim scene in the kitchen, but exhaled with relief. It could have been so much worse. "Oh, nothing, I promise. Father startled me in the kitchen last night and I dropped a glass and it must have cut my hand. No, no, there's no need—"

There was no point in saying there was no need, Mrs. Pennington was already hustling off for water and a bandage.

don't you tell her i won't have her meddling any longer.

she isn't meddling, mother. she wants to help she wants me happy she wants me to get along with father.

she wants you wrestled wrenched wrapped stuffed in a lovely box just like your father does.

Sometimes the one thing Iseult truly wished for was that her mother would give her some straight instructions. And then sometimes Iseult thought perhaps this was too much to ask of the dead: a solid message from someone who had lost corporeality. But it was like grabbing at an object that seemed real enough, only to find yourself falling through a shimmering mirage. You could tell yourself all you liked that it wasn't real, but when it was what your brain thought it saw, which part of you was the winner? And that's why Iseult asked for clarification, every time, even though she had never once received it.

mother. can't you stop confusing me i don't understand what it is that you want. would you like me to obey him? obey him and marry? pretend that you aren't here, forget you? be a good little wife? or shall i keep defying him? fight and kick and swear and scream?

oh don't swear my dear. a lady doesn't swear.

—

just. just. get me. just get. JUST GET—

"Now let's see to that hand." Mrs. Pennington's mouth was bunched and colorless, which meant she thought Iseult had done it herself. Iseult currently had a number of self-inflicted wounds that the housekeeper was unaware of, and she was not going to be caught out by one that wasn't even her fault.

"But I promise you, it was an accident. I promise." Iseult fixed her most earnest expression on Mrs. Pennington. She knew it was very earnest: she'd practiced it in the mirror.

Mrs. Pennington's eyes shrank back to their normal size but

kept searching Iseult's face for any sign of a lie as she wiped off the traces of last night's blood.

"Your father is very upset this morning. What do you know about that?"

Iseult thought, not for the first time, that it was a shame women couldn't work as police detectives; Mrs. Pennington would have made an excellent one, ferreting out the truth from wily, hardened criminals. But Iseult was well versed in this interrogation process.

"I'm sure I've no idea. Perhaps he is upset that the glass was broken. I believe it was a wedding gift. Why do you say he is upset, anyway?"

"He's walking about the house like a madman, mumbling and wild-eyed." She dropped her voice, as if there were someone else in the room listening. "I believe he's been drinking since last night. His bed wasn't touched."

"Oh, is that all?" Iseult said airily, although in truth the breath had left her lungs. This behavior was too agitated for her liking. It was especially odious because she knew it didn't result from concern for her, but from pity for himself. Something was about to happen, and she knew from experience that it wouldn't be anything good.

The household saw nothing of Mr. Wince for the next week. The first day's absence was not out of the ordinary, until he failed to appear for dinner. The second was tense and uncomfortable, as he could arrive at any moment. The third felt joyous, as if they had received news that he was never coming back at all, but his salary would continue to pay for everyday expenses.

The fourth day Iseult roamed the city, light and easy, stopping at an open-air market with Beatrice on her shoulder like a good angel.

look there iseult such beautiful flowers my mother used to fill our
house with bluebells

would you like me to get some, mother? now that father
seems to be away, i daresay we could fill a room at the very least.
darling you know he will be back though

Iseult leaned over a display of peonies inhaling their scent. She
was too happy to let any thoughts of her father intrude.

wouldn't it be lovely, though, just you and me and the house full
of bluebells?
of course it would of course but
but what?
but could we have anemones too

Iseult laughed aloud, startling a policeman who looked her up
and down disapprovingly, as if a woman in mourning dress had
the right neither to laugh nor to smell peonies. When he turned
away, she stuck out a smidgen of her tongue at him. She bought
four large bouquets of anemones before adding a posy of bluebells.
And a very large peony plant.

She set off toward home with what could have been described
as a flounce, relishing her arms and legs that felt strong and pur-
poseful and confident. She nodded and smiled at the other pedestrians, wanting to share her good mood as she so often wanted
to share her bad. She even stopped and gave a cornflower to a
winsome baby in a pram.

it would be so wonderful, mother.
what would my dear my darling
if he were dead.

For a strained moment, Iseult thought she'd gone too far.

it would solve a good many of our problems

It was one of those times when Iseult wished she could hug her mother. She longed to know how Beatrice would feel: Would she be thin and birdlike and breakable, or more substantial? Would she return the embrace with any strength, or remain passive? Iseult knew that she was taller than Beatrice had been, but by how much? Would she be able to see over her mother's head, or could she rest her chin on top? It was too hard to tell from just two pictures.

Back at the house now, Iseult hugged the damp and fragrant bundles to her chest and was about to kick the door with her foot when it suddenly opened, Aunt Catherine on the other side and on her way out, as usual.

"Always passing like the proverbial ships, aren't we, Iseult? You must come round for tea soon." Catherine paused a moment to scrutinize her niece over the flora. "I must say you're looking remarkably well."

Iseult leaned in as far as the bouquets would allow and kissed her aunt's powdery cheek. "Thank you. And I will come for tea. I promise."

At the time, she even meant it.

Day five dawned temperate and beautiful, but it was as if a gray, shifting cloud roiled above the house. By the afternoon of the sixth day, Iseult was nearly catatonic with panic. Even Mrs. Pennington couldn't sit still, and the house itself felt as if it were about to snap from tension.

And then he walked into the house as though he had never been gone. He gave Mrs. Pennington his hat and overcoat and asked what was for dinner. She muttered, "Lamb," her button eyes racing over him, looking for . . . what? A sign that he'd been kidnapped or mugged, maybe a suitcase he'd hidden behind his back somehow?

"My dear Mrs. Pennington," he said, with a disturbing hint of a smile (his smile was as rare as his daughter's, and he certainly never referred to his housekeeper as "my dear"), "I can see you have been fretting over my absence. I have merely been staying at my club because I had some very important business that I simply could not afford to be distracted from. Please tell Iseult to dress for dinner, as I've some wonderful news."

Mrs. Pennington gawped after him as he walked smartly off to his study. There wasn't even the faintest whiff of alcohol on his breath. He reached the study and then, hand on the doorknob, turned back. "Lamb, you say?"

Mrs. Pennington nodded. "Yes, sir. We'll be having lamb."

Again, the smile that didn't even believe in itself. "Wonderful. Just wonderful."

Later in the afternoon, an envelope slithered under Iseult's door. She was sitting stiff and motionless in her mother's faded arm-chair, as she had been for hours, staring at but not seeing the mottled gray sky out her window.

The sound of the sliding paper was a shock to the silence, a sort of aural papercut, but Iseult did not flinch. She breathed shallowly through her mouth, since a cold several days in the making was blocking her nostrils. Her right hand floated to her left shoulder.

you don't know it's something bad my darling read it first give your father a chance.

he hates me he has always will always hate me. is it because he loved you so very much?

i think that is not it.

—

he did not love me he did not know me even couldn't have told you my favorite color or dress or flower or how i smelled or what my hands felt like iseult never marry a man who does not know these things.

yellow. the lace with the high square neck and pearl buttons. gardenias. soap and milk and clothes shut up for too long and the taste of blood from a bad tooth. my hands are rough and raw but if you feel the bones underneath they are ladylike and fine. as if someone would ever feel them to notice, or indeed to care. mother—

Iseult's longest fingernail found the seam of her scar through the neck of her dress and dug fiercely downward. The red skin blanched white then back to red like the frayed skirt of a lazy jellyfish as the nail worked stealthily back and forth, seeking a new opening. An opening to let something in, to let something out. A weak trickle of blood smushed under her fingertip, but that's not what it was seeking.

—mother what do i do? i know i know he's determined to be rid of me at last but what is it that *you* want me to do? i never know you never tell me just this once can't you tell me?

you should go and read the note my dear. perhaps it is nothing after all.

you are a riddle mother. obey father or disobey? marry or not? free you or free myself?

A little tired, a little stumbly, Iseult approached the envelope. It had been sealed with wax. Only her father would write a letter to his daughter, in his own house, and seal it.

She bent herself in half at the waist to retrieve the offending missive. Even his stationery was like him: heavy, ostentatious, and of a creamy blandness that was somehow distasteful. She flipped the envelope over. At least he hadn't addressed it to her, although if he had, that wouldn't have surprised her. She slid a finger underneath the flap, willing a paper cut that didn't materialize. She pulled the card out with a rasp; it fit too tightly in the envelope, but of course her father was aware of that. There was nothing he liked better than knowing he'd caused someone unnecessary trouble and irritation.

We are expecting guests at luncheon. I take this opportunity to express the importance of your behaving with the utmost discretion and tact. Everything depends on it. I trust you understand my meaning.

Signed,
Your father.
Edward Wince.

Iseult gave a rare laugh. He had included his full name, in case she had him confused with some other Edward Wince, some other father.

She was lost. Her mother would give her no instruction, her father had no thought but to bend her to his will, whatever that meant for her. She decided.

She fumbled for hopes to cling to: an invalid husband who would forever be convalescing elsewhere, or a business-minded gentleman too obsessed with finances and futures to grace the family home very often, or even a man who had desperately wanted to marry someone else, and now preferred to pine alone and leave Iseult to her own devices. Surely there were even more palatable possibilities than those she could think of so hastily. And in any case, she would no longer experience every moment as a millstone around her father's neck.

She would not be headstrong, for once. She would do what he asked, no matter how odious. And see where it took her. She was a tiny vessel on the sea, no sight of land, no hint of wind, no hope of rescue. What else was there to do?

9.

The drawing room interlude was always the worst. The black collar that she suspected had been starched with iron ore, considering how it stretched her neck to unnatural lengths; the shoes that pinched but made her an appreciable inch taller; the stifling air; the furniture arranged in a way that signified that no one ever sat in that room with ease; the seconds ticked off by a clock that had a grudge against time. The waiting. He always made her appear in the drawing room half an hour before the guests were meant to arrive. She wondered if he knew how the ticking of the clock drove her mad.

And it was hot. How could it still be so hot at this time of year? She felt that autumn should have come and gone a hundred times, and still the summer lingered on. Her fingers felt for the spot on her shoulder where the blood had stuck to her dress. She shuddered and ground her teeth again. If it was what her father wanted, she would marry. She would marry the man who came today. If her mother would not consent to guide her, she would make her own way, rather than be cast out onto the streets. (Did she really think such a thing would happen? It was hard to tell. Once when she was ten and she had continued speaking aloud to her mother despite constant admonishments, he locked her in the back garden overnight in the rain. Of course, to other people he behaved like a perfectly reasonable man. That was the problem. There was no telling, there was no warning.)

It was hot. And Iseult was not one of those dainty English roses who turn all kiss curls and fetching blushes in the heat. Beads of sweat bubbled on her forehead and upper lip; her dress beneath her arms was stained a darker black. At least, she reasoned, this suitor would have ample reason to refuse her if he had half a brain in his head. Half a brain was the most she could hope for at this point. She would take half a leg, gladly. A hook instead of a hand. As long as he was decent and left her alone. But she didn't know whether that was something a girl in her position had any right to hope for, decency. She had no friends to conspire with, no sisters to whisper with in the dark.

She had only Mrs. Pennington. She assumed that Mrs. Pennington had a husband, or had had one at some point in her career, but for all she knew Mr. Pennington could have been a fabrication to secure her position in the house. Every few years or so there was a veiled reference to him, and there were children—that, Iseult had been assured of—but of course, children could be gotten without a husband. But such intimate things were not to be discussed.

And after all, she'd never even met the children; she'd taken Mrs. Pennington's word for their existence. She paused momentarily in her sweaty shifting, eyes widening at the realization that Mrs. Pennington could have made up Nigel with his troubles at school and his lustrous hair, and Elizabeth with her fine embroidery and her penchant for sweets; but then, it wouldn't have been worth all that trouble, now would it? And if there was one thing Mrs. Pennington loathed, it was having too much on her mind. No. There were children. Relieved, Iseult relaxed and slouched, then bolted upright again. The sweat on the back of her dress had caught a breeze and was now chilled and slimy. It felt nice on her skin, but there wasn't a chance that the heavy black fabric was stuck to her shoulder blades in an attractive manner.

She jumped from her seat, seeing in horror what she knew she would see: a damp patch on the pale upholstery. Her eyes darted about for a doily that could be repurposed, but the only one of sufficient size to cover the stain was underneath a largish potted plant.

Panicking now, breath coming short and fast through her nostrils, she looked at the wet spot and then at the plant, the spot and the plant, faster and faster, and she was just beginning the mad dash for the plant when the door opened.

Of course. The guests had arrived.

Three people stopped short in the doorway as Iseult tried to right herself. She managed it with only a slight bobble against the table, but the potted plant reacted with some violence, the faux-Chinese porcelain complaining against the wood. Iseult could see her father's disapproval rising over the faces of a dignified-looking older gentleman, a gray-haired woman whose forehead spoke of someone perpetually unsatisfied, and a man who looked to be in his twenties or thirties.

Their eyes met, Iseult's and this man's, and the trepidation clearly visible in all four eyes eased as they took each other in. Suddenly everything made sense, and all was revealed. Their faces relaxed. *Ah,* their expressions said. *This is why we have been brought together.*

The youngish man looked at Iseult and saw an uncomfortable, black-clad woman trying to stand in one place. She was sweaty and twitchy and held herself oddly, one shoulder arching higher than the other as if headed for escape. Her mousy hair was a little unkempt, and her large, washed-out eyes blinked too often.

The pale skin of her not unpleasant but not remarkable face was blotchy; hives, perhaps? You could tell she was gnawing at the inside of her lip, and what she was thinking no one could tell.

Iseult looked at the youngish man. He was of a good height, taller than her father. Well dressed by an excellent, subtle tailor. He had an open face with a warm expression, and dark, kind eyes. Thick brown hair waved attractively from his brow. He looked the perfect gentleman.

One more pertinent detail: his skin was silver.

Iseult was always at a loss during these meals, but usually it was from boredom or self-consciousness or repulsion. This particular meal was remarkable, not for the routine, dull conversation, but for the fact that Iseult was in a state of high confusion, which made her act like a nervous coquette. She was obviously avoiding looking at Jacob, but the repression of her natural instincts sometimes burst at the seams, and she stared openly until the whole table was uncomfortable, and then she blushed a mottled red, all the more furiously when she wondered what color embarrassment would turn his skin.

Early on he quietly asked her to pass the rolls, and in her agitation she upset a glass of water over them. She knew better than to look at her father. She was already familiar with his customary visage of anger and disappointment, so she just pictured it as she knew it would be. The three proper grown-ups chatted mindlessly. Jacob's father was a relation of a business colleague of Mr. Wince's. He was a lawyer, and it sounded very much as if his cases were all very dry and complicated and uninteresting and lasted, oh, for years and years. "Jacob here"—he gestured toward his son with a mild whiff of distaste—"is a clerk in my office. In the back library."

"Yes, in the back," Jacob's mother murmured, poking her fork at a morsel of beef Iseult suspected she had no intention of eating, although she did look longingly at the place where the sodden bread basket had been before Sarah whisked it away.

Jacob's parents asked about the steelworks, and Iseult's father asked about the law courts, and then the conversation moved to the weather, and whether Surrey was an interesting enough place for a trip of several days. After the "back library" comment, Jacob was left out of the proceedings, and Iseult was never mentioned at all. She wondered whether this was how it felt in foreign countries where aristocrats arranged the marriages of their small children, talking over them, not even pretending they had a choice in the matter. In fact, she and Jacob had been so utterly forgotten that no one noticed when he said softly, "They don't like you much, do they?"

Iseult nerved herself to look at him properly. It was fascinating, really. Even the whites of his eyes were silver, with spidery red veins running through them, and Iseult wondered whether they were as sore as they looked. She looked away again.

ask him iseult ask him how he got to be this way because you don't want to marry him you want to see this one off quick

"No." Iseult looked at his silver hands sitting next to her ruddy ones. "Nor you."

and what if he's the last one, mother? what if there are no more to see off? father is done with me, no matter what. and they won't let me into the convent. i know this one won't love me they never do never will but i think he is the last. there are no more from today.

"Always silence." Iseult spat the words out like a spoiled piece of meat. Jacob made a gesture she could not interpret with his silver hands, but he said nothing. She wondered whether she could look at him every day until one of them died. She looked back at her lunch, rapidly cooling under a layer of grease. Something between her shoulder and her neck twitched and Iseult scooped up a massive forkful of congealed potatoes and crammed it into her mouth.

"Well, I suppose that's one way to deal with things," Jacob said in the same level tone as before, a gentle smile on his face as he regarded his parents and Iseult's father. He looked for all the world as if he were having a perfectly normal conversation with the woman next to him, with cheeks puffed out with food and tears beginning to stream from her eyes. Jacob's parents and Iseult's father smiled blandly back and continued with their benign conversation.

"Do you ever feel like a window display?"

Iseult swallowed the last bit of potato and straightened herself in her chair. She tilted her head in an approximation of normalcy, but the last eye contact was still too recent, so she looked at the buttons on his shirtfront. "How do you mean . . . exactly?"

"As if you were some curious or exotic good of unknown provenance set up in a shop window, gathering dust."

"And people walk by on their way to somewhere else and stop for a moment to stare and say unkind things that they don't believe you can hear?" Iseult said, raising her eyes to Jacob's collar, which met his silvered skin.

"Precisely so. And later they tell someone of the oddest thing that they saw in the window that day, and wasn't it funny?" Jacob spoke lightly, but Iseult listened closely and could hear the tinge of bitterness.

oh iseult i think not he is not for you for us so strange. people will laugh at you. better to be shut up in a convent than to be laughed at.

"I am laughed at already," Iseult said to her mother, but she met Jacob's eyes as she said it. Jacob looked as if he was about to speak, but thought better of it.

"Miss Wince, do you have . . . hobbies?" Jacob's father barked. Iseult looked up, startled, but Jacob seemed to accept it as a matter of course. Iseult tried to swallow, but there wasn't enough saliva in her mouth.

"I . . ." She looked at her father for help that she knew would not be forthcoming. His eyes had grown very bright; he tapped his fork on his plate once or twice, and Iseult knew that her answer was crucial to whatever was going to happen next.

tell them darling that you are quiet and good and a quiet good girl needs no exemplary hobbies as long as she has her mother with her

"I am . . ."
   devoted to my mother
"I am a great . . ."
   listener who listens to my mother
She could feel everyone at the table leaning forward in anticipation of something meaningful, and she found herself leaning forward too, waiting to hear what came out of her own dry mouth. She felt a great tug inside her pull her back, and the words burst forth. "I am a great walker, sir. I love to walk. That is my hobby. That is one of my hobbies. My greatest hobby, I do believe. Sir. I . . . read. And I sew. And I enjoy"—curse the liar!—"sitting with my father of an evening. But mostly sir I do love to walk whenever and as much as I can."

Iseult sat back in her chair, out of words. That number was usually her store for an entire week. She noted that while both of Jacob's parents looked mildly alarmed at the force of the words that had come out of her, they did not look displeased, exactly. She was breathing heavily from the exertion, but felt a sense of satisfaction. Her father looked baffled, but hid it well. She did not look at Jacob. As if rewarding her for a job well done, the parents resumed their banal small talk and left Iseult and Jacob well out of it.

There was a long silence, and Iseult's thoughts had drifted away into a pleasant nothingness, when Jacob said, "Where do you walk?"

She looked him full in his silver face and had to bite her tongue, hard, because the words "why are you silver?" almost slipped out. She concentrated instead on a little imperfection on his left cheek, maybe a dimple, maybe a twitch, it was hard to tell. She looked at his eyes again for a moment before she remembered that a question had been asked. "What?" She sat on her hand, because otherwise it would reach for her neck.

He smiled a polite, removed smile. "You said that you were a great walker, and I asked where your walks take you."

"As far away as possible," Iseult said. He seemed like a decent human being. He didn't seem slow, or sly, or cruel. She would try telling him the truth. Not too much truth, not so much truth that he turned and ran, but enough truth so that she wasn't hiding. Much.

"As far away as possible," Jacob repeated, in what Iseult thought was a presumptuously amused manner for someone who was the same color as the forks on the table. "And do you always return?"

This felt like a challenge, and Iseult was not used to being challenged. She was used to being fussed at or shouted down or ignored. And it was a silly question. "I always have so far. I'm here, aren't I?"

He again smiled as if she had said something amusing. Iseult was sure she was missing something, but she wasn't sure what. He didn't seem altogether real. He was polite and apparently in control of all of his faculties, but he was laughing at her, however gently. And who was he to laugh at her? He was silver. But . . . could it be . . . she liked him? She didn't hate him. That much could be said.

"Will you accompany me on a walk one day? I know that it is impolite for me to ask you something like that, impolite and overconfident, so we had better pretend that I didn't."

Jacob smiled again, a small smile this time. "I could pretend I asked you, and come to call one afternoon. Or we could plan to meet as if by accident, as if we were in the middle of a mad love affair."

Iseult could feel her mother writhing inside her and hoped it didn't show. It didn't, but a hot blush crawled up her neck, out of her collar, and clutched at her jaw like hands. Iseult's free hand twisted the napkin in her lap until she thought it might rip apart.

"Yes. I think we could do that." Iseult nodded, a small, sharp bob, and stood up, knocking her chair over with a bang and startling the entire table. "You must forgive me; I feel slightly unwell."

Without a backward glance, she walked out of the dining room with as measured a pace as she could muster, narrowly avoiding slamming into Mrs. Pennington and Sarah, who had been eavesdropping behind the door. She raced up the stairs to her own room, flung herself at the ivory basin by the mirror, and threw up everything she had just eaten.

When every trace of her lunch was gone, she pulled "The Unsuitables" from underneath the mattress and prepared to make an entry under "J." She sat at her desk for close to an hour, pen in hand, before admitting to herself that she did not have the heart to make the entry, on anyone's account.

10.

Iseult spent the next two days locked in her room, pleading ill-ness. Mrs. Pennington cajoled and begged, but she was not let inside. The rumblings in the house caused by her father stomping and slamming doors made the case that he was angry, or possibly more confused than angry. The only true predictor of Mr. Wince's anger was a deadly silence.

For those two days, Iseult sat curled in the corner of the room. She was in her nightgown, in a nest of blankets, but she did not sleep. The sun rose and set, rose and set, and she watched the shad-ows chase each other across the walls and ceiling. She had her small army of tools laid out in front of her: hairpins and hatpins, sewing needles and bits of wire, embroidery scissors, penknife, and even a nasty little cheese knife. Iseult liked it because it had both a serrated edge and two little prongs on the end, ostensibly for spearing a piece of cheese, not for jamming into one's flesh. But to each his own.

The current hiding place for her little bundle was inside a large bouquet of dried flowers, a souvenir Elspeth had given her from a wedding Iseult had not been invited to. At other times she hid her tools inside the lavender sachets in her dresser, in her stationery set (hiding needles in the inkpot had resulted in a permanent spot above her knee), or behind the back lining of a painting of geese that hung on Iseult's bedroom wall.

She lined them up and then she rearranged them, as if it mattered to someone besides herself. From smallest to largest, from pointiest to least pointy, from aesthetically pleasing to merely functional. From the least silver to the most.

Perhaps she would never see Jacob again. Perhaps she minded that, perhaps she didn't. It was hard to tell at this point. This exercise in complete on-her-own-ness was meant to determine that. What would happen after that determination was less certain.

She did know that she needed her mother to be quiet so she could get her own thinking done. There was an eerie almost-silence in her head already; the only sound was a rasp that told her that her mother was drawing in her breath before a tirade, the way a small child will inhale deeply to increase the power of an impending sob.

no, mother. i am cutting you off before you begin.
iseult! iseult. iseult

When you have said a word too many times, it begins to lose its meaning, its shape, its very wordness. Try it. Say "orange" aloud. Say it again and again. Write it down and stare at it. It has morphed into something unfamiliar, an arrangement of letters you cannot recall having seen in that particular formation before. If you were to see an orange right next to the word, then connecting the two would be a guess rather than a certainty.

Beatrice said Iseult's name over and over, questioning, threatening, pleading, until it became just a statement, and one that no longer had any relevance for her daughter. It was the middle of the night; Iseult propped a small mirror up against the enormous window looking out at the back garden.

Nothing was really in bloom. Nothing was ever really in bloom. There were a few elderly, wizened trees, a sickly rosebush planted by Beatrice, a lone violet pansy in a flower bed sporadically tended by Mrs. Pennington.

Weak moonlight spilled into the room, but it was enough for Iseult to see by. She opened the neck of her nightgown and yanked it down to her shoulder, while her mother continued to drone her name.

She started with the hatpin. It wouldn't inflict gratuitous damage. If a little would suffice, then it would. There was no need to overdo things.

She jammed the hatpin into the seam of the original scar, relishing the reassuring sting that radiated farther than the needle could reach.

iseult stop. stop please. you needn't. we can talk, surely.

Not working yet, then. Move onto the next. She pulled the hatpin out. It slid easily through the scar tissue and left only the tiniest speck of blood. She put it back in its place, at the beginning.

Next was a delicate penknife she had taken from an old desk of her father's, which he had obviously forgotten to check for contraband. She felt along her shoulder for a softer spot, fingers tapping up and down, listening for a less hollow sound, something fuller, more swollen. She found it in a dip in her crooked collarbone.

wait wait iseult wait

She gave the knife a swift, sharp tug, wondering if her father had ever imagined this while he cut the pages of a book or opened letters. The bead of blood became a bubble that grew over a ridge of skin and then trickled downward, edging toward her pristine white nightgown. Too late to take it off now; she would just have to wash it out herself. She waited.

And still. She could hear Beatrice repeating her name. Her voice was softer, perhaps, but still petulant and insistent. Iseult had thought silencing her might be easier. Maybe this was all more important than she had realized. Her hand hovered over several implements in their tidy row, rejecting each. No need to overdo it, but prolonging the process was not practical either.

The embroidery scissors. She had been allowed to keep them, because what young lady is complete without her embroidery tools? Iseult felt compelled to dedicate herself to immaculate sewing, in thanks to the gods of social niceties, whose praises she did not often sing.

She wiggled her left arm free of the sleeve to have more space to maneuver. She glimpsed a flash of her breast in the mirror and shuddered. Her body largely disgusted her, although she was not entirely sure why. She had received the usual sex education of a moderately privileged Victorian woman—that is to say, none. Having no mother, she couldn't even expect a timid lecture on the eve of any forthcoming wedding night. She hadn't had the luxury of whispered conversations among schoolfriends. No one ever whispered to her, unless it was to pass on a rumor that *accidentally* made its way back to her ears.

She had found some pictures hidden away in a book in her father's study about financial practices in the Far East. Her suspicions that her father would hide his worst secrets from her in what he imagined she would find the dullest place were well founded. She scanned the shelves until she found the most deadly title. Odd proof that she and her father thought alike.

These were hardly scandalous pictures. Not that Iseult knew that, though. She peered at them through squinted eyes and slatted fingers with a mixture of revulsion and . . . something else. It wasn't actually as bad as all that. A few heaving bosoms, uncorseted; one or two plump coquettes looking over their shoulders at their bare bottoms.

Mostly, she didn't understand what these pictures had to do with her father. Mostly, she didn't want to know. She tucked the pictures back into the book and thenceforth avoided that particular section of the study.

Now there were two voices to silence: Beatrice, and the voice that sometimes spoke to her of those pictures, and of what they might mean.

She wiped the scissors on her nightgown, to rid them of any tiny snips of thread that clung to them. She wiped her hand across the cut made by the penknife, smearing the half-clotted blood across her chest. She would tidy up later. She opened the scissors slightly, with her first two fingers gripping the handles.

The points of the scissors touched her skin; she raised them, about to strike, but then her nose itched and she had to stop to scratch it. It didn't do to be distracted. She could be scattered, yes, but she was not sloppy. If she meant to do something, then she meant to do it well.

Nose scratched, she returned to the task at hand, completing it with the least fuss. She liked the one-two punch of the scissors, liked that there was a formula to be followed. Stab snip, open stab snip, open stab snip. The proper order must be observed. Pins were easy, uncomplicated. Any type of blade was tricky, ambiguous. Could easily go wrong. But the scissors. If you followed the formula you had nothing to worry about.

She stabbed snipped and opened five times. She liked even numbers, but also fives. A heaviness was beginning to settle on her head, pressing her down, warming her neck and shoulders and beyond. She pressed a towel to her shoulder and curled up on the floor, making sure none of the blood would get to the rug. As said, Iseult learned her lessons. Once she had made a mistake, she did not make it again. Unless she chose to make it.

She could hear Beatrice still, but far, far off. She thought. No. Not far off. A place that was close but sounded far. One sailor to another on cantankerous voicepipes on a ship in the middle of the sea; they had seen nothing but the sea for days and days and they were too bored to listen to each other, too bored to say anything of consequence. That was how Beatrice sounded. Far off but still somewhere in the ether around Iseult. Inside her.

Iseult woke up the next day to silence, still curled up on her towel. She could tell by its crunchiness that getting up was going to be a trial, so for the moment she decided to stay put. There was an emptiness in her head and in her body—not loss or hunger, but lightness, as if gravity had only the merest hold on her. She could still hear Beatrice like a hovering bumblebee, but the bee was stingerless, the kind you could walk by and go about your day. A stingerless Beatrice. Oh, that was dreadful.

Iseult heard the scraping sound of another envelope underneath her door. Merciful heavens, what was it to be this time? Dinner with a man with no eyes? A man with fur? Siamese twins?

She could hear Mrs. Pennington panting away down the hall. She could tell by the fragment of color on the floor that the envelope was not from her father. It was gray. No. It was silver.

She jerked upright, knowing what a bad idea it was the whole time. She quashed a small "mrmphl" of pain with her right hand over her mouth. Her left hand was all rubbery pins and needles. She had tried to bring the towel with her, but part of it was wrenched away, the dried blood sticking to her skin and the floor in unequal measures.

A voice seemed to rise up over the wheezing pneumatic tube—not her mother's, for once, but her own.

Jacob? Could it be Jacob? Surely silver was too obvious. Was it Jacob?

She awkwardly crawled to her knees, then her feet, using her elbow to rise against the chair as a toddler might, armful of half-stuck towel coming with her. She shuffled barefoot across the floor, flinching as rug gave way to chilly wood.

As she bent to pick up the envelope, she heard a shrill shriek from Beatrice. "Oh, hush," she said aloud.

It had her name on it, Iseult Wince, but no address, so he must have come to the house. She hadn't heard the bell, but she hadn't been paying attention.

It was an ordinary envelope, just silver. As Jacob was ordinary, but silver. The handwriting was ordinary, apart from a marked disparity between the size of the first letter of each name and the rest. The result was ostentatious and stylized, and Iseult frowned. Jacob received his first minus in a list of pluses. She turned the envelope over. He had sealed it, which gained him a plus. Secrecy was a good sign. And he'd obviously come when Mr. Wince was out; otherwise the seal would have been broken.

She shuffled back to sit in the armchair and plucked a knife from her little arsenal on the floor. She slit the envelope's edge. She peered inside, sniffing the paper experimentally. No great clue. It smelled papery. Before pulling the letter out, she checked her fingers for bloodstains. Clean.

It wasn't technically long enough to be considered a letter. More like a memorandum. There was no salutation; her name was absent. Unorthodox, Iseult thought, not sure whether that was a plus or a minus.

I shall wait on the bench by the butcher in St. James's Square at two o'clock every day this week. Jacob.

And that was all. She turned the card over. Nothing. She held it up to the sunlight, not sure what she was expecting to see, but whatever it was, she didn't see it.

She assumed he was insinuating that he would be waiting for her arrival. That was plain enough. After all, she had been the one to suggest it at dinner. But she hadn't been thinking then, had she? If they went walking, they would be expected to converse. She had never been alone with a man other than her father. She wouldn't know how to behave. Would she be expected to take his arm? How would she know which arm?

She squinted at the small clock on her vanity table. It was after one. She couldn't be expected to go *today*. There wasn't time. And perhaps she didn't even want to go. She hadn't decided yet. She would decide tomorrow. Or the day after that. There was no rush. He said he would wait all week.

Iseult glanced down at her nightgown and saw the caked dried blood. It would have to be thrown away, along with the towel. She took the nightgown off, replacing it quickly with a dark robe, stuffing the ruined nightgown and towel underneath her mattress until they could be disposed of properly. She slid the letter in there as well. She moved toward her array of tools to hide them away, then hesitated. Maybe the letter should go under her pillow? No, that was too intimate. It would stay under the mattress.

It was only Monday. She had plenty of time to decide. And Beatrice was held at an appreciable distance for the time being. Iseult went off to scrub the blood from her skin, feeling a rare sense of self-satisfaction. Someone was waiting for her decision, and for once, the decision was entirely hers.

11.

The rest of Monday passed quietly for Iseult; still pleading illness with Mrs. Pennington, she rested and read, her mind feeling uncluttered. Tuesday she awoke and wondered whether she should go and meet Jacob at the bench by the butcher in the square at two o'clock, but she didn't want to come across as fast. Her shoulder was sore, but Beatrice had fallen completely silent, so she forwent her usual walking, preferring to nestle in the puddle of sunshine at her window and embroider. She liked to embroider with the same needles she used for other purposes. Not that she didn't clean them in between—she wasn't an animal—but there was a sense of putting a secret something of herself into her work, and any compliments on said work seemed instead to be directed at a crucial part of her Self, rather than at a mere means of combining fabric and thread.

Wednesday's dawn was so sluggish that it was only just recognizable as morning. The soupy sky put her in no mood for company. It did put her in the mood for walking, though. At one o'clock she slipped furtively out the front door and bolted in the opposite direction from the bench by the butcher in the square. She walked in as straight a line as possible, marveling at the silence in her head, reveling in it. She let thoughts of Jacob in, but only a little bit. It was still only Wednesday.

She would have been hard-pressed to describe *how* she was thinking of him. He was there, in her mind. The way Beatrice was, but also not like that. More benign. He wasn't a strong presence, more of an infusion. He was background. She saw a group of businessmen trickling out of a restaurant, slapping one another on the back. Jacob was one of them. A crowd of tourists craned their necks at a cathedral dome; he was one of them too. When Iseult paused to take in the bright colors of a sweet-shop window, she could see Jacob's reflection, next to the lemon drops. He was everywhere and nowhere, and Iseult walked on.

She wasn't ready to turn around when the skies unleashed a downpour. She tried to hurry home, but she had walked so far, and a pedestrian with an umbrella somehow moves faster than a pedestrian without. Iseult seemed to be the only one without. She was jostled by a hundred scurrying shoulders, and doubly drenched by the dripping from their black umbrellas racing past.

One of her cuts had been red and puffy since the evening before, and now it began to ache fiercely. She passed a nondescript church with a decrepit graveyard, and took advantage of the fact that the congregation clearly did not employ a regular gardener. Picking her way through wild shrubbery that slapped at her wet skirts, she reached the patchy cover of a small weeping willow, and perched atop a ledgerstone, murmuring her apologies to a certain Mrs. Thistlethwaite. Surely Iseult wouldn't have minded if the situations were reversed, and a wet and weary traveler sought shelter over her bones. *Welcome!* she would shout up through the clay.

She didn't think of suicide often, and then only abstractly. She would have been surprised to hear someone suggest that she might consider it. She saw no connection between what she did and a genuine desire to die. She wanted to live, of course; who didn't?

She just wanted to live in a different way, and it was difficult to achieve, and most didn't understand the means to her end.

It had been mentioned to her over the years, by cruel schoolmates (and her father), that her death would be more beneficial to others than her life. She'd never cared much when other girls sneered this at her, and from her father she took it as a challenge to live as long as possible.

The rain showed no signs of stopping, but she was largely protected underneath the tree. Soggy rain spots on her black dress looked like seeping blood, although possibly only to Iseult. She tried to think about marriage. She honestly didn't know much about it, hadn't witnessed many marriages firsthand. Her father had not, to her knowledge, even considered remarriage. Mentions of Mr. Pennington were few and far between, as well of being devoid of much detail. Her aunt Catherine had a husband, Fordham, who was wide and overbearing. He behaved toward everyone with a forced familiarity that made Iseult squeamish, and whenever she had to submit to a kiss on the cheek in greeting or farewell, she would leave the room as soon as possible to wipe away his saliva. He often chastised his children publicly in a way that embarrassed those who witnessed it. Mr. Wince found him boorish. It was one of the few opinions that father and daughter shared.

And Iseult saw very little interaction between Catherine and Fordham, who communicated mainly through their servants, their children, and a complicated series of sighs and coughs. She had never seen even the smallest affections exchanged. Her cousin Elspeth she saw showered with somewhat sickly affection by her husband, and that did not appeal to Iseult either—to be fawned over and pawed at; both of them always had an eye on the rest of the room, as if gloating at their good luck.

Other than that, other than married couples at the dinner parties she loathed, and people she saw from afar, the only marriages she had any knowledge of existed in books. Iseult was no fool; those weren't real. Although she knew herself to be more unhappy than many people, she was sure that no one was as happy as people in books appeared, and there were even a great many people more unhappy than herself.

If the stars were to align somehow. If Jacob did not wholly object to her, nor she to him. If both sets of parents could agree. If suitable housing could be found. If. Ifififif.

She had to go and meet Jacob. She knew that. She was certain that to do otherwise would mean to be condemned forever to her father's house. And when her father died, what then? No one had ever discussed that eventuality with her. But as uncharted as that future would be, would the alternative—being married off to a stranger—not be worse? She would be condemned to that companionship for much longer, unless the husband were to die young. And that couldn't be the correct way to begin a marriage, gauging how long your prospective partner might live.

It was at such times that Iseult did contemplate suicide. Each choice was the devil's choice: continue to live with her father, or be sold to a stranger.

She realized the sky was beginning to darken as evening fell, and she didn't know what time it was. She looked up at the church's crumbly, sooty tower, but the church bells were still.

There was a rustle amid the wet leaves collecting at the corners of a nearby grave, and Iseult saw a hedgehog poke out his nose, sniffing the air, bobbing up and down, beady eyes reflecting the autumnal gloom. Iseult poked her toe out from under her great skirts, and the sudden movement startled the little fellow so that he snapped right up into a ball. How Iseult wished she could do the same.

It was a defense mechanism she had affected for years, making herself impervious to input from anything outside herself, shooting out prickled barbs when the world came too close, relaxing only when the danger had passed and all was quiet. She didn't know why, but it seemed to be the end of the road this time.

Something was about to end. She felt her heart gallop, crashing about in her ribs. Whatever was about to happen was not what she wanted, although if you'd asked her what she did want, she would have had nothing to say. She wanted to go on unnoticed, unbothered, unperturbed. But her time was up.

She slunk in before dinner, and it was remarked upon that she was bedraggled and more out of sorts than usual. She refused help in dressing, even though she knew that would lead Mrs. Pennington to suspect mischief on her part.

She was chilled and sneezy all through dinner, wiping her nose with her napkin because she knew it would irk her father. But he remained undisturbed.

"Excellent of you to join me at last, Iseult," he said, scraping his spoon along the bottom of the soup bowl to irk *her*. "I haven't seen you since our lunch. I trust the food did not disagree with you?"

"No, Father," she replied, snuffling mightily.

"Would you care to guess whom I lunched with today?" The long sighing scrape of his spoon on the china shot a shiver through her neck, so Iseult rolled her head slightly until there was an audible crack.

"I've no idea, Father; with whom did you lunch?"

"With our guest from the other night, Mr. Vinke." He paused, waiting for a reaction that was not forthcoming. "Jacob's father."

Iseult felt a tremor of unknown provenance, but kept it out of her voice. "Did you? Was it . . . enlightening?"

Mr. Wince looked blankly at his daughter. "I would have said pleasant, interesting, but . . . enlightening? I'm not sure any new information was presented. We discussed Jacob's prospects, of course, his relevant skills and education, whether or not he could be suitably employed in the steelworks, he's really more progressively educated than I'd like, you see, we don't want him thinking he can implement anything, well, experimental—"

"And why, exactly, is it suddenly a foregone conclusion that Jacob will be employed in the steelworks? Because you lunched with his father? This is how you interview your workers now? Nepotism?" A fury had grabbed her, and she wondered if there mightn't be a fine steam rising from the top of her head.

"Frankly, I wasn't aware you even knew the word 'nepotism.' I underestimated you. Well done."

Iseult slammed a fist onto the table, making the dinner, the dishes, the cutlery, the candle flames, and her father jump.

"Would you care to tell me the cause of this particular outburst?" Mr. Wince said, his voice turning dangerous and low.

She could easily match his warmth. "Are you giving Jacob a job in exchange for his willingness to take me? He can't get a job elsewhere looking like that, I'm sure. So it's not as I've always feared, exactly. You haven't sold me. You've bartered me."

Mr. Wince threw his napkin on the table. "Look here, my girl. This man is possibly willing to marry you. It is immaterial to me whether I have had to bribe him with all manner of riches. I will be rid of you in any case. I should think you would thank me for taking the time and care to find a man who is at least morally decent. Believe me"—he spat, a finger in her face—"I could have made arrangements that would have been far more beneficial to me, and far less pleasant for you. If I'd have known you would be this ungrateful, I wouldn't have bothered. Although I don't know why I'm surprised. You were born ungrateful."

The two of them sat there, heaving, not looking at each other.

Despite herself, Iseult's voice broke on the next words. "He's silver."

Was there, possibly, just possibly, a tinge of regret, of something like sympathy for his only child in his response? He exhaled. "I know."

Iseult looked at her soup; a scum of oil was forming on its surface. "But why? Do you know . . . why?"

Mr. Wince rose, and Iseult could see him slide his hands into his pockets. "Does it matter, Iseult? No one . . . no one else will have you. Iseult. This . . . this is all there is. You will marry him."

She felt so at sea that she didn't even flinch when he placed an awkward hand on her shoulder. Not her left shoulder; he knew better than that. There was nothing more to say, and Mr. Wince left the room, so there was no one left to say it to.

So she had one more morning. One more day in which to . . . plan? Plan an escape, a façade. No. She had one morning to wait. Her father sent her a note telling her that they would dine with Jacob's family the next week and formalize the engagement, make plans for the wedding. She had the morning, and then she would meet Jacob, and find out what sort of person he was, or what sort of person he chose to present to her.

She didn't undress at all that night. She left the house before Mrs. Pennington was up, almost before the sun peeked its tired eyes over the dingy skyline. As she marched along the streets, she noted a faint stench, a sourness, arising from her. She did not care. No one could bother her this morning, her last morning.

12.

After hours of traipsing up one street and down the next, she had come to a decision. She made her way to the bench by the butcher, pleased to find that her resolution strengthened with each step. She practiced her lines. She would begin with a no-nonsense handshake, and say, "It appears as if our parents have already decided. It will be easier if we offer no resistance. Let us treat this marriage as a business arrangement, as our parents have. I shall expect nothing of you if you expect the same of me."

Her resolve wavered as she turned a corner to see that he was already on the bench. An elderly man passed by, openly staring at him. Jacob looked back at him unperturbed, and she felt surer as she approached him. She was still a few steps away when he turned his head and saw her. He brightened perceptibly and stood. She stuck her hand out too soon to seem natural, and was inhaling to unleash her prepared speech when he grasped her hand in both of his.

"Miss Wince," he said, smiling. "I'm so pleased that you've come. I was beginning to fear you would not."

Iseult's train of thought was utterly derailed. She stood dumbly, staring at her chafed pink hand between his two silver hands, and thought it looked like an animal caught in a trap.

"Are you all right? Perhaps you would like to sit?" He looked at her with concern, and Iseult felt a ripple of irritation.

"I am quite well, Mr. Vinke. And I prefer to walk, if you don't mind."

He bent his silver face in acquiescence, and the two of them started off down the road. Iseult's mind churned furiously, trying to remember what it was she had come to say, while Jacob remarked upon various things in shop windows, the weather, and a number of other banalities. They paused crossing a street to let a carriage pass; there was a silence a hair's breadth too long to be comfortable, and Iseult felt compelled to speak. So she blurted out the question that had been hovering on her tongue all day.

"Why is your skin that color?"

A small boy passing them snorted, and his mother shushed him and hurried him on, although not before sneaking a furtive glance herself. Iseult felt hot with shame, both at her rude question and at her own embarrassment at being seen in public with Jacob, for the knowledge that people assumed some relationship between them. "I'm sorry. You needn't answer that."

"But it's a perfectly natural question, Miss Wince. If your hair had a violet hue, I would certainly question you as to its provenance. If we are to marry, you've every right to know why I look as I do."

Iseult stumbled on the pavement at the word "marry," and Jacob took her elbow to steady her. She flinched, but managed not to shake him off.

"Since childhood I have suffered from a mild, noncontagious, but very irritating skin condition. It made every waking moment very uncomfortable for me. The only treatment that has been able to keep that sensation away contains a good deal of silver, which unfortunately does have one very obvious side effect when swallowed. But I find the stares of strangers much less intrusive than skin that feels perpetually aflame."

Iseult was unused to honest answers to honest questions, and merely said, "Oh."

They moved along in a slightly more companionable silence, Jacob ignoring their fellow pedestrians' curiosity, Iseult pretending to ignore it by concentrating on the ground. They turned through the gate of a small park, which was blessedly empty, at least.

More words popped into her mouth. "Are . . . are we to marry, then?"

It wasn't the way she'd meant to phrase it, but maybe she should cut through the niceties and get to the point.

Jacob sighed and stopped walking, so Iseult stopped too. There was a very large, very dead rosebush in front of them, which they mutually, tacitly agreed to stare at.

"I think we must. My parents have presented it to me as my only option, which I assume is how your father presented the matter to you."

Iseult nodded and reached out a finger to a bright yet forlorn inchworm on the dead bush. She felt a twitch at her shoulder warning against it, but she let the tiny thing wobble its way on.

"It isn't that I hold anything against you, of course. I know nothing about you. I had just always hoped that this was a decision I would make for myself. But look at me"—he extended a hand in her direction—"who would have me?"

"Only a misfit such as myself," Iseult said, flicking the hapless inchworm to the earth and grinding it mercilessly under her boot.

Jacob was quiet, obviously embarrassed. "That's not what I mean, Miss Wince."

"Of course it is," Iseult spat out. "I am well aware of my reputation after my father's numerous failed attempts to pawn me off on someone, anyone. I am thought strange at the very least, silent and odd. At the worst I am thought possessed by some demon, most likely with blood dripping from my teeth. Believe me, Mr. Vinke, you have a much easier time of it. I am reminded every step of the way that I am not what anyone wants."

"I admit that I had heard things about you before we met." Jacob still wasn't looking at her, but at least he was speaking more in her direction. He coughed to get through the next words. "Unflattering things. But thus far I have seen no evidence of there being any truth in such rumors."

Iseult peered down at the earthworm's mortal remains, waiting for Beatrice to pipe up with an opinion, a directive. But there was nothing.

"Miss Wince?" Jacob ducked his head slightly so their eyes were on the same level. "I hope I have not said something to upset you."

Iseult stared at his lips. They would have been a nice shade of red, but the silver dulled them to a dusky, sickly shade, making a flake of dry skin at one corner stand out all the more. She wondered what it would be like to be kissed by those lips. She wondered what it would be like to be kissed at all. She didn't imagine that it could be very pleasant. She preferred not to be touched.

"Do you not find me . . . abhorrent?" Iseult asked, bracing herself for an internal pinch from her mother. None came.

"Abhorrent? Not at all," Jacob smiled and crinkly lines appeared around his eyes, making him look very old. "You are very different from anyone I have met before, I will say that. I have the feeling that you always speak your mind, even when it is not polite. And you do not see the world in the usual way, I believe. But abhorrent? No."

Iseult considered smiling, but wasn't sure it would be appropriate. A fat sparrow flew onto the branch of the dead rosebush, which rustled its dryness violently in response.

"It's a strange situation we find ourselves in, isn't it?"

It seemed more definitely appropriate to smile at that, so Iseult did, making sure to keep her mouth closed. At school she had been mightily teased for her sharply pointed teeth, led by an especially keen right incisor. Her father had once taken her to an exhibition about primitive cultures (presumably because Mrs. Pennington and Aunt Catherine were so vociferously against it). There had been a portrait of a group of pygmies, which in itself would have been startling enough for a ten-year-old British girl, and their broad grins revealed mouths full of sharpened teeth like miniature daggers. Iseult was convinced that her father had brought her to show her this particular likeness, even though he didn't mention it again afterward. But she was ever after conscious not to smile widely, lest people suppose she had been raised in the Congo.

"I do not expect . . . love, Miss Wince. In either direction." Jacob poked the remains of the poor inchworm further into the dirt with his toe, which struck Iseult as kindly, a rough burial after the brutal murder. "I have never loved anyone, and no one has ever loved me."

"Your parents?" Iseult asked. "Surely they must care for you, and you for them."

"No, I don't believe there is affection on either side." The inchworm rites completed, Jacob extended a hand toward the path and they began again to walk. "We tolerate each other. There is perhaps even a grudging respect at times. But at this point all I am is a hindrance to my sisters' chances at marriage. I have two younger sisters, and I am standing in their way."

"Do you not love them?"

"No."

Iseult was surprised, impressed at how matter-of-fact these admissions were.

"They are naïve, silly girls, and they are ashamed of me. They would not survive a moment in this world without my parents' money."

"My father hates me," Iseult said. She was aiming for the same lackadaisical tone, but there were slivers of venom in her voice.

"Why does he hate you?"

Iseult was pleased that he didn't ask why she *thought* her father hated her, but rather trusted her judgment.

"There are many reasons, but the reason for all the other reasons is that I killed my mother." Iseult concentrated very hard on walking in a straight line and not seeming as if she were bracing for interference, which only caused her to bump into Jacob.

"Why should he think such a terrible thing as that? Pardon me," Jacob said, taking her elbow, most likely thinking she had forced a stumble in order to bring them into physical contact. Iseult wasn't skilled enough in feminine charm to effect such a move. But he looked at her and smiled, taking her hand and wrapping it into the crook of his elbow. She willed herself to keep moving, speaking, breathing. She had better get used to this, if they were to marry.

"Because I did," she blurted, and the admission gave her the curious sensation of her hair being pulled at the roots, from inside her head.

"I'm sorry, Miss Wince; I have tired you, and you are unwell." He stopped their progress in the middle of the pavement, forcing other pedestrians to walk around them, and making them even more conspicuous than they already were. Her heart was pounding and she tugged him forward.

"Please keep walking," she heard herself sputter. Her eyes darted about for an escape and found it in a narrow lane that she knew to be secluded. She was ashamed as she hustled him down it, but they simply could not keep standing in the street like specimens in a carnival sideshow. Iseult pressed sharp shoulder blades into the cold wall behind her. Jacob looked at her solemnly.

"If it is so dreadful a thing to be seen with me, then perhaps this is not going to work after all," he said quietly.

"Can't you understand?" Iseult felt, as she often did with people, that she was conversing with someone very ignorant if the truth was not plain to them. "They stare at you as if you were a carnival monstrosity on display, but don't you know yet? I am more monstrous by far."

Jacob laughed the short, sad laugh of a man defeated, and backed away from her until he leaned against the wall opposite. "You are strange, I will grant. You have spent perhaps even more time alone than I myself, which could make anyone strange. But I do not see anything which would warrant the label of monstrous."

There was a jagged chunk of brick behind Iseult's waist, and she worked her left fist into it, finding some measure of relief in the pain. "My mother . . ." she began, but couldn't find it in herself to continue.

why don't you speak? you must be aching to.

"Your mother . . . passed away in childbirth, I believe?" Jacob again bent his head to bring her eyes up from the ground. "So I cannot see that it was any fault of your own. Although if you know otherwise, please do enlighten me."

There was a tinge of amusement in his voice, a shade of mollification, and Iseult jabbed her fist again at the broken masonry, feeling a strip of skin leave her hand like peel from a carrot.

"I hope that I will not alarm you with my indelicacy, but what happened was that a bone broke here"—Iseult's right hand smacked at her collarbone as her other fist scraped away at the wall again—"and it cut my mother inside and she bled to death."

It was Jacob's turn to look at the ground, and Iseult felt a sense of triumph, although over whom she didn't yet know—Jacob? Her mother? Her father? It would come to her later. For now, she felt as if she had won. "So, Mr. Vinke, if her death was not at my hands, pray tell me who is responsible. My father has always considered me to be at fault, and I must confess that is one thing upon which we are in agreement."

Her hand began to throb, but the sense of impending victory kept her head high. This marriage wasn't going to work; how could it? It would be akin to leaving two cripples alone in a house where everything was on the fifth floor. No. She would prefer a convent to this public humiliation. She would be damned if her father was rid of her so easily.

Something inside her curdled in disgust and, again wondering where Beatrice could have got to, Iseult grasped her head in her hands. Her fingers threaded their way into her hair and she wondered idly how long it would take to pluck every single strand from her head. As she stood looking at the cobblestones, she saw rather than heard Jacob's feet come close to hers.

"What has happened to your hand?"

Iseult straightened up immediately, thanking her aunt silently as she plunged the wounded hand into her pocket, and attempting to smooth her hair with the other.

"Mr. Vinke, I believe that you were correct before. I should very much like to go home. You are right. I am unwell."

"Of course," Jacob said. There was silence, and Iseult realized that he was holding out his arm for her to take. For her to take with her left hand.

Iseult wanted to go home. She didn't care if she never married. She didn't care if her father locked her in her room and stopped feeding her. She didn't care she didn't care she didn't care.

She took her hand out of her pocket and wrapped it in the crook of his elbow. He looked calmly at the wreck she had made of her poor fingers, reached into his pocket for his handkerchief, and wrapped it gently around her hand, holding it in place with his own.

They walked back to the Wince home in silence.

The walk was a blur for Iseult. Was she glad it was over and she had driven him away? Because it was surely over. Surely.

Her father would certainly do his worst. In a way, she was curious as to what his worst would be. He had never raised a hand to her. Not even the time when she was twelve and bit his hand, although on that occasion she could see that he longed to thrash her. She wished he would, so their mutual hatred could at last be tangible instead of just another ghost in the house. Maybe thrashing her would relieve the awful tension between them, and they could coexist peacefully in their ignorance of each other. One ghost fewer, two more, did it make any difference?

They had nearly reached the front gate when Iseult remembered that members of her household would be more than a little surprised to see her swan up to the door on Jacob's arm. Trying not to be abrupt but failing, she removed her hand, handkerchief and all (she suspected it was now part and parcel of her fingers) and gave what she supposed to be an Oriental bow of apology.

"I will see that the housekeeper returns your handkerchief to you, and I am very sorry about the whole . . . business." She looked for a better word but couldn't come up with anything. Business was what it was, anyway; they had at least agreed on that much.

"Nonsense," Jacob said, smiling. "You are feeling unwell and we shall simply continue our conversation another time. There is nothing to apologize for."

Iseult pursed her lips, annoyed now. One of them was misinterpreting the situation. She believed that it was him.

"Mr. Vinke, I don't think you understand." She spoke slowly and clearly, as if he were deaf or elderly, or merely not very clever. "I am releasing you from any . . . obligation that we may have discussed earlier."

He continued to smile pleasantly at her, not saying a word.

"Look, I promise you'll get the handkerchief back, and we'll consider the matter settled."

"Miss Wince, the return of the handkerchief is immaterial." And still with the bland smile. He just stood there, smiling as if they had shared a pleasantly banal afternoon. She waited for him to say goodbye. And waited. She didn't want to be any ruder than she needed to be after the disastrous afternoon, but he didn't seem to be leaving her with much of a choice.

"Well," she said slowly, giving him one last chance to release her from what was sure to be an embarrassing farewell. "I do appreciate your taking time to discuss this with me, and I truly am sorry for any inconvenience and . . ." How long was he prepared to let her keep going? She longed to be elsewhere and to be done with the whole stupid thing, to tuck it away in a drawer like stockings she never meant to wear again. "And I have enjoyed . . . knowing you, and our walk, and . . . good day. Goodbye. I am sorry to have wasted your time, but surely you agree it is better this way."

Here Jacob wrinkled his largish silver nose, as if he had just been dropped into her speech and wasn't sure which bit she was at. "Better which way?"

Iseult huffed in exasperation. If she hadn't exactly disliked him before, she was beginning to now. "Better that we know that we are ill suited, Mr. Vinke, and we can regretfully but respectfully inform our parents that the attempt at a match has failed."

He shook his head as if genuinely surprised. "But, Miss Wince, I did think that we were in agreement earlier. That we thought we might as well try it as not. Didn't you say . . . ?"

He had a pathetically questioning tilt to his eyebrows, making him the double of a stray dog.

"Well, yes, I did, but . . . but don't you see now it would be of no use?"

"I don't see that at all," he said, stepping closer while his voice grew quiet, which in turn made Iseult feel that she should step closer and speak more quietly as well. Whatever it took to put an end to this ridiculous charade.

"I think we had a fine time. A few hiccups, some understandable awkwardness, you aren't feeling your best, but what I can surmise from both today and our previous meeting, Miss Wince, is that I like you, and that is far more than I can say for any other of my prospective brides." Iseult's shoulder twitched at the word "brides" and she realized that they were standing close enough that she could feel the edges of his breath float by her face. She began to breathe through her mouth, feeling that it would be unseemly to know what his breath smelled like.

"But I don't think that will last very long, you liking me."

"Let me worry about that," he said, and then the nose wrinkle again, but sadder this time.

She inched backward, edging along the iron fence until she felt the space of the open gate at her back. She gave a highly perfunctory curtsy.

"Again, thank you, and good day, and my apologies," she said too loudly, as a pedestrian was passing and she didn't want them to assume some sort of lovers' quarrel. A shiver of something ran through her at the appearance of the word "lovers" in her head. She was aware that Jacob was saying something, but she had already decided not to listen. Stumbling slightly over her own feet, she turned and ran to the front steps, which had rarely looked so dear. As she banged the door knocker, she threw words over her shoulder, more to drown out the sound of his voice than to provide any real information: "Try not to worry about the handkerchief!"

He was still saying something when Iseult fell inside the door as Mrs. Pennington pulled it open. She crashed to the floor, a tangle of knees and elbows and fabric. Mrs. Pennington was gathering her resources to fuss when Iseult cried, "Close the door, close the door!"

Mrs. Pennington did hastily close the door, but immediately her fists went to her hips. "Now, Miss Iseult, you are going to explain to me exactly what is going on, and don't even think of trying to tell a lie. You're no good at it and you never have been."

Iseult stayed in her heap on the floor, wanting to wait until her joints stopped echoing with pain, rubbing a knee exaggeratedly with her undamaged hand, hiding the other hand, and trying to think of a lie that wasn't too far from the truth. Mrs. Pennington's eyes became small and beady, and for a moment, Iseult felt relief when she heard the knock on the door. But that lasted no more than a moment, until she realized that there was only one person who could be on the other side.

Iseult scrambled to her feet as if she'd been pinched and tore off up the stairs. Mrs. Pennington was either too stunned or too angry to call after her. Iseult slammed the door shut to her room, but she wanted to keep running; she ran across her bedroom to the armoire. She could hear voices downstairs. She opened the doors and climbed inside, pushing her way past the winter coats and dresses, stiff with tissue paper and reeking of must, and she wrestled the doors closed behind her. It was chokingly warm, but that felt about right. Squashed behind everything like that, she discovered that all sounds from below were so muffled that they weren't recognizable as human voices. They might have been squeaking mice or barking dogs, for all Iseult knew.

She thought she could hear her mother's disapproval, though. A silent censoriousness with which she was intimately familiar. Was she imagining it? She sank to the floor, knees coming up to meet her chin. The handkerchief was still stuck to her bloody fingers. Iseult felt stupid and embarrassed; surely things couldn't get any worse than this. But she had felt that before, and things almost always got worse afterward. She rubbed some spit into the dried blood on the handkerchief to loosen its grip.

It came away with blessed ease. Iseult sniffed the fabric to see whether it smelled like Jacob, but there was only the rusty scent of blood mixed with her own saliva. Her knuckles were bare of skin, and would take ages to heal. When she was small and had hurt herself, Mrs. Pennington would laugh and say, "You'll be better before you're married." A thought that had always made Iseult uneasy. Marriage at that time had been so far in the future. Would she be hurt for so long? Mightn't things heal sooner than that? Now, with the specter of an actual marriage (however unlikely) hovering in her field of vision, she wanted her skin to stay raw. Maybe injury could stave things off a little longer.

Iseult moved to press her ear against the back wall of the armoire, jamming a hole in a hatbox with an elbow as she did. The collapse triggered a puff of dust and she stifled a sneeze. She could hear the faraway hint of a conversation, presumably between her father and Jacob. She pulled herself in smaller and smaller, pressing her face into her knees, and her eyeballs began to throb pleasantly. The blackness behind her eyelids changed shades, rippling with charcoal and grays, shot through with bruised yellows. Iseult thought she might stay in the armoire indefinitely. She was getting used to the heat.

13.

Iseult's father's footsteps grew louder and faster, and Iseult's heart-beat sped up to match itself to to their rhythm. As he walked toward the bedroom, Mrs. Pennington's footsteps could be heard bustling alongside his, and Iseult's heart pounded loud to drown them out. She resisted the urge to press her knees further into her eyes. She started to see small silvery worms wriggling back and forth across her field of vision. She wished there were more dresses in the armoire to put between the outside and herself, and she tucked in her feet so her shoes weren't visible.

There was a knock on the bedroom door, unnecessary since Mr. Wince had never grasped that the point of knocking was to determine whether there was someone on the other side who wished that you come in. Or not. Mr. Wince merely knocked and entered, even when he visited other people's homes. Iseult had seen him surprise a number of servants and housekeepers while on social calls, entering homes as if they were his own. Iseult was surprised now.

"I don't understand; where is she?" he said. Mrs. Pennington's sigh sounded like a weighty thing, which Mr. Wince ignored. "She's not here. Did the little fool climb out a window?"

Iseult pressed her knees so hard against her eyes that her ears began to hurt, and colors she couldn't name flashed against her eyelids. She thought she might be sick.

"Iseult, your father wants to speak with you. Please come out," Mrs. Pennington said in a thin voice. Mr. Wince opened the door and began pawing through the clothes, a whoosh of air signaling that he had moved the correct ones to uncover her hiding place. She let up the pressure on her eyes and raised her head, blinking until she could focus again.

"Get up, Iseult, for Christ's sake."

Iseult looked up sharply. Her father was not one to swear. He did not extend a hand to help her rise.

Mrs. Pennington sidestepped him and reached into the armoire to pull her out. Iseult's knees didn't want to straighten; she stumbled.

Mr. Wince breathed noisily through his nose. "Mr. Vinke, for whatever reason, has asked for your hand in marriage. I have given it to him. You will marry in two months. And you will no longer be my concern."

Iseult looked hard at her father's shoes. They were plain black. Elegant yet simple. They had most likely been expensive, they were sturdy, and they would last him a long time. She didn't know where he had gotten them. But they seemed to be very nice shoes. Anyone seeing these shoes might think their owner a reasonable, thoughtful man. It was likely that he saw himself as a reasonable and thoughtful man. But Iseult was thinking that she knew very little about her father, and that he knew very little about her. It was probably for the best if they were to part ways for good.

She could feel Mrs. Pennington's sweaty palm through her sleeve, could sense that everyone was waiting to hear her speak, but she didn't feel like speaking. She noticed that the stitching on her father's shoes was so delicate and deft that she had to squint to see it at all. The man who had made the shoes was probably a much better man than her father was. She felt Mrs. Pennington nudge her with a round, warm hip. Iseult raised her eyes to meet her father's, and began to say what was expected.

"Thank you, Father. I will marry him. I promise . . . I promise that I will be . . ." Iseult felt the words slowing down as they came out of her mouth like sludge, and she had forgotten what was supposed to come next.

She tried to imagine what Beatrice would say if she were there.

"—willbeadutifuldaughteruntilthen." The last words of the sentence shot out like a starter's pistol, loud and clear and sharp. She worried that it might have sounded as if she had said "beautiful," but it didn't matter. He would hate her no matter what she said.

They stood there looking at each other out of identical eyes, too angry and self-pitying to have any pity left over for each other. He wanted to slap her face, which wasn't enough like her mother's to be pretty. She wanted to claw out his eyes, so hers would be the only ones left. Neither of them felt like expending the energy this would have required.

His mustache twitched, a thing separate from the rest of him. "You can do what you like until then. Dutiful or not, I don't care. You can live in the armoire for the next two months. Only know that on the day I designate, you will marry him and you will leave this house for good. I will be polite and civil. I will do whatever needs to be done to avoid scandal. Dinner parties, christenings, weddings, funerals. But no more."

Iseult felt compelled to curtsy for the second time that day. Wasn't the day over yet? It was taking a very long time to reach its conclusion. Iseult swayed but didn't bend, and the tightness in her throat relaxed. Mrs. Pennington's arm stayed resolutely around her, firm and sweaty, but it was small comfort.

"Do you require a response from me?" Iseult asked her father, who didn't seem to be in a hurry. "Do you want me to plead with you? To let me stay here, unmarried? To let me go but stay always my loving father? I won't plead with you. You wouldn't listen anyway."

He moved slightly as if to go, lifting a foot from the carpet but putting it back down again. Opened his mouth and closed it. Was something softening in him? Even a little? Again the dragon-like breath through the nostrils, the slightest disruption in the mustache hair. He made himself taller, somehow. "Perhaps your mother would have loved you."

He turned and left so quickly that he likely did not hear Mrs. Pennington gasp. Iseult shrugged off the dead weight of that hot arm. "It would only have been surprising if he had said something kind," Iseult said, putting on the chilly smile she reserved for company. Mrs. Pennington looked heartbroken, and Iseult could not bear it. On a better day Iseult would have tried to cheer her somehow, but this was not that better day.

14.

For the next week, Iseult considered the prospect of drowning as if she were in imminent danger of it. Her bed was her life raft, the floor the sea. Mrs. Pennington brought her meals on a tray. It was easy to plead sick because she could only get down the slightest morsels of food. She was hungry, but she didn't care that she was hungry. She couldn't maintain the feeling of caring long enough to complete an action. A spoonful of rice would leave the plate but then hover in midair, until it began to feel cumbersome and she put it down.

She was afraid. Of marriage. Of Jacob. Of leaving the only home she had known. Of leaving her father. As odious as he was, he was her father, and in the times when neither of them needed something from the other they coexisted as easily as if they each lived alone. She was afraid of what her mother's place was to be in this new arrangement. She was afraid of telling Jacob about her mother.

It wasn't that she had spent hours discussing her mother's presence with Mrs. Pennington and her father, but Iseult knew that they knew. They might not agree with her assessment of the situation, but they knew. Mrs. Pennington accepted it as best she could, and would even awkwardly ask after Beatrice on occasion.

But Beatrice was gone.

Since the day after the lunch, she had been quiet. Iseult knew that this was her own fault, and she now regretted silencing her. She wasn't sure what to do, as she'd never been in the position before of *needing* to hear her mother's voice inside her.

So Iseult did the only thing she could do, and she went to see her mother.

As she entered the churchyard, the groundsman nodded to her and she nodded back. They often greeted each other thus at hours other people would regard as unsuitable. No one bothered her here. The minister, the parishioners, all knew of her, even though she and her father attended services infrequently, and apart from polite pleasantries they spoke to no one.

She wove her way through the graves, through the grass that tugged at her skirts like tiny hands. Not yet, she said to them silently. Not long, perhaps, but not yet.

Beatrice Wince's tomb lay off to the side. The churchyard was very old, and shortly after her death there had been an all-consuming fad for the new. Beatrice was one of the last to have been interred there. They had been running out of room anyway. Several streets away was a more popular church and cemetery, with a new building and headstones that were guaranteed not to erode. There were graves here where the words were worn smooth by the weather, and only the mildewed records book inside the church could tell you whose body lay beneath, whose body was once wept over in a given spot.

Iseult hoped that by coming to the grave she would earn forgiveness without expressly having to ask for it. But she sat and sat, and that cottony stillness inside her head persisted. She chewed on her lower lip, pulling off a flake of dead skin and pondering her next move. She stared at her mother's name. The letters had been traced by Iseult's fingers in the way that other children love a favorite doll or bear until its hair falls out and its eyes become dull.

When she was small, she had believed that she could find out all sorts of secrets about her mother this way, and had spent so much time tracing the letters that she had dreams that consisted of nothing else, just her hands moving over the grave. And it was true that when she did this her mother spoke to her, but she spoke only of Iseult and never of herself as Iseult longed for her to do. It had made Iseult angry. She would ask endless questions but they were always deflected.

When she was ten or eleven, this had made her wonder whether it was true that, as everyone else said, she merely had the delusion that her mother was inside her. But she wasn't crazy. She knew that. And her mother's voice had always been there, she remembered its presence in her earliest memories, telling her not to pick up a stone at the seaside because it was dirty, whispering to her to slide her chubby child's body under her bed while her father raged over some paltry misbehavior. Those thoughts hadn't come from her own consciousness; she was certain of that.

And sometimes (not terribly often, it must be admitted), when Iseult was still in school, Beatrice would whisper the answer to a question, something Iseult wouldn't have been able to know, about the number of bones in a blue whale, something like that. How Beatrice knew the answer herself was just another question, one that Iseult chalked up to the mysteries of the afterlife.

(It was a shame that Mr. Wince hadn't known his own wife better, or he could have told his daughter how much Beatrice had enjoyed natural history, and the whole matter could have been cleared up. It might have even proven to Mr. Wince that his daughter wasn't lying when she insisted that her mother lived inside her.)

mother please. it was wrong, very wrong of me to try and get you to go away. i needed a little time to myself, a small space in which to think. i wanted to know my own mind for once, and only my own mind. you are always in it. i wanted to make a choice on my own. but now i am not allowed even that. and it's not right of me to change my mind about your opinion now but mother i need your help very badly. i have no one else and i realize that now. father says i must marry jacob whether i want to or not. i really think that he means to force me this time, and i am frightened of what that means. i don't know what to do and i don't know if it even matters what i do but i know if i don't have you there have you here i will lose my mind. if i must see him again and you don't go with me i don't know what will happen. i will go down on my knees if i must only please do not deny me this request.

She paused for breath, eyeing the flagstones in case she would be required to lower herself onto them, but in that pause came a sound so welcome she nearly wept with relief.

from now on do you promise to listen to me iseult
    yes mother of course i will. thank you. thank you. thank you. i don't want to be without you i don't think i can. i'm sorry.
    i know you are. we will figure out what to do together i won't let you be hurt my poor iseult so many times you've been hurt because of me i wish i could truly be where you are i wonder what your life would have been like with a proper mother to guide you.
    don't think of that mother it doesn't matter it doesn't bear considering. regret is not a worthwhile emotion. none of it was your fault. there's nothing to make up for. you came back for me. and you're here now. i need your help now so please tell me what to do i promise promise i will listen i will be good from now on.

let me see your hands when you say that

mother it has been years since i crossed my fingers to lie to you. . . . oh very well.

mind you clean under those fingernails before you see him again he will mistake you for the gardener.

so you aren't angry that I met him? on my own?

you will not be alone again. you will never be alone again. i will be with you. nothing can part us now. if your father insists upon your marrying him then you must but you will not go into marriage alone. i am here i am there to protect you.

you think i should just let father have his way? shouldn't i . . . scream and wail until he sends me to an asylum? shouldn't i throw myself from the roof to teach him a lesson?

Icy fingers thrust upward from Iseult's stomach and clutched at the inner workings of her throat. She identified a wet, choking noise coming from her head as the noise she was making as her mother shook her from the inside. She felt her eyes bulge, although whether from lack of air, or pain, or shock, she could not have said. She tried to close them so they wouldn't fall out of her head, and she gripped the side of the tomb with one hand, the other flailing about her throat, but there was nothing on the outside to be removed.

never say that again never think that again iseult never never if you die i die and i am not ready yet to die a second time.

Iseult tried to speak but it was no use with no air at her disposal. So she tried hard to think.

of course i won't mother i spoke foolishly rashly i couldn't i wouldn't please stop.

As swiftly as it had started the grip released and Iseult felt she'd been dropped from a great height.

This had never happened before, her mother as such a physical manifestation. It was something she had always longed for, it was just that the manner was different than she had hoped.

your life is not your own not just your own. you must always consider the consequences that your actions have for me i have never chastised you for your foolhardiness always saved you from your errors and i see now that i was remiss in my duties. i will not make that mistake again.

Iseult was afraid to move a muscle for the next hour. She was afraid to think. Her mother was unperturbed. She was not silent, but neither was she upset. This comforted Iseult somewhat, but the earlier outburst had come from nowhere, so how was she to know what another one might look like, were it to come along?

She emptied her mind as much as possible of suppositions and fears. If impending marriage was truly unavoidable, then it was, and there was no use struggling in vain. If drowning was a surety, why fight? It would do you no good. Iseult at last rose shakily from the tomb and brushed off a few dry leaves.

Come along, said Iseult to her mother. Or maybe Beatrice said it to Iseult. Iseult was not sure.

Iseult was tired, but she didn't think she was sleeping. She certainly didn't remember sleeping, and she wasn't any less tired. The clock never stopped ticking. She was never unaware of its presence, its insistence.

But she must be sleeping, because she is dreaming of Beatrice. In the dream (there was only the one), Beatrice flickers toward her in the snow, in the black and white of a photograph, in the wedding dress in which she must be freezing. She is talking, but Iseult cannot hear her, and she is talking too fast for Iseult to read her lips. But they must be conversing, for Beatrice pauses and listens and nods and responds. Then Beatrice starts to walk away, and Iseult sees a gaping tear in the gown's left shoulder. Iseult runs toward her and she knows that she's running because she can hear the *crunch crunch crunch* of her feet in the snow. She touches Beatrice's shoulder, the skin so cold it is tinted blue, and she turns. Beatrice looks momentarily surprised, but then smiles shyly as if posing for her portrait to be painted, except her teeth and gums are coated in fresh red blood, and as she starts talking again, little driblets fly out over her lips and down her chin, spattering the bright snow. And then she is gone and Iseult is alone in a barren landscape under a hard shell of frost, and a forest of skeletal trees smudged into the horizon meets the gray sky, and spots of red blood are dissolving the snow with their heat.

And that's how Iseult knew that she was asleep, because of bloody Beatrice in her dreams. She tossed and turned on her bed that was a boat and the spots of blood smeared throughout the dream made her seasick. Or was it the wedding dress causing her nausea?

She knew she was awake because Beatrice was talking again.

What did she say in this perpetual unchecked monologue? She talked about the wedding, about Jacob, about the entire Vinke family, about how to run a household, about what shade of ivory might flatter Iseult's coloring best. Iseult could not escape the clatter of Beatrice's voice, so she tried to let it wash over her like bathwater.

There had always been periods of Iseult's life during which Beatrice's voice became overwhelming to the point of madness. But just to the point. Every word was a drop of water in her ear, and Iseult sometimes tentatively prodded at her ear canal, making sure it wasn't slowly widening or leaking moisture. Sometimes if she shook her head, quick and hard, she could shatter Beatrice's voice, flinging it to the distant corners of the room, giving her a few minutes of respite. But the words returned without fail, each one assuming Beatrice's ghostly form creeping on hands and knees, belly low, until she was back.

Oh, yes, at times Beatrice became almost, almost a physical being outside of Iseult. Iseult could get almost, almost close enough to touch her. On several occasions she even had gotten within reach, but the almost, almost certain knowledge that her hand would come up clutching only air prevented her from traversing the last few millimeters. After the bloodstained dreams began, Iseult averted her eyes from Beatrice's physical manifestation, however slight.

And then one morning Mrs. Pennington broke in upon Iseult's torpor, having spent the week tiptoeing in and out more quietly than the best nurse on record. Suddenly the drapes were pushed open, and Iseult could tell without opening her eyes that there were hands on hips, and that this was the end of her nonsense and that time was moving forward and was slipping through her hands. She opened her left eye, with effort, the lashes crusted with sleep and idle tears. Something like "What?" croaked from her throat, but it was parched and cobwebbed from disuse, and the word caused a fit of coughing. Mrs. Pennington's blurry form made no move to offer her a glass of water. She waited until the coughing stopped.

"In two hours your aunt is coming to take you to the dressmaker, so we had better start making you look presentable." The blurry form loomed in front of Iseult's open eye, and a hand lifted a limp hank of Iseult's hair, slippery with grease. There was a grumble. "Though Lord knows how I'm to be expected to pull off that miracle."

Iseult rubbed her right eye free and sat up, swaying. Mrs. Pennington hustled Iseult into her robe, over her filthy nightgown.

Iseult found herself being led to the bathroom, the path to which was already being worn out by Sarah, running back and forth to ensure that everything was in order. Iseult coughed the last of the dust from her throat and said, "Why the rush for the dressmaker? I don't need any new dresses. My old ones are just fine."

Mrs. Pennington jerked Iseult to a halt. She had to reach up slightly to put a hand on each side of Iseult's face, Iseult having passed her in height the year that she turned twelve. "Darling girl," she said. Iseult squirmed at the direct affection but didn't wrench herself away. Mrs. Pennington's eyes were darker than usual, full like the moon. "You are not going to escape this time."

Iseult shuddered and backed herself out of Mrs. Pennington's hands, bumping into the doorframe of the bathroom. The older woman made a helpless gesture, of comfort that could not be given. They stood in silence, not looking at each other; then Iseult turned her back, walked into the bathroom, and closed the door.

The bathroom filled with steam. Iseult shrugged out of her robe and nightgown, which slithered to the floor even more easily than usual, there being little flesh to impede their progress. She looked down at her feet as she extricated them from the puddle of fabric. They were visibly dirty. They usually were. Iseult wondered if this was something she would have to pay more attention to when she was married, and as usual, when that word ran through her mind, a drum began to beat in her stomach. She plunged a dirty foot into the bathtub.

There was a knock on the door and Iseult grunted her assent, pulling her legs in closer, trying not to be revulsed at the feeling of flesh against flesh, squashed and hot. Mrs. Pennington came in all brusqueness and control, the sentimentality of a few moments ago banished entirely. She launched into a steady stream of gossip as she dealt with Iseult's hair.

The scent of lavender firmly overtook the sweaty, sour scent of her own self. Mrs. Pennington nattered on about the trouble with the new maid at No. 4, working up a lather on Iseult's scalp that rocked her head in a slow rhythm. She relaxed her grip around her legs, and let herself imagine that no one was getting married at all.

don't iseult don't pretend to yourself you must accept that things are how they are from now on for us for both of us
    can't i for a moment, mother? just a lovely moment where i am myself and beholden to no one, not even you?

"Stop fidgeting about, Miss, you're splashing water all over me and the floor!" Mrs. Pennington hopped up with a shriek, and a lock of wet hair slapped Iseult's forehead, which she felt she deserved. She straightened up her back and stiffened her mind while the rinsing continued in silence.

you think i ruin everything it isn't a very nice way to think about your mother.

—

    i want what's best for you and me for both of us

—

    if you don't marry now what life could either of us have with your father hounding us and he would you know would hound us to death

"Please leave me the soap, I can handle the rest," said Iseult.
    Mrs. Pennington slapped the bar into her hand, red-faced and annoyed.
    "All right, but don't you be thinking you can spend all day in here. You're not going to be even a moment late for your aunt," she said, wrapping Iseult's wet hair in a towel so tightly that she felt her pulse banging away at her temples.

Iseult took the bar of soap in one hand and attacked until her skin turned red. How much of the life she knew was about to change beyond recognition? There would be her father's absence, but she was pretty sure she could bear that. She would live in a different house. She looked around the bathroom as she went at her fingernails with a brush. It was a room she had been in every day of her life, but it held no particular charms for her. She assumed it would be no trouble to take her mother's chair, and Mrs. Pennington. She did not know which of the two she would fight for if it came down to one or the other.

Jacob's family was very well-off, so there would likely be a good many new servants to remember. The food would be different in this new house. She might not be so close to her mother's grave, but distance would not stop her.

The water clouded with grime. She did a cursory job on her limbs the closer they grew to her torso. Quick swipes of the soap under her arms sufficed. She worked the soap into a lather between her hands, and, holding her breath, plunged her hands into the water and between her legs. There was that flash of skin again in her head white silver silver white.

Iseult rinsed the soap off, not doing a very good job. She got out and ran the towel briskly over her body, not doing a terribly good job of that either, and when she put on her robe it grew wet in patches.

A slight rattle of the door handle was her signal to Mrs. Pennington, who she knew had her ear pressed to the wood. When Iseult opened the door, she found Mrs. Pennington waiting in the bedroom, rearranging herself. Even though they both knew perfectly well what was going on, it pleased them both to pretend that they were each of them ignorant of each other's actions.

Mrs. Pennington hustled Iseult into her underthings, covering up her shoulder, then recruited Sarah to help things go more quickly. The two women worked in near silence, Mrs. Pennington's breath coming quick from exertion, and Sarah's from nerves. Iseult was well aware that she made Sarah nervous, but she couldn't help it. She tried as hard as she could to make her body pliable for Sarah, but when Iseult was an awkward jumble of angles and wings, Sarah was as bad if not worse.

All the while that Mrs. Pennington tugged and tied and jerked and buttoned, she kept up a running lament under her breath at the state of Iseult's physique, asking questions that wanted no answer. "Less than two months until her own wedding and the clothes are like to fall right off her. Am I supposed to force-feed her? She's not a child, and I'm sure it's no business of mine anyway. But won't I be blamed? Oh, yes. Blamed by the father and the aunt and the little snip of a cousin and the dressmaker, oh the dressmaker. Are we to make a wedding dress for this bag of bones, or hope that we can fatten her up by then? Lord only knows." Iseult silently thanked her for not mentioning the state of her neck, which was also not good. The dressmaker would surely have some choice words on the subject.

Finally she was dressed, clothing pulled in a hundred different directions (and secured with pins to obscure the fact that it no longer fit). Sarah stood by, studying the rug, as Iseult's hair received a very stern brushing and was swept back so severely that it made her skull look as if it were trying to get to the other side of her skin. But she was presentable. Unattractive, but presentable. And that was the best that could be hoped for today.

Venturing out into bright daylight was an assault on her eyes, but Iseult thought better of complaining. She struggled to keep up with Mrs. Pennington, whose legs moved along the sidewalk like tireless pistons.

Mrs. Pennington's mouth, always on the thin side, had a particularly tight set to it today, and as Iseult looked at her, trying to pretend that she was not looking at her, she saw with surprise how old the housekeeper looked. She had always been possessed of a double chin, but it had lost its cheerful buoyancy. Her neck sagged sadly into her collar. A plush brown mole just beneath her jawline, that Iseult had thought as a child looked very like a scrap of velveteen, now had a wiry gray hair protruding from it. Iseult felt a shock of guilt in her sternum.

it's my fault. every life that brushes up against mine, i drag down into misery.

nonsense iseult nonsense what sort of a life would she have had without you you are her livelihood and she cares for you in her way her way that is not what my way would have been but still she has done well by you i know you have brought her much joy

as i have brought joy to father?

you have you have he doesn't show it but he will come around i know my own heart once you obey him and marry and are happily settled he will come around i am sure that he will

why change things now? he hates me; i hate him. if we never see each other again in this life i'll not complain.

"Ow!" A muscle in Iseult's shoulder twisted viciously and she shouted, causing an elderly gentleman to drop his newspaper in alarm. Mrs. Pennington looked mortified; she rushed to pick up the paper and hand it back to him. The mortification was too much for her to even speak—a rare occasion—and she merely grabbed Iseult's arm and propelled her onward.

They came to a stretch of empty street outside the dressmaker's shop and stopped. Mrs. Pennington was breathing through her nostrils, a sure sign that she was attempting, and failing, to control her temper. Iseult, looking down at the woman who had been saddled with raising her, wished that she could tell her the truth. *My mother pinched me. She talks more than ever now. And I am starting to feel her all the time, physically inside me, pinching and grasping and poking and squeezing. And I am afraid. I am no longer sure whether she is trying to stay in or to get out. Sometimes I am sure I can feel her teeth just under my skin. They are hungry.*

"I know you are unhappy." Mrs. Pennington had pitched her voice low in order not to give away her emotions. "I understand. I've seen the young man. I'd be unhappy too, betrothed to a young man of that color. And I won't throw it in your face by telling you that you've brought it upon yourself by misbehaving in front of every young man your father ever brought home." (Which is exactly what she was doing by saying it, but Iseult forgave her.) "But we women must do what we are told and no mistaking. You have no choice, Iseult. From here on out. But it will be so much easier on everyone if you go along with it, if you stop making these scenes. You know how to act like a lady. Please do what you're told, do the things that you should, or you'll . . ."

A slight commotion coming from the corner announced the arrival of Iseult's aunt and cousin, waving and carrying on.

Mrs. Pennington regained Iseult's arm and whispered into her ear as she steered them both in the direction of the cacophony. ". . . or you'll end up in the madhouse."

"Good afternoon, my dears, isn't this the most wonderfully exciting day? And Iseult, you are as radiant as a bride-to-be should be." If there was one thing that could be said for Aunt Catherine, it was that once she committed, her enthusiasm was flawless. She pressed a joyous kiss to Iseult's wasted cheek, and while not ignoring the obvious, pretended that no one knew the reason: "Oh, my sweet, you are simply wasting away to nothing! Nerves and excitement, nerves and excitement. Why, don't you remember that before Elspeth's wedding, the dress had to be taken in at the last minute because the poor child was simply too lovesick for even a bite of food?"

Iseult plastered a rictus of agreement on her face, noting both Mrs. Pennington's relief that Aunt Catherine was participating wholeheartedly in the deception that everything was fine, and the semi-horrified look in Elspeth's eyes. "Yes that's right," Iseult said in a voice she hoped wasn't too mechanical, "I've just been overly excited and it has been difficult to remember to . . . to . . . it's been difficult to eat."

All three women smiled in relief as Iseult finished her sentence. Seeing things through to their conclusion wasn't one of her strengths, after all. As the four made their way into the dressmaker's, Catherine and Elspeth twittering like birds, Mrs. Pennington squeezed Iseult's arm. The right arm, of course. And Iseult tried not to think that Mrs. Pennington had been as good as a mother to her, because she didn't want to be pinched again. There was no pinch, but she could feel a space open up in her shoulder. Not a large space, but then again, a chasm often begins as a fissure.

15.

Iseult never enjoyed the dressmaker, but this visit was ghastly. She sat in stiff silence while Aunt Catherine and Elspeth discussed the changes in bridal fashion since Elspeth's wedding four long years previous. How many ruffles, how much lace, how many buttons, how much must you adhere to fashion mores and how much could you bend to personal taste? *I have no personal taste,* Iseult thought. Or was that Beatrice thinking? Iseult wasn't sure. She tried to look into her mind, to draw a dividing line, thinking, *you stay on your side, i'll stay on mine. things are difficult enough right now without me being confused.* She concentrated, trying to hear an answer, but the *of course, dear, of course* she received sounded watery and thin.

A seemingly infinite number of fabric swatches were held up to her face, and there was much worried chatter over her pallor, and would it necessarily be improved in time for the ceremony? Aunt Catherine assured the company that her own cook would prepare as many rich and restorative recipes as were required to put the requisite roses into Iseult's cheeks. Iseult imagined frayed and biscuit-colored roses. She tried to muster up an opinion, but there was so little difference from one color to another. She made weak excuses for her poor eyes, and left the choosing to Elspeth, who everyone said had a most discerning eye. Elspeth demanded that she be left alone with the swatches: she required concentration and peace. As the rest of the women retreated to the fitting area, Iseult remembered a childhood afternoon when Elspeth had banished her from her room while she took over the the costuming of their dolls, shouting, "I'll not have my doll looking ridiculous just because yours does. I'll fix everything, you go away and let me do what needs doing!"

There was an unpleasant sensation of déjà vu, as Iseult could recall her doll being returned to her with many more frills and furbelows than before, which she did not consider very attractive, but which pleased Elspeth enormously. "Promise you'll keep her like this forever?" As with so many things that Elspeth lisped so attractively, it might have been presented like a question, but there was a look in her eye that said the matter was not up for discussion. And indeed, Iseult's doll wore her flounces steadfastly and without complaint, until the ribbons grew bedraggled and Iseult was too old for dolls. The doll was still in the attic somewhere, laden with dust.

The next phase promised to be especially grim, as there began to be talk of necklines. It was not as though Aunt Catherine was completely unaware of Iseult's disfigured neck and shoulder, but Mrs. Pennington had masterfully concealed the fact that Iseult had been continuing and worsening the disfigurement for years. Mr. Wince himself naturally never mentioned it. Anyway, Aunt Catherine had a horror of blood, and the mere mention could send her into a swoon. The plan for so many years had been to keep Iseult as unobtrusive as possible, and given that she never attended anything so gay as a party or a ball, fashion had hardly been an issue.

"I'm sure that you know there are some . . . reasons that we cannot display too much décolletage," Aunt Catherine said to the dressmaker, with a prim set to her lips and a prim nod toward Iseult's flat chest. The dressmaker, who had seen the self-inflicted damage to Iseult's skin, smiled graciously and nodded, already anticipating how she would tease this story out in gossipy tidbits to her husband over dinner.

"Of course," the dressmaker said, moving Iseult to the small dais at the center of the room. "I should think it all the more striking if we were to go against the current distasteful trend of exposure"—sharp moralistic nods from Aunt Catherine and Mrs. Pennington—"and create for Miss Wince a much more tasteful, demure gown than so many young ladies are choosing at the moment. Perhaps even a high neck . . . ? To set her apart?"

Aunt Catherine chewed on the inside of her lip, a nervous habit. "We don't want her looking like a nun, do we? I agree that those thin little shoulders should be covered, but as long as certain . . . areas are not on display"—here she gestured toward the flat bosom and, belatedly, the natal wound—"there is no reason why that lovely swanlike neck should not be the centerpiece."

The dressmaker rubbed at her right eyebrow with the back of her hand, which was her nervous habit. She had last seen Iseult's swanlike neck not three months earlier, and she wasn't sure how to say that an open, oozing wound was a sure way to ruin a bridal gown. She hustled over to her lace cabinet, looking for something with such a heavy pattern that it would obscure any scars beneath. "Now, mind you, I am just ensuring that, should this poor appetite continue, we won't have anyone the wiser that she's on the frail side. I think we can highlight this lovely neck with some beautiful lace."

Iseult and the dressmaker were aware of Mrs. Pennington letting out a breath, but Aunt Catherine was not the sort to notice such things. She looked up at Iseult, perturbed, although if she had been asked, she would not have been able to put into words the reason why. She didn't exactly like Iseult. Did anyone? She'd been a prickly baby, and a prickly child, and she had grown into a prickly woman. Her own Elspeth had always been a warmly affectionate child, smothering everyone and everything with kisses. Iseult had always remained distant and watchful.

It wasn't that Aunt Catherine thought Iseult was exceptionally intelligent. Did anyone? But there was an air about her that suggested something, a feeling that the child knew things that she should not know. Oh nothing wicked or salacious, just something . . . beyond. Along with her generally bad behavior, she often said things that chilled your blood; she always had, even as a small child. It was unsettling. She made comments about (and to) her mother Beatrice, whom of course she had never known, in a discomfitingly knowing manner, as if Beatrice were right there next to her.

Aunt Catherine had not been fond of Beatrice, truth be told. Altogether too wispy and insubstantial, both in person and in personality. She was lovely to look at, no one could deny that, but she was always nursing some ailment or another. Her lungs were weak and she couldn't walk any great distance. Mr. Wince had been quite a walking-holiday fanatic in his school days, and didn't she put a stop to that. She was always chilled, and kept her gloves on from September to May. Once, after Beatrice gave in to repeated exhortations to remove them on an uncharacteristically fine spring morning, Catherine had been horrified to see that those slender fingers were tinged with blue. She did not mention the gloves after that.

There had been a few family discussions wherein they had attempted to dissuade Mr. Wince from his choice of bride, but there was no talking to him. He was headstrong for the sake of being headstrong. He was spiteful, as Catherine often remarked to her husband.

Catherine firmly believed that if a colleague (friend was too strong a word) of Mr. Wince's hadn't been so lovestruck over Beatrice, the marriage would never have come about. Mr. Wince had, since childhood, turned peevish when watching anyone get what they wanted, and would feel compelled to go after it himself. It wasn't that Mr. Wince wanted the same thing, and that was precisely the trouble. Mr. Wince resented feeling all that keenly about anything, and it irritated him when other people did. He often said that his goal in such matters was to prove that whether or not people got what they wanted made no difference in the grand scheme of things. But in truth Mr. Wince just liked winning, even if the other person felt their life was destroyed in his pursuit of it.

Of course, as regarded Beatrice, there was the allure of her father's steelworks as well as that of besting someone in the game of love. Surely he regretted winning this particular game almost immediately. If ever a man was temperamentally designed for life-long bachelorhood, it was Edward Wince. He was perfectly competent at play-acting love when he could drop it after an evening's conversation and retreat into his solitude at home. But when love moved in after the wedding, Mr. Wince was annoyed by Beatrice's constant presence. She made no real demands on his time, but there was always some petty issue that needed discussion: the menu for a dinner party or new curtains for the drawing room or the price of a new spring gown. It was beyond him why she was interested in his input. He certainly wasn't interested in giving it.

But catastrophe soon visited the newlyweds. Not only was it unexpected, it was horrific, and it was made even more so by the fact the entire family witnessed it, at a lovely ceremony recognizing Beatrice's father's contributions to the community as a leading local businessman.

Mr. Wilkinson had hired a young man to photograph the

occasion for posterity, and it was this unprecedented excitement that brought about poor Mr. Wilkinson's untimely demise. He was a stickler for safety; he was famous for it. But if Mr. Wilkinson had one character trait that exceeded even his scrupulous carefulness . . . the man was impossibly vain.

It wasn't an unwarranted vanity. He was strikingly handsome, even in his later years, with lustrous black hair that had only begun to thread with silver, a mustache waxed into symmetrical perfection, dark, attentive eyes, and a figure that still had the power to turn a much younger lady's eye. (Of course he was faithful to his wife, no question. But a man can enjoy attention, can't he?) He was routinely heard to boast that he could still wear his wedding suit. And him married thirty years or more. (He was coy about his age.) A pretty wife on his arm whose face also belied her (never mentioned) age, delicate daughter Beatrice, and feckless son Henry completed the family portrait. Henry was a bit of a wastrel, but what handsome son wasn't? Especially when spoiled so by a doting mother and older sister. There was plenty of time for Henry, there were plenty of schools he hadn't yet been kicked out of, plenty of positions he could still be apprenticed to (his father had washed his hands of that nonsense when the far superior Mr. Wince entered their lives), plenty of young women of means who could be fooled by his looks and charm long enough to embark upon an unwise marriage. Henry wasn't bad; he was just used to having his own way.

But enough of Henry. The ceremony had gone off without a hitch, and only the family remained. Photographs had been taken of all of them, including Mr. Wince as the heir apparent. (Even though he hated this sort of thing, he gritted his teeth rather than suffer Beatrice's pouting for the next month.) The young newspaperman fancied himself a real artist, daring, avant-garde. He had the stiff family portrait in his pocket. For the solo image of Mr. Wilkinson, he had something bolder in mind.

"What, *in* the foundry?" Mr. Wilkinson exclaimed.

"Oh, yes. To show you at your work," the young photographer said earnestly. "To get a true sense of a man, we must see him in his element."

Mr. Wilkinson wanted to clasp this young man to his bosom. But he didn't—not because Henry was in the room, but because Mr. Wince was. It would be bad form. However, he did escort the young man into the foundry itself, the family trailing with visibly less excitement.

Various parts of the foundry were scouted in order to find the safest and most dramatic setting. Several were rejected due to the noise and the possibility of soiling the ladies' garments or their persons. After much animated negotiation (and much teeth-gnashing from Mr. Wince, who had been promised this venture would be completed within an hour), the perfect place was decided upon.

There was a crucible of molten steel which one could look down into as if into the very mouth of hell, via a convenient set of stairs and a platform. If Mr. Wilkinson arranged himself in the corner of the platform, the photographer would be able to capture a fiery glow and wafting smoke behind him. The family arranged themselves below in an attitude of anticipation.

(Mrs. Wilkinson was fretting that the roast would be dry when they finally reached home, and thus Mr. Wince would be peevish, which would set off the chain reaction of Henry needling him and Beatrice weeping. In hindsight, though, a dry roast would have been quite the preferable outcome.)

"Back a little further, Mr. Wilkinson, back just a little further, that is almost the very thing!" the photographer shouted from underneath his hood as Mr. Wilkinson worked on maintaining his preferred expression of dapper nonchalance. Annoyed that the railing wasn't situated another inch to the left to allow for the best view of the jaw he was angling toward the camera, he gave it a vicious nudge with his hip, which would leave him with a terrible bruise. Unbeknownst to Mr. Wilkinson, the railing had been put up carelessly, in contravention of his stringent safety regulations, during the week before Mr. Wince and Beatrice's wedding, when he had absented himself to ensure that the wedding tent was up to the highest possible standards. Just as the photographer got what would have been the prize photograph of Mr. Wilkinson's personal collection, the railing gave way and Mr. Wilkinson fell into the enormous crucible of molten steel not six feet below.

For a moment, not unlike a photograph, nothing changed. The family on the ground, Mrs. Wilkinson, Beatrice, Henry, Mr. Wince, everyone still looked at the space where Mr. Wilkinson had been. The photographer underneath his hood remained unaware, temporarily blinded by the phosphorescent flash.

The next instant was sheer chaos. Mrs. Wilkinson charged up the stairs, followed by Henry and Mr. Wince, and then by Beatrice, who had a new and uncomfortable petticoat to negotiate.

Mr. Wilkinson had not uttered a sound when he fell. His backside made a noise as it hit the contents of the crucible along with the poorly constructed railing. Beatrice recognized the sound from childhood. She had once chased Henry round the nursery after he had stolen her hard-boiled egg. He climbed up on the table and held it over his head, then dropped it into the large pot of oatmeal which had yet to be divided between them. The sound was a wallop, but a muffled one. Beatrice never told anyone of this connection between the two sounds. Nor did she ever eat another bowl of oatmeal or another hard-boiled egg.

When Beatrice and her petticoats reached the top of the stairs, she bumped into Henry, who had been held back by Mr. Wince, who attempted in vain to put a hand over Mrs. Wilkinson's eyes, but too late, too late.

By some miracle Mr. Wilkinson had been able to stand up, and he reached his hands, dripping molten liquid, up to his wife who, as a wife is wont to do when a husband reaches out to her, reached down to him. Luckily for Mrs. Wilkinson, it was from her that Beatrice had inherited such cold hands, and she had not removed her gloves; otherwise her hands would have been much more badly burned. As it was, the liquid instantly ate through her gloves as she tried to clasp Mr. Wilkinson's hands, but when she did the skin of his hands and arms slipped off like meat from a bone that has been simmering for days.

He fell back into the crucible and slipped beneath the surface. Mrs. Wilkinson was too busy shrieking to see what was happening, as the hands that had so recently been her husband's charred spots into her dress as they fell sizzling to the ground. Beatrice fortunately had her eyes shut tight and did not see any of this; there are things that are hard to unsee. Unfortunately for Beatrice, there are also things that are hard to unsmell.

Henry took one look at his father's hands, emptied of his father, on the platform and promptly vomited. Mr. Wince was trying to stop Mrs. Wilkinson from screaming and injuring herself further; he almost carried her down the stairs. The photographer had run for help, all the while wondering whether he had enough money saved to beat a hasty retreat to his mother's house in the countryside. Beatrice was left swaying on the platform with that smell in her dainty nostrils. Eventually, she got it over with and fainted next to the still-retching Henry.

A difficult few months ensued. Henry was more useless than ever, but at least he was rarely home. Beatrice spent most of her days at her mother's house, although it did neither of them any good. Beatrice wept piteously while her mother stared at the wall, constantly brushing an imaginary something off her hands. At first everyone assumed that this was a reaction to the bandages, but several weeks after the tragedy her hands had healed well enough for those to be removed, and still she did not stop. The doctor informed Mr. Wince that she most likely was attempting to wipe off the memory of her husband's ghastly hands in hers, and that since she showed little sign of doing so, she should be given up as mad and institutionalized. (This was the sort of behavior that Mr. Wince liked to point to whenever Iseult acted up, saying to himself, "It didn't come from *my* family!")

Beatrice was loath to have her mother confined thus, and Henry's consent could not be obtained because he was always either absent or too intoxicated. Mr. Wince was beginning to fray at the seams. Although he appreciated the advantage of having Beatrice largely away from home, visiting with her mother resulted in Beatrice weeping every night upon her return to Mr. Wince.

And then a stroke of luck, at least as far as Mr. Wince was concerned: Mrs. Wilkinson died. There was no one clear reason, but many possibilities. She hardly ate, she hardly slept, and she hadn't said one sensible word since she was carried off that gruesome platform. She was like Beatrice, too, in that she didn't have a hardy constitution. Mr. Wince thought it was excellent timing, as now they wouldn't need to shoulder the expense of a private sanatorium. Beatrice was practically comatose herself by this point, but that would pass in time. There was only the difficulty of what to do with Henry. And as it turned out, that sorted itself out beautifully as well.

Not two months after Mrs. Wilkinson's death, which had come three months after her husband's, Henry's body was discovered in an alley in very insalubrious conditions. Mr. Wince luckily had a friend in the upper echelons of the police force, so the worst details were not released to the press, but it seemed that Henry had had the bad taste to involve himself with not one, not two, but three married women. And thanks to Henry's brazen behavior, it didn't take long for all three cuckolds to catch on. No one was ever arrested for the crime. Mr. Wince declined to press charges, as he frankly believed that Henry had gotten what he deserved. It wasn't entirely clear what had caused Henry's demise in the end, but it was either the worst of the head wounds (inflicted, presumably, with one of a number of bloody bricks found near his person) or blood loss from the violent removal of a piece of his anatomy (this was not found near his person, nor was it found anywhere else).

Mr. Wince never breathed a word of this to anyone. Henry was buried without the company of friends or family, in a church-yard several towns away. Beatrice was mostly still in bed during those days, and hardly competent to ask what was going on. Mr. Wince intimated that something heavy had fallen on her brother in an alley (which was true, if you consider that all three husbands happened to be men of above-average size). Beatrice had been grieving for three months. There simply wasn't any grief left over by the time Henry died.

Two months later Beatrice was expecting Iseult, and her family receded into the past.

16.

"Is there anything you can do to disguise these bony areas? Ruffles, perhaps? How puffed a sleeve is too puffed?" Aunt Catherine gingerly touched Iseult's shoulder, afraid it might cut her.

The dressmaker pursed her lips. "Too much puff and she'll be overwhelmed. I think the simpler the better—don't you, Miss Wince?"

All eyes turned to Iseult. She was unaccustomed to having her opinion asked, and unsure as to how to show the small burst of pleasure she felt.

"What do you think would be Mr. Vinke's preference?" Elspeth said. Having known her since infancy, Iseult could detect the subtle tone in her voice which laughingly said not only that Mr. Vinke's preference would be for something ridiculous, but also that Iseult would have no idea what he would prefer.

puffed puffed puffed
>**i would be humiliated**
>>*puffs as big as your head you'll look like a fairytale*
>>**you don't care about my humiliation, do you**
>>>*i've dreamt of this and you should look beautiful*

**but i'm not, mother, i'm not beautiful. and i won't pretend
to be for your sake.**

Iseult was half prepared for the sharp twist she felt inside her—
only half, because although she knew it was coming, she didn't
expect it at the base of her spine, so far from her mother's usual
purlieu. It nearly threw her off the dais, but Mrs. Pennington's
solid body was there to steady her. Everyone else gasped, but the
stout woman just shook her head and lied, "She's so excited she
can hardly think straight."

"Simple would be best," Iseult said a little too loudly, cutting
off Elspeth and Aunt Catherine before they could begin cooing
too much about her maidenly excitement. "I think Jacob would
prefer simple. I know he would. That is how he likes me best."

Their coos became murmurs at her boldness. Iseult seemed
on perilously intimate terms with her fiancé, certainly on terms
more intimate than anyone had expected. Iseult knew that
she was meant to blush prettily and say that that was what she
assumed he might like, but whenever society manners looked
to push her in one direction, she would set doggedly off in the
other. She knew everyone thought it would be best to disguise
her looks and her gauntness with frilly distractions, but in a
burst of clarity she decided that if she were going to marry Jacob
(even if that still didn't seem realistic or possible) she was going
to do it honestly.

"I want it to be very plain," Iseult said clearly, addressing herself to the dressmaker, holding her chin above the waves of disapproval that were coming off Elspeth and Aunt Catherine. "I don't
want lace or bows, and I don't want a veil."

A sharp gasp from Aunt Catherine. "No *veil?*"

Iseult took no notice, but continued with her sharp chin even
higher. "And I don't want a low neck but I don't want a high one

either. If it shows my scars, then it shows them. He'll see them anyway. I see no reason why I should hide from him."

Iseult had to hold herself very straight and firm as Beatrice tried to twist her spine from side to side. Mrs. Pennington kept a hand on her shoulder, and Iseult gave her a quick grateful glance. Catherine, Elspeth, and the dressmaker were expressing their discontent, each trying to make her disapproval heard over that of the other two.

"And"—Iseult raised her voice above the fray—"the dress should be ivory, as far from white as possible. That will look nicest against his skin." She looked pointedly at Elspeth. "His skin is silver. I don't know if you know that. Jacob's skin is silver."

For the first time in her life, Elspeth looked as if she was on the back foot. She looked uneasily at her mother before meeting Iseult's eye, and she stammered, "Y-y-yes, I . . . I believe I knew that his . . . that he was . . . It's a medical condition, I believe?"

Iseult peered down with what she hoped was a withering look and did not respond. She turned her attention back to the dressmaker. "I assume new measurements are to be taken?"

The dressmaker nodded mutely. She had never heard Iseult speak so many words in a single visit.

"Then let us take them. I should like to be by myself for a moment first. I will let you know when I am ready," Iseult said, stepping from the dais and past the four women staring at her open-mouthed. Without a backward glance she went into the small dressing room and closed the door behind her.

There was a long silence.

"We'll have a veil, in any case," Aunt Catherine said.

17.

Iseult's fingers were shaking so hard it was difficult to put the hook into the latch on the door. Her spine ached from top to bottom, and she arched it uselessly, trying to get out of her mother's grip.

so you've chosen him over me already have you his wishes over mine is that how it is going to be iseult from now from now on am i to be an afterthought a thought a dream you try to shake off a nightmare you cannot will not wake up from

stop it, stop it please. this is hard enough i need you on my side. you are the one who is making me do this—

don't you try to blame your father's decisions on me i am only helping you as well as i can i know it isn't much god knows—

Iseult had to move quickly. Her right hand shot out to grab a pearly-topped pin from the dressmaker's pincushion. The dressmaker would be on her way in soon, requiring Iseult to bare her neck, so that was off limits. She didn't have time to unlace her boots. Beatrice's voice was rising like a river bursting its banks, building in shrillness and intensity to the point where the words were blurring into one long howl. Iseult hoisted up great handfuls of skirt and quickly jabbed the pin in and out of her right thigh. A bead of blood was just visible through her black stockings, and there was a perceptible dip in Beatrice's mania. There was a timid tap at the door. Without a thought in her head other than to smother her mother's voice, Iseult shoved the pin into her leg right up to its pearly top. Beatrice's voice cut off like a door slammed shut, and Iseult let out a deep breath. She dropped her skirt and straightened up; the feeling of the pin in her leg made her feel stronger, bolstered. She checked the mirror briefly to see that her smile was pasted on correctly, and she opened the door.

Iseult knew from experience that the dressmaker would get through the measurements as quickly as she could. Buttons were undone, laces untied. The whole affair was conducted in silence, save for the *zzzzip* of the dressmaker's thumbnail against the tape measure as she extended it, the dull scratch of her stubby pencil making notes. Iseult focused her eyes on a water stain on the wall and enjoyed the quiet flooding her head. She would have to apologize to her mother later. In her dreamy, muffled state, even though she could see in the mirror that her bones were trying to poke through her underthings, she didn't think she looked so terrible. Even her eyes felt comfortably packed in gauze.

She floated through the rest of the appointment. Her clothes were put back on her; she raised and lowered her arms like a docile toddler. The dressmaker held out examples of fabrics and patterns and necks and sleeves, and Iseult pointed out her choices as if drawn to them by magnetism. She brooked no discussion, and the tsks and sighs of Elspeth and Aunt Catherine floated over her head unheeded. Iseult decided every last detail of the dress, with a clarity she rarely felt. It wasn't that she'd suddenly developed a strong fashion sense, but simply that the right choices felt blessedly obvious.

She felt lovely until she reached home and went to sit alone in

her mother's armchair to wait for Mrs. Pennington to bring her
some tea. Suddenly she felt very alone. The room felt larger than
usual, the air seemed thick and hot. Her thoughts, which were so
used to bumping into her mother, were left to their own devices,
swimming around stickily, uselessly in her head.

mother. . . .

No response. Iseult felt strange, but not strange enough to apologize. Not yet. She didn't like this new mood of Beatrice's, she
didn't trust it. The anger had frightened her. She would try it this
way a little bit longer. She could always apologize later, after all.
It wasn't as if Beatrice was going anywhere. Surely not . . . ? Iseult
stood and paced back and forth by the window, arms crossed,
fingers rhythmically stroking her elbows. A sharp pinch in her leg
brought her up short. Startled, she looked down. There was blood
on the wooden floor, and she had been traipsing through it, leaving footprints in front of the chair. She felt the bulbous head of
the pin. She had forgotten it. She pulled her skirt up to where she
could see it again. Blood ran down to her boot in a thick stripe,
and the stockings, which would be difficult to take off, were a
total loss.

Still. She was surprised to have forgotten the pin completely.

There was a knock on the door and Iseult dropped her skirt,
shuffling about to see if the blood was still wet enough to smear
into the floor any better (it was), and then she stood over the worst
part. "Come in," she said, finding she enjoyed the clear sound of
her voice without Beatrice's static in the background.

It was Sarah with her tea, not Mrs. Pennington. The two
women eyed each other warily, like dogs meeting on the street.
Sarah did what she always did, standing awkwardly with the tray as
if perhaps she expected Iseult to relieve her of it. Mrs. Pennington

said that Iseult was under no circumstances to do this, and that if Sarah wasn't prepared to do the duties of a proper maid, well then, she should have been born into a family with fewer daughters so she needn't have gone into service. Still, Iseult stutter-stepped toward her, but then remembered that she needed to stay where she was to keep the bloodstain covered.

Prompted into action by Iseult's movement, Sarah rushed forward and clanged the tray onto the table next to the armchair, milk sloshing out of the pitcher and onto the envelope that was propped up next to it. A silver envelope. Iseult's stomach lurched, and there was a blank space where Beatrice would usually have been.

"Thank you, Sarah," she said, again beginning to move forward but remembering too late. This time it was her torso rather than her feet that swayed forward and had to be recalled. To distract attention from her curious movements, her voice rose to a shout. "That will be all, please!"

Sarah turned tail and fled, thankfully remembering to slam the door behind her. Iseult first grabbed the napkin, dipped it in the glass of water, and wiped the blood smears from the floor before they got sticky or dry. She felt a twinge in her leg; she thought maybe she would take the pin out, but then she thought maybe she should read Jacob's letter first.

She felt very composed as she opened it, and only slightly less so after she read it.

If you will consent to walk with me again, I will wait in the same place at the same time every day this week until you come. We should get to know each other better.

He had written neither his name nor hers. She checked the back of the page, in case they had fallen to the other side. She even looked inside the envelope, even though she knew they were unlikely to be there. "Miss Iseult Wince" was written tidily on the front of the envelope, but there was nothing inside. It wasn't that she was such a stickler for epistolary etiquette, but the note seemed too intimate this way. She had been hoping this marriage could be conducted on an entirely formal level, with as much distance and chilliness as possible.

So here she was again, required to make a decision, with no one to ask for input. She searched briefly inside herself, but her mother was still wherever Iseult had sent her with the pin. *Oh yes,* Iseult thought, *the pin.*

She hoisted her skirts as high as she could on her right leg and observed the situation. The stocking would have to be ripped. She began, little rips, and her mind wandered where it wanted to, with no one and nothing to contradict it.

What would Jacob want to know about her? What was there to know that would please him? From listening to other girls talk when she was young, at school and with her cousin's friends, she had the impression that the consensus was that it was unwise to be entirely yourself with someone of the opposite sex.

She couldn't think there was terribly much about her worth knowing. He knew the basic facts. She had no real hopes or dreams, other than to live in as much peace and solitude as possible. There was nothing she felt she couldn't live without. Did she have favorite things? Not really. Certain things moved her, but not in any way she could express except to her mother, who knew her feelings before Iseult knew them herself, so there was rarely any need to try to express them.

Maybe she was looking at this from the wrong angle, asking the wrong question. Instead of "What can I share with him?" the question was "What will be impossible to conceal?"

The stocking came free of the pin, although it was still gummed to her leg with a clot of blood. The pin came out easily, and clean, as when Mrs. Pennington checked a cake with a knife stuck in the middle. Iseult placed the pin on the floor on a napkin, to be disposed of later. She unlaced her boot and removed it along with the shreds of bloodied stocking.

Ah, there was something she would not be able to hide. Iseult wiggled the four toes on her right foot. As a squalling infant, Iseult had lived in the home of a wet nurse, a great bosomy girl who loathed babies, but was too indolent to earn money any other way. She would leave Iseult screaming for hours, only picking her up when she was scheduled to be fed. One day when Iseult was about six months old, Mrs. Pennington visited to check on her. (Not that Mr. Wince had asked her to visit; she went completely of her own volition.) She found the wet nurse sprawled on her sofa, asleep, as in the next room her own child slept as well, and Iseult in the crib beside him was hoarse and red-faced in screaming distress. Mrs. Pennington scooped her up and ran with her to the doctor, not even pausing to wake the slovenly nurse. The doctor examined the wailing child patiently. He was surprised to find that her collarbone, apart from the expected nasty scar, was healing on schedule and didn't seem to be the cause of her immense discomfort. The contents of her diaper were nothing that would cause alarm. Her lungs were certainly healthy. There didn't seem to be anything wrong with her at all. As a last resort, he thought a bath might soothe her, and she smelled as if she could use one anyway. He called upon Mrs. Pennington to assist, and when they removed the tiny knitted booties (completed by Beatrice mere days before the birth and her subsequent demise) the mystery was solved. A single strand of hair had gotten wound so tightly around the middle toe on Iseult's right foot that no blood was getting to it at all. The hair functioned as a crude, cruel tourniquet, and the doctor suspected it had been in place for some days, as the poor baby's toe was quite black, and he could catch a faint whiff of the sweet smell of gangrene.

Mrs. Pennington burst into tears. The doctor tried to gently explain that it was not an entirely uncommon occurrence, as babies weren't very good when it came to communicating what troubled them, but that most parents and attendants noticed before so much damage has the chance to occur. Mrs. Pennington was positively inconsolable and wept right along with the now naked Iseult when the doctor told her that they could not possibly remove the hair themselves, but she would have to be taken to hospital where the toe could be safely removed. Mrs. Pennington promptly fainted, and the doctor, not for the first time, wished his practice would prove itself more successful, at least to the point where he could employ a proper nurse.

The amputation went smoothly. Mr. Wince was more upset about Iseult's return to his home than he was about her missing digit. But once a suitable concoction was found to render a wet nurse unnecessary, she was such a quiet presence that Mr. Wince regularly had to remind himself that she was in the house at all. Mrs. Pennington was never to forgive herself for leaving her with that heinous woman, a woman she had vetted herself!

Since the toe was long gone by the time Iseult learned to walk, it never affected her balance. Very few people knew about it at all outside of her own home, and she was relatively certain her father had forgotten that particular detail years ago. Elspeth had teased her about it in childhood, but had not been cruel enough to tell other children.

So that was something she would need to tell Jacob, so as not to surprise him. But . . . Iseult nibbled her lower lip. Was he going to see her bare feet? If he saw her bare feet, how much more of her would he see in that state? The old revulsion flooded her stomach. She grabbed her teacup and took much too large a swallow of very hot tea, which then dribbled out the side of her mouth as she tried not to choke. But at least the tea shook her brain hard enough to shake away the thoughts that had arisen.

But only for a moment. *What else?* Iseult thought. *What else must I confess before its inevitable discovery?* She looked closely at the tiny dark red hole in her leg where the hatpin had resided so recently. She knew from experience that this would not leave a scar, if she refrained from picking at it. And she could restrain herself, if she put her mind to it.

Her mind started to race, running up and down her body, scanning for the marks of her own making. How many could be hidden forever? By her clothes, by her hair, by never venturing into sunlight? In truth, she didn't know a thing about marriage. Surely there were some husbands who had never seen their wives' bare shoulders? Weren't there?

Things were going to be expected of her, that much she knew. Things above and beyond the economical running of the household and a pleasant attitude toward his family. Goodness knows those would be hard enough. But she had only the dimmest of ideas as to what else might be entailed. At school, once, the girls had spent a rainy afternoon discussing whose parents shared a bedroom and whose kept separate quarters. Iseult assumed that those who shared a bedroom were less prosperous, but then why did the girls look down on the girls whose parents had their own bedrooms? Iseult did not ask. Iseult never asked. And thus Iseult remained in the dark about a good many matters.

It was at times like this that Iseult most regretted not having a mother of flesh and blood and bone. Someone she could look at across a table, instead of probing her neck while watching in the mirror for some reaction. She often glimpsed moments of something like maternal affection from Mrs. Pennington, but Beatrice was always there to make her regret those moments.

But there was no one to tell her, and no one to ask. There was

Mrs. Pennington, of course, but as much as their relationship had blurred the lines between house and help, this was a bridge Iseult did not think should be crossed. At least, she did not know how one would begin to cross it.

She wondered whether Jacob would know. And would he expect her to know? The answer was surely yes on both counts. Blood flooded her head at the thought, and she put the backs of her hands to her cheeks, cool against the now-hot skin. Iseult squirmed in her chair, trying to exorcise the feeling of her pulse in places on her body that she would prefer felt nothing. And the more she tried to stop it, the more her pulse beat.

She felt seasick, and knew that she would probably continue to feel that way until the wedding. At least until the wedding. She should meet Jacob again, if only to assuage the nausea. What was it Mrs. Pennington liked to say? "Better the devil you know." Her father was fond of saying that you should always know your enemies better than your friends. Iseult could grudgingly see the wisdom in that, even though she was not in possession of either.

18.

Dinnertime. Iseult had not made an appearance at dinner for weeks, but had her usual thought upon entering the dining room: it was never not dinnertime. She was sure that at least a quarter of her life was spent sitting at the table, waiting with trepidation for her father to appear. Fidgeting in the heavy wooden chair, knowing that nothing would make the time go faster. Wishing there was at least a loudly ticking clock in the room to mark its passage, no matter how slow. There had once been a clock, but Mr. Wince had it removed in her adolescence, annoyed that she kept her eyes fixed on it as they ate in silence.

She wondered what the dining room at her new home would look like. She didn't even know whether they were to live with Jacob's parents and his silly sisters or on their own. She made a note in her head to ask Jacob. She wanted to be able to picture her future accurately, even if it was to be terrible. She wasn't sure which would be more terrible. The most important thing would be to set a precedent wherein she dined alone in her room. This would be easier to accomplish if they had their own house.

She was lost in thought and did not register her father entering the room, but snapped to attention when he dragged his own heavy chair away from the table. She knew that he made the noise on purpose, because she recognized the same streak of petty vengefulness in herself. The key was to act just upset enough for Mr. Wince to know he'd had an effect, but not so upset that he felt encouraged to go on. She winced, as befitted her name, but threaded the expression through with a weak smile. Mr. Wince gave her a look a step or two above a sneer, and sat down.

"I didn't believe you were truly ill, but now I can see that you were." Mr. Wince's mustache twitched in anticipation of a direct hit as he spread his napkin in his lap with exquisite care. "Your pallor, my dear, is simply cadaverous."

Fight back just enough to protect yourself, not enough to prolong the battle. Iseult paused, waiting for the predictable voice of her mother to jump in and encourage her to back down quickly, but then she remembered there was only silence.

"I have indeed been ill, Father; I would not lie to you." She held back a remark about the pleasure of his company. "And I am confident that the resumption of regular meals will return me to my former bloom of health. I hope for Mr. Vinke's sake that I will not make too piteous a bride." And she tried to resist, but without her mother to hold her back, she found she could not. "Since we are being so rudely forced upon each other."

Mrs. Pennington burst through the dining room doors, red-faced and laden with plates. She was practically psychic in her ability to sense impending turmoil and thrust herself between the opponents.

"Now, Miss Iseult, you are going to eat every last bite of these greens so you get your strength back," she said, far too loudly, placing a towering plate of dark green leaves in front of her. "And Mr. Wince, here's some for you too, so you don't feel left out."

Mr. Wince grimaced, although Iseult was never sure whether the expression he was making wasn't meant to be a smile that simply came out wrong. Iseult often practiced her expressions in the mirror, so she could at least mimic the face she should be making.

She would not have been surprised to learn that her father did the same thing—not for her benefit, of course, but more in a business capacity.

Mrs. Pennington swept out of the room, restoring the atmosphere to its previous chilly temperature.

"I am told you were fitted for your bridal attire today," Mr. Wince said, although it was impossible to tell whether the distaste in his voice was directed to Iseult, the concept of bridal attire, or the profusion of vegetables before him, which he seemed unsure how to attack. This was one of his favorite conversational tricks with his daughter. Instead of asking a question or voicing an opinion, he merely stated a fact and left it to hang in the air to see whether Iseult would take the bait. She had just stuffed a great forkful of food into her mouth, and it was *her* trick to chew every bite slowly and methodically, as if she wanted to wrangle every last trace of flavor from it before swallowing. Thus it was common for both father and daughter to be rendered frantic with rage by the other during the course of dinner. It was rare for them to both finish the meal.

Iseult swallowed at last and heard her father's breath catch as she took a dainty sip of wine. Usually Beatrice would be moaning pitifully about obedience to one's parents by this point, but Beatrice remained silent. Iseult wondered whether Beatrice was all that had been restraining her from constantly telling her father exactly what she thought. Perhaps. Was she coming into her own voice after all this time? Perhaps.

"You heard correctly, Father. It all went well, I think. But I couldn't help but wonder something. Would you tell me what you thought of my mother's wedding dress?" And she shoved another large quantity of greens past her sharp teeth.

"It was . . ." Mr. Wince began, but paused to calm himself

until the clamor of Iseult's chewing subsided. ". . . It was, I was told, a very typical wedding costume for the time. You have seen the portrait yourself. I can assure you that your mother had no pretensions of grandeur. She did not aspire to fashion. She was simple and level-headed and did what her parents asked of her, as daughters are meant to do. Mrs. Pennington thought that you made some unusual choices regarding your style of dress. I'll thank you to remember that until I hand you over that day I am regretfully still responsible for your expenses. Once you are married you may drape yourself liberally in gold and diamonds, but until then I expect you to behave with decorum, and within the strictures with which I believe you are well acquainted."

Iseult found herself out of greens, but Mrs. Pennington was coming through the door with lamb chops and potatoes. Mr. Wince sat back smugly and waited for Iseult to volley the shot back to him, while Iseult smiled beatifically (and uncharacteristically) at Mrs. Pennington, who grabbed the plates from the previous course and headed back to the kitchen with great speed, taking cover before the gathering storm.

Beatrice's absence echoed. Iseult found herself wondering, as she did when she was small, if Beatrice could still hear her when she didn't seem to be present. She wondered whether she would get into a rip-roaring argument with her father to find Beatrice suddenly on the attack. She decided to put the thought to the side.

"Would you prefer I don sackcloth and ashes instead of the traditional white or ivory, Father?" Iseult said brightly, slicing her knife through the pinkish meat on her plate, feeling a twinge in her leg where the needle had been earlier in the day. She chewed slowly. The meat was dry, and formed a gloppy paste on her tongue.

Mr. Wince scraped his utensils against his plate deliberately. "That witticism doesn't work, Iseult. You'll not punish me with social humiliation; you'll only punish yourself. Once this debacle of a wedding is over I intend to wash my hands of you. Although yes, I admit I would prefer you didn't dress like a bejeweled strumpet. Call it my greatest wish as your loving father."

The eyes of father and daughter met across the table. Mr. Wince pulled a piece of meat from his fork, teeth clamped and shrieking against the metal. Iseult held his gaze and steeled herself not to shudder. Why did it always end this way? Mr. Wince triumphant, Iseult furious and sputtering. She had a moment of sharp loneliness for Beatrice, her absence a vacuum. No mother to soothe her, no mother to prod her to flee to her room, no mother to pop something into her head to say that might temporarily appease her father, at least until the end of dinner. No mother to anything.

Was Beatrice gone for good? Had the needle vanquished her once and for all? The vacuum threatened to swallow Iseult whole. That wasn't what she wanted. She wanted control. She wanted to be able to go into her room and close the door on the world, including Beatrice. Had she accidentally locked her out forever?

"You look paler than before, Iseult. Don't tell me you're still ill."

"I'm fine," she said mechanically. "Just fine. But the day has been tiring, since I've been so unwell of late. I think I shall go to bed early."

She pushed her chair back from the table. Mr. Wince made no move to rise.

She closed her eyes, a thing she did sometimes to feel herself sway with the earth's rotation, a simple reminder that time was passing, that this moment would turn into another moment, and another, and another, until it was finally all over.

She opened her eyes. Her father continued to eat his dinner as if she were not still standing there. It wasn't that Iseult was unaccustomed to the certainty that her existence in the world was of little importance to anyone, but sometimes it smarted more than other times. If she fell down dead at her father's feet he would rejoice, although he would likely grumble that even though he was being spared the expense of a wedding, there were now funeral costs to contend with.

Iseult left the dining room and headed for the stairs. She heard Mrs. Pennington hasten after her and say . . . something, but she interrupted without turning or pausing, saying, "No, thank you, I shall see to myself tonight. Good night."

Her knowledge of Mrs. Pennington's affection for her, however small, however secondary to her love for her own children, made Iseult feel even worse. Iseult had long battled with herself over whether it was better to live hungering after the scraps of affection she had from Mrs. Pennington and her fickle mother, or to have nothing. After all, her father had not a shred of love in his life, and he was content. She couldn't deny that his life had a cleanness to it that hers lacked. He was never caught up in trying to please someone who was ultimately unpleasable.

She felt as if the journey to her room was very long tonight, and darker than usual. She ran a hand along the gloomy wall-paper, flocked with something she'd never been able to figure out, just blobby shapes. Had Beatrice picked it out? Maybe while still in mourning for her family? It was wallpaper that spoke of misery; it would have been at home in a funeral parlor.

She locked the door behind her and, gathering her skirts, curled herself small into her mother's chair. She tried to feel as penitent as possible, to let her mother know that she hadn't meant it, the transgression still so recent that her leg began to throb anew. She knew she should clean the wound, but she hoped that leaving it a mess might prompt her mother to realize the confused, anxious state of mind that had led her here.

With a jerk, Iseult realized that she hadn't thought of Jacob for hours and hours. How could he flood her mind so completely at times, and at others be so totally absent? She had read her share of romantic novels, and she'd never read about anything like this. Oh, it wasn't that she wondered if what she felt was love, nothing like that. She didn't think love was something that she was capable of giving or receiving, not even for Beatrice: for all they felt, they were merely in thrall to each other, their strange circumstances thrust upon them.

She did, however, wonder what Beatrice thought of love. Had she loved her husband? Iseult felt restless, smoothing her skirts over and over. She decided that she would meet Jacob tomorrow, and felt the thought roaming around her head, looking for Beatrice and not finding her.

She couldn't sit still, so she got up and paced the room. She felt hot, so she began to divest herself of her clothes, button by button, hook by hook, discarding each item on the floor. The mess wouldn't make her very popular with Mrs. Pennington or Sarah, but that couldn't be helped. Maybe she would feel like picking it all up later.

It was unpredictable, this . . . Beatrice-less-ness.

Iseult came to rest on the seat at the vanity table, long fingers spread on the tabletop, and looked soberly at her reflection.

What would she have to do to make herself more attractive? Or at least, what a man would find attractive. She'd never found any need for prettiness before and didn't know how to go about it. She studied herself in the glass. Paleness of course was to be desired, but the paleness of her cousin Elspeth, all sweetly peach around milky-white edges, soft and blurred. Iseult's edges had points, and the skin over her cheekbones, chin, and forehead had a weak blueness, like the milk of an unhealthy cow. She rummaged through a drawer until she found a small pot of rouge that she had stolen from an apothecary as a child. Not because she had wanted it, exactly, but because she had found that she could.

She had opened the jar at the time, touched it hesitantly, and immediately felt wicked. So there it had stayed at the bottom of the drawer, until now. The gold was flaking from the lid, and it stuck to Iseult's hand as she opened the jar. She sniffed the contents but smelled nothing. Had it gone off? Did such things even go off? It looked the same as she remembered from all those years ago, and still a part of her was tempted to jam a finger all the way in.

She swiped her little finger gingerly against its sheen, inspecting her fingertip for evidence. Nothing, other than some grime under her nail. She smushed harder at the rouge, and the surface splayed under the pressure, like butter. She rubbed finger and thumb together and peered closely at the result. It was very red, although not unpleasantly so. Dubiously, she held her thumb up next to her cheek and leaned closer to the mirror. Even at this proximity the color made her face appear fairly ghastly. Well, more ghastly than before. What would happen when the rouge was on her face? She removed her thumb from the mirror's gaze. It couldn't look much worse.

She dabbed a little on her right cheek, then her left. She squinted in the dimness. The effect was not unflattering. Was she, though, beginning to detect the faint, clinging scent of roses? She disliked roses; she thought they smelled sweetly of decay. But the smell was very faint, almost unnoticeable.

With no mother to chastise her out of it, Iseult decided then and there that she would indeed paint her cheeks with rouge before she went off to meet Jacob in the morning. She was tempted to go to bed with the rouge on and not have to start again, but Mrs. Pennington might see, and she was not sure what effect it might have on the bed linens.

19.

She woke in the morning, wrenched into daylight from her dreams by an unseen hand, sweating, her mouth gummy and tasting like too much wine.

Mrs. Pennington was opening the drapes to a beautiful day. Too beautiful. Suspiciously beautiful.

"Are you all right?"

Iseult jumped at Mrs. Pennington standing suddenly beside her.

She put her motherly hand on Iseult's forehead. "You don't feel warm but . . . your cheeks . . . are you feeling ill?"

"No, no, I'm fine. I feel fine," Iseult said hastily, scooting herself out the other side of the bed. "Please help me get ready, I should like to go for a walk."

She could hear Mrs. Pennington summoning up the breath for a lecture as Iseult hurried past and shut herself in the bathroom. She was afraid to look in the mirror, and instead looked at the cold tiles at her feet while she tentatively touched her left cheek. It didn't feel right. It felt bumpy, swollen. She touched the right. It didn't feel any better.

Peering through her hair, Iseult grabbed a small disc of mirror that had belonged to Beatrice. She looked somberly at one cheek, then the other. Maybe rouge did go off, after all. Both cheeks were a strange shade of red, the color of roses that had not only been dead for some time but were also coated in a layer of dust. And underneath the terrible color were uneven raised patches, like those on a topographical globe of the kind found in gentlemen's studies. And all this made the rest of Iseult's face even more sickly pale than usual.

Her heart sank, although thanks to her stubborn, pragmatic resistance to hope, it didn't have far to sink. She momentarily congratulated herself for self-protection. But it was a small victory. A very small one. Although she hadn't been silly enough to hope that nothing would go wrong, she had still been hopeful that the thing to go wrong wouldn't be her face.

But she wasn't going to let this stop her from meeting him. After all, she was the one who had succumbed to vanity. It was right that she should suffer for it.

Iseult felt nauseated as she set off to meet Jacob, but consoled herself with the fact that the weather was at least cool enough that she wouldn't sweat, and that the veil Mrs. Pennington had arranged over as much of her face as possible wouldn't look too terribly strange. The housekeeper had fussed and fretted and wondered aloud what could have caused Iseult's cheeks to catch such dusky fire as they had done. She had a very suspicious look in her eye, and clearly believed there had been some mischief on Iseult's part, but Iseult did not budge, refusing to meet her gaze. She also did not answer questions as to her destination, instead waving a hand vaguely in the direction of the blue outdoors.

The door closed behind her; Iseult thought of how, when she was small, Mrs. Pennington had followed her on her walks. As Iseult got older, she got faster, while Mrs. Pennington got slower, and eventually Iseult was free to roam without looking over her shoulder. No one cared where she was.

She had left too early, so she took a circuitous route that would probably result in her being late. She had never mastered being perfectly on time. She bounced one hand off her thigh to see whether it still hurt from the most recent wound (it did not; not much), while her other hand fiddled with the veil tumbling from her hat. It was old and gray; it had belonged to Beatrice. Veils were not much in fashion at the moment, so Mrs. Pennington had had to sift through a number of boxes before she came back with it, sneezing. Finding that it wasn't terribly easy to see where she was going, Iseult took advantage of a moth hole in the veil, and she worked her little finger into it to give her a wider view.

She was well aware that this was causing people to stare at her, but she reasoned that they would stare harder if she fell in the street. It was going to be her third time seeing Jacob, again without Beatrice there to tell her what to say. Not that she always went along with Beatrice's suggestions, but it was still comforting to have a little bit of input.

She could hear by the church clock that she was late, but restrained herself from going any faster. Before rounding the corner that she knew would reveal Jacob in the distance, she stopped to put a steadying hand on the stone wall next to her. It was cool and pleasant to the touch, and she was tempted to lay her cheek against it. She could imagine her mother telling her not to. She longed for Beatrice's voice, longed for it with a physical pain in her hands. It was an emptiness pressing against her from the inside.

Come back, she thought. She looked around, but she was alone. She leaned against the wall, tracing a crack in the stone. She got close enough so she could feel her breath returned to her.

"Come back?" she whispered, through her veil, to the wall.

Her eyes felt warm and swollen, stinging tears building up somewhere behind them.

She heard someone walking on the pavement toward her, and she stepped sharply back, smoothing her dress as if she were in the middle of doing . . . something. It wasn't a very good impression of a normal person, but it was serviceable enough. The gentleman passing didn't turn and stare.

Her head still felt thick, but it was time to go. She gave it a quick, sharp shake and walked around the corner in an imitation of resolve.

There he was on the bench, as she knew he would be. Her heart gave a lurch that was instantly transmitted to her feet, and she briefly tripped over them. To smooth out the trip, she walked faster, and must have been something of an alarming sight looming in Jacob's field of vision, for he looked up from his newspaper, startled, and jumped to his feet.

"Miss Wince! Hello—I wasn't . . . expecting you," he said, trying to refold his paper with one hand while taking hers with his other. Unfortunately, he was folding with his right hand, and therefore only the left was available to extend itself to her. Iseult had stuck out her right hand, so they ended up awkwardly patting each other's elbows before the whole gesture was simply abandoned.

"Oh, but I thought your letter said that . . . Would you prefer that I go?" Iseult couldn't tell whether she was embarrassed or relieved.

"Not at all!" he said, much too loudly. He was obviously trying not to stare at Iseult's veil.

"But . . ." Every fiber of Iseult's being told her to pick up her skirts and run. Was married life to be constant embarrassment? She could tell that passersby were staring at them. That was one benefit of the veil, though: she couldn't actually make out any plainly curious expressions, but she could perceive faces turned toward them.

"It's just that I didn't think you were going to come." Jacob cleared his throat and put his newspaper, which was refusing to be folded, into a nearby dust cart. "You didn't seem to be very excited about the prospect of . . . all this."

Iseult's panic must have translated into her body language, because Jacob took her arm and began to walk her down the street. "I did not expect you, but I am glad that you came. Pleasantly surprised, as it were."

Iseult searched herself frantically for Beatrice's presence. She knew that a compliment was most likely expected, but compliments were not a thing which she was accustomed to giving out, receiving even fewer. She did not even merit the compliments she received from Beatrice. She sometimes wondered if all mothers lied as much as her own.

However, she would have been highly grateful for a lie from her mother at the moment.

"What's that?" Jacob's silver face loomed up through the hole in the veil. Her father had often admonished her for muttering under her breath. Perhaps marriage was just a repetition of the current state of affairs, but worse. Husband instead of father, new house instead of old, complete solitude instead of her mother's companionship.

"I said, I . . . I am not excited." The words tumbled out, and Iseult was mightily glad of the veil covering her face, which was surely now even brighter red than before. "I mean, I am . . . not . . . used to being married."

She gave it the inflection of a question, then shook her head as if to do so were a means of rewinding time. "No, obviously, we are not yet married. And I have never been married. I am not used to . . . acting. To acting married."

She groaned, and moved to pull her hand from his arm. He kept a tight hold on her fingers, though, and didn't seem at all bothered by her stupidity.

"Neither am I, Miss Wince, neither am I. I think we will learn to act married together." He said this with a smile, much to Iseult's surprise. "And maybe then someday we won't even have to act anymore."

Again, what was she supposed to say? So she stayed quiet as they walked several blocks in not completely uncomfortable silence. It was only when he guided her toward the door of a tea shop that she found her tongue.

"What, do we mean to . . . go inside?" Iseult thought quickly and employed a trick that had always served her well with Mrs. Pennington. She wiggled one foot around until her heel slipped into a crack in the pavement and sank as much weight on it as possible. Mrs. Pennington was stout, but she was a poor match for a wiry child who didn't care to be moved.

"If you are ashamed to be seen with me, I can assure you that while we will be more visible to a small number of people inside the tea shop, we will be less visible to the larger number of people on the street."

He said this with such an unflappable, even tone, as if he were not discussing the presumption that his future wife would prefer that not even strangers be aware of their connection. Iseult felt shabby and small, and she wished to express that she hadn't meant that, but what had she meant? And if she had, why wasn't he upset?

"People must have been very unkind to you," she said, feeling not quite herself. It certainly wasn't what Beatrice would have instructed her to say. She didn't want to wait for his response. "I think they have been unkind to me as well. Perhaps this is why we have been . . . entangled." (She knew that was not the word that should have been put in that place, but it was too late to retrieve it now.) "Of course we will go inside. Of course, of course."

And she put on what she hoped was a decent approximation of a smile (surely the blurring effect of the veil would come to her aid in making it more realistic) and made for the door with something like confidence.

Naturally she had forgotten that one heel was tightly wedged into the ground.

She pitched headlong into Jacob's chest, dislodging her veil and the hat along with it. Jacob managed to grab her about the waist before she could topple any farther, and he righted her before fetching the hat and veil, which had fled her head in the breeze. He walked back to her, smiling. She was ashamed of herself for so many reasons that it wasn't even worth trying to categorize them. The not-smile was still frozen on her face, and it didn't help matters when the smile fell from Jacob's.

Her mind went blank until he reached a silver hand up to her cheek.

"Oh, God," she said aloud, batting his hand away without thinking.

"Are you all right?" he said, only retracting his hand a little, leaving it hovering in the air between them.

"Yes, of course, I just, I don't like to be, my face, I mean, I think I must have eaten something that didn't agree with me. I suppose." The thought flitted through her that it was strange to sometimes have so much trouble formulating words in the mind and getting them out through the lips, and to sometimes not be able to stop the words from pouring out, to have them spring fully formed from she knew not where. And sometimes both of those things seemed to happen at the very same time. Jacob was still staring with concern at her cheeks. She couldn't stop herself from asking, "Does it look so very dreadful?"

She thought a smile twitched at the corner of his mouth, but it could have been a muscle spasm as well, for it was only there for a moment. "It is not so very dreadful. Some tea might improve the situation, don't you think?"

Was he teasing her or was he in earnest? She decided that she did not care. She was tired. All this being in the presence of another person was draining. She nodded. She would like some tea.

20.

Whether Jacob had planned the setting or whether it was by mere luck, the tea room was dimly lit, and as he mentioned, there were not many people dining. As they were seated, Iseult felt anxiety careening about inside her, bouncing off her bones. Anxiety about her face, anxiety about an afternoon of conversation with Jacob, anxiety about having a public meal with a man. She tried to remember the last time she had eaten a meal with her father in a restaurant. Not since childhood. She was glad it was only teatime so she would not be required to consume multiple courses.

The waiter took up a blessed amount of time, and Iseult wanted to cry at how much he was acting as if she and Jacob were both normal people, and not, in reality, a silver man and a red-faced scarecrow. (She did not know how her hair looked, and even though there were several dainty mirrors scattered about the walls, she preferred to remain unenlightened.) Jacob ordered what Iseult thought was a ridiculous amount of food, but he seemed accustomed to it.

The waiter had to leave eventually, and silence fell. Iseult decided she had better say something sooner rather than later, because the longer she left it the less control she would have over what words came out.

"Mr. Vinke," she said timidly. "Our housekeeper, Mrs. Pennington. She has been with my father since before I was born. And I . . . I would like . . ."

She had started out so well, but as usual, a few well-crafted and spoken sentences were the most she could muster. Her mouth felt dry, and the waiter had not yet arrived with the tea. Jacob smiled, as if this was just fine. "And you would like her to come and be our housekeeper, is that it?"

Iseult mutely nodded.

"Well, as long as your father has no objections, I don't see whyever not. I should like you to have every comfort possible." His smile was disarming. It was a very nice smile, once you got over the silver. Although you had to get over the silver each time you looked at him, Iseult found. "What else would make you feel that our house was to be your home?"

Iseult was unaccustomed to having questions directed toward her that were not either rhetorical (from Mr. Wince) or overly simple (from Mrs. Pennington).

He was being so kind that she was tempted to be suspicious, another feeling that she tried to quash. She tried to think. "I have a chair. It was my mother's. Maybe I could bring that?"

Jacob opened his mouth and Iseult was seized by a fear that he would say no, so she kept talking, faster and faster.

"It's very old and shabby and we could keep it somewhere that visitors would never see it. Although I don't know if we will have visitors. I can keep it somewhere that you don't have to see it, in a small room that only I go into. You never need look at it."

Jacob laid his silver hand on hers. Iseult forced her muscles to swallow the flinch. "We shall put it in whatever room you prefer."

The waiter arrived with a tray laden with an immense number of small dishes, which he began to transfer carefully to the table, necessitating the removal of Jacob's hand and so enabling Iseult to relax. Everything looked immensely appetizing, and things weren't going too badly. The waiter departed like a shadow, and Iseult felt emboldened.

"What will make the house feel like a home to you?" she asked, picking up a dainty fork with confidence. She did not always choose to have impeccable manners, but could have them when she chose to.

"*Our* home," Jacob corrected her, and she was sure the red blotches on her cheeks were standing out in ever more furious relief. So as to avoid having to respond, Iseult shoveled a farcical amount of cake into her mouth. Jacob seemed content to continue. "I have a desk I am very fond of. It is heavy and cumbersome but I shan't be parted from it, even if you despise it."

Iseult thought how different the same words would have sounded in her father's mouth. Mr. Wince had certainly never had such a jolly smile as Jacob currently wore. She wondered whether the inside of his mouth was silver as well, and tried to sweep the thought quickly into oblivion.

"Perhaps we could set your desk and my chair facing each other, and thus be set up to glower at each other from across the room." Her words came out so smoothly and coquettishly (what!) that she could scarcely believe that she had said them.

"I think that is a wonderful idea," Jacob said, and Iseult noticed that his manner of drinking his tea was altogether more agreeable than her father's, with no noisy slurping or gulping. "Oh, I should tell you: I believe my parents have found a prospective house for us. I told them that no decision should be made until you have seen the property and approved."

Iseult felt blank, and, after the unexpected confidence of the last few minutes, felt the old familiar plunge. She groped about inside herself for her mother, groping in the dark and finding nothing. "I'm sure . . ." She faltered. "I'm sure that whatever they have chosen will be agreeable."

"Miss Wince." Jacob set down a small tart. (Truth be told, it was a small tart that Iseult had had her eye on, and only one such tart had been brought. There were two people at the table; why not bring two of everything? Iseult disliked clashes between odd and even numbers. They required too much negotiation.) He put his hand on hers again. (This time her hand had a fork in it, and she felt her pulse lurch. Should she put the fork down? Etiquette dilemmas of this ilk had not been covered in school.)

"Iseult," he said quietly. In a movement of sheer awkwardness, she dropped the fork, pulled her hand away, and pretend her nose needed scratching. Then she regretted it, because his face turned a darker silver than usual.

"Iseult," he said again, more firmly. "I know that our beginnings have been . . . not exactly ideal. I know that our *lives* have not been ideal. But you should know that I intend this to be a real marriage. I want to know what you think about things, your preferences. I want us to be honest with one another. It might not be easy, but . . ."

When he wrinkled his nose in frustration, little white lines appeared, and Iseult wondered if that contrasting paleness was the color that his skin was supposed to be.

"Wouldn't you like an ally in this world? God knows I've never had one, and I assume you haven't either—"

"Where did you hear that?" Again, it was definitely not Beatrice speaking, but Iseult felt as surprised by her voice's ferocity as if it had come from another room.

He looked uncomfortable and she felt sorry, but only for a moment.

"Where?" she demanded. "And what?"

"People say you are strange," Jacob said, straightening in his chair and meeting her eye, but just barely. "Strange and willful and—"

"And what?" Iseult had somewhat unconsciously got hold of a plump strawberry and was on the verge of crushing it.

"And they say that you are out of your mind. *I* don't think so, but—"

"Is it because of my mother?" Iseult was dimly aware that the strawberry was now a pulpy disaster in her fist.

"They say you think she is still with you. In you. Something like that. It's just what people say."

"It's true," she said simply. "Although not lately. She seems to have gone away. I made her angry."

"How did you do that?"

She looked up at him. No one had ever responded to her talk about her mother with questions, or with interest.

"Sometimes I wish she would leave me alone to have my own thoughts," she said, drawing a circle in her strawberried palm with her finger. "But then she does, and I realize that she thinks all my thoughts, speaks all my words, and I have nothing of my own to think or to say."

She began to surreptitiously look about to see if there were any extra napkins to wipe her hands with, and wondered whether Jacob would break off the engagement or grit his teeth and go through with it.

"Is it like hearing another voice in the room?" he said.

Iseult looked up, startled. He was continuing to eat his tart, as if things were perfectly normal.

He looked at her expectantly, chewing, not looking as if he was going to change the subject.

"Well . . . no," Iseult said, glad of the generous tablecloths in the tea shop, which allowed her to be fairly certain that no one could see her wipe her sticky hands on the underside. Still, she was suspicious of his motives. "Do you really want to know?"

He nodded.

"It's her voice in my head." She took a bite of cake, hoping that he would understand that it was now his turn to say something.

"Does it not just sound like your own voice? I hope this isn't rude, but how would you know what her voice sounded like?" And then he put a large bite of sandwich in his mouth. Iseult felt her eyes narrow. She didn't like it when someone used her own tricks against her.

"I know," she said icily. "I may not have heard her voice for long, but surely, one has ears while still in their mother's womb, doesn't one?"

If Iseult had expected him to be unsettled by her frank use of the word "womb" (she had), then she was to be disappointed. He sipped his tea, and Iseult strained to catch any hint of a slurp so that she could be doubly disappointed.

"And what does her voice sound like?"

No one had ever asked her this, so she had never thought about it. Which annoyed her. But she was also at a loss for how to explain. "What does your own voice sound like?"

Jacob dabbed at the corners of his mouth with a napkin, Mr. Wince–like, and she hated him. "My voice? You can hear it, can't you?"

She was beginning to fear that he was an idiot. "Not to me," she said, scraping a curl of icing onto her fork, and licking it off as she would have done had she been alone. "How does your voice sound in your head? When you are not speaking aloud."

She realized that this must sound confusing, but if he was too stupid to understand she was not going to explain further.

He tilted his head to one side. "I suppose there's no real sound. It's just there in my head, the thought."

"And how do you know it's you?"

"Well . . . I just do."

"That's how I know it's my mother."

Now *he* looked annoyed. "What sorts of things does she say? When she is speaking to you, that is."

"Just . . . conversation." She would have thought that would be obvious. "How does your mother talk to your sisters?"

He smirked. Iseult loathed smirkers. "She nags them, and she fusses over them, and she rages at them, and she tells them how beautiful and perfect they are."

"It's the same with my mother," Iseult explained patiently, having told herself that her fiancé (shiver) had the mental competence of an infant in swaddling clothes, and that she would have to accustom herself to explaining things that didn't need explaining if she was going to make herself understood.

"And so it's different from the way your own voice sounds?" Fork scraping.

Iseult bit her tongue until she tasted salty blood.

"Of course," she said, barely opening her mouth, trying to unclench her teeth. "Don't you think you could recognize another voice in your head?"

Iseult had abandoned her cake and was gripping the sides of her chair in an attempt to steady her emotions, which were swinging like a pendulum, each swing wider than the last. She thought maybe he was all right; she didn't find him too bad. She thought he was terribly nice; she disliked him. Perhaps marriage would be wonderful; she wished she could stab him with that scraping fork. The blood would look striking against that silver skin.

It took her a very long moment to realize that there was one other relationship in her life that included such wild swings of emotion, and the realization hit her with such force that she jumped in her seat.

Jacob either didn't notice or chose to ignore it, polishing off one sandwich and casually selecting another. "That sounds reasonable. I suppose that one would be able to tell the difference."

21.

Once the conversation left Beatrice, though, the rest of tea was uneventful, and Iseult would have been hard-pressed later to name the subjects they discussed. The banality of topics like preferred foods, books, and ways to spend a rainy day was calming. She was stuffed with rich food—that was certainly a contributing factor—but also, conversation with Jacob had been easy. It hadn't been intellectually stimulating, but then Iseult would have been baffled by intellectually stimulating conversation. She had not been as comfortable as she was with Mrs. Pennington, but she perhaps could imagine reaching that level with him, someday in the future. She was not entirely relaxed, but she was nowhere near as on edge as she would have been with Mr. Wince. She was not even as on edge as she felt with Elspeth or her aunt and uncle. Taking his arm as they walked didn't feel natural, exactly, but neither was it repellent. By the time Jacob had paid the bill and was escorting her home, Iseult felt a pleasantly hazy sense of calm.

They shook hands politely at the gate, and arranged to meet a few days hence. She slowly walked up the stairs to her front door, thinking.

i do not believe i shall ever love him, not the romantic love married people are meant to feel for one another. but i can imagine us being allies, as he said. even friends. someone to share a small joke with, just we two.

She banged the knocker, and after a wait, Mrs. Pennington opened the door before rushing off again, throwing over her shoulder a hasty explanation about something burning. Indeed, Iseult could smell a faint whiff of smoke coming from the kitchen.

One more thought occurred to her as she climbed the stairs to her room.

now that i have jacob, maybe i don't need my mother anymore.

Iseult was flung off her feet. She had hardly reached the staircase's small landing when she was propelled forward with such vehemence that her cheek collided with the wall before she could raise her hands to try to catch herself. She lay in a heap, too stunned to move or register any meaningful thought beyond the suspicion that fresh bruising would make her mottled cheeks look even worse.

"Everything all right? What's all that thumping?"

Iseult's brain felt rattled. Her palms had scraped along the surface of the carpet, and they felt raw and skinned.

She heard the scurry of Mrs. Pennington's feet running from the kitchen. She tasted iron in her mouth where she'd bitten her cheek as she hit the wall. "N-nothing!" she shouted, clambering to her feet. She hadn't counted on the wave of dizziness that sent her stumbling right back into the wall. "I'm fine! Stay downstairs!"

The scurrying paused, but the pause did not sound confident. "Are you sure? Did you drop something?"

Iseult scrunched her eyes tight, leaning against the wall, willing the room to stop spinning. "Yes, yes—I dropped a . . . book. I dropped a book. You can go back to the kitchen now; everything is all right."

She held her breath until she heard a great sigh from below, and the footsteps began to move off, accompanied by grumbling under the housekeeper's breath.

Iseult began to breathe, and the world began to still. She waited another long moment; then, heaving herself over to the banister and gripping its smoothness with both hands, she began to slowly, carefully, walk up the remaining stairs, like an unsteady toddler. One foot, two feet. One foot, two feet. Once she reached the top, she pressed her body against the wall and used it as a support on the way back to her room.

She locked the door behind her. A glance at the mirror hinted at the disaster her face was to become, but she couldn't bear to look more closely. Her bed was farther away than she would have liked it to be, so she decided on her chair. At least it was raining. A step away from the wall, and another wave crashed in her brain, so she slid down to her hands and knees on the rug. She crawled halfway to the chair before stopping to gingerly touch her cheek. It was hot and sore and swelling fast, but the bleeding seemed to be only on the inside, so at least she needn't worry about dripping on the rug. She crawled the rest of the way and pulled herself, shuddering, into her mother's chair.

a girl never stops needing her mother

Iseult didn't feel upset when she heard Beatrice's voice, dripping with ice. She didn't feel surprised or alarmed. She felt numb. She carefully leaned her head against the chair's worn back. It still hurt, but she didn't care. She stared out at the rain as Beatrice raged inside her.

ungrateful wretch! where would you have been all these years if not for me? at the mercy of your father, that's where. if not for me, you'd not speak a single word all day, little mouse. little mealy mouse with no will of your own, no thoughts of your own, not a thought in your head that didn't come from me first!

She kept going, on and on. Iseult didn't interrupt, didn't ask her to be quiet, didn't say "I have a headache; please leave me be." It wouldn't have done any good. She couldn't think about something else, couldn't shove the voice into a small corner of her mind; she heard every cruel word with crystalline clarity. Beatrice's verbal attack was much more vicious than the physical one had been, and even as Iseult could feel her cheek swelling, the words hurt more.

you are as spiteful as your father. you are as ugly inside as you are outside. such an ugly little thing you are and have always been. i rue the day i gave you life. i am glad that i died. they should have killed you i would have killed you had i lived little bitch little harlot you think you can just leave me. i am the only reason you have survived this long and now i know that you have always been using me. i am ashamed that i ever loved you you will never ever be rid of me i will never let you rest.

What could she say? Iseult sank down in the chair and curled herself up like a dormouse. She thought of taking her nails to her shoulder, but in the face of her mother's newfound force, she decided not to press her luck. The rain outside the window was coming down so hard that everything was obscured. It was cozy and warm inside, but Iseult felt cold and miserable, as if she'd been sleeping in wet clothes.

Was her mother going to scream like this for the rest of her life? Iseult didn't even know whose life she was referring to. Her face hurt.

mother?
    mother.
    please mother.

Beatrice's diatribe did not pause or slow or change tack. She called Iseult names that Iseult had never even heard before; she used words that could not be construed as anything other than obscenities. Beatrice was wild and furious, but possessed of a newfound precision. As horrified and beaten-down as Iseult was by these words, the sheer surprise of them broke her out of her stupor.

mother you must keep to words that i am familiar with in future. where did you even learn to pronounce such things?

Finally Beatrice paused for breath, and Iseult swore she could feel her mother bare her teeth inside her neck. Pointy little teeth like her own, scraping against her skin. She was afraid to touch her neck in case she could feel them jutting out from the other side.

you think you know everything don't you little madame but you never think to ask a question you know nothing nothing nothing at all while i know your every thought and conniving desire you have not had a single moment not a breath of life that i didn't breathe right here inside you you have no right to ask me a question i'll not answer you

Iseult eased herself up into a sitting position, wondering, as she had often, whether her mother was affected by the positions of Iseult's body.

don't start pretending to care now it won't do you any good and i am well acquainted with the trickery of your mind. you pretend my comfort is of importance to you when i know you would kill me in less than a heartbeat

It had been such a short period of time that Iseult had had without her mother's thoughts intruding upon her own, and she didn't realize it at the time, but she could see now that those unfettered thoughts had had a clarity to them that she should have appreciated.

you wasted it though didn't you you wasted your escape you assumed i would just leave you just leave you alone do you not know me better than that after all of these years if i had lived i would have smothered you in your crib
    what do you want me to say, mother? i only ever have tried to please you. i am sorry that sometimes my temper gets the better of me and i wish i could just have a moment to myself to think, a moment when you don't know my thoughts.
    what is the point of having a mother who doesn't know what you're thinking? i told my mother everything everything and i was glad to

Iseult eased herself up and began to pace the room, pausing every few seconds when her head began to whirl. Sometimes she concentrated better the more things there were to concentrate on, so she walked carefully, trying to make the distances between footsteps impose a little order in her brain.
    Beatrice had fallen silent, and Iseult was hesitant to risk angering her again, but something was going to have to be untangled if she was going to live in peace.

mother. could you tell me simply, plainly, what you want from
me? i love you. you know i love you. but i am always going to do
the wrong thing, even when i try to do what you want, because
i never know what it is that you do want! wouldn't it be better
for everyone if i knew what you wanted? so i could see whether
i could give it to you?

Iseult walked the length of the room two, three, four times.

what do you want from me?

She heard Beatrice draw in a breath, a gust of wind rushing
between her ears. It grew louder, and louder, and putting her
hands over her ears did nothing to stop it.

everything

Iseult gripped her neck as if to smother what was inside.

mother. i am going to be married. i think you would like him.
he is kind to me. i think it might be all right.
   *then what is the matter i shall go with you wherever you
go and we three shall live together it will be like it is with your
father you and i together i am sure he is a decent man if you say
he is and if he is he will be as content as your father to leave us
alone*
   but . . . but. . . .
   mealy-mouthed child what is it spit it out

Iseult leaned her cheek against the cool window, watching the
raindrops trip over each other in their haste.

could i have some time on my own? when i am talking with jacob, if i could be on my own with him, then i promise i would come and talk to you about everything.

Beatrice's voice went cold as steel, and the hinges of Iseult's jaw stung as if she'd eaten a lemon.

no i don't think so iseult i know you don't trust me well i no longer trust you not to try to get rid of me forever to get me out out out you're trying to kill me your mother you're trying to kill your mother
    i am not mother i swear to you that i am not.
    oh no iseult you won't trick me again with your needles and your knives you can stab me to death but you'll only kill yourself i won't leave you again not when you need me so much that you no longer know your own mind i won't leave you ever my darling and you are going to love me as a girl should love her mother as the best girl would you are the best girl you are my best girl

Sometimes in life you are beaten, and there's nothing more to say about it. Iseult had never won an argument with her mother by trying to speak reasonably, by convincing her that she was wrong. Iseult had never won an argument with her mother at all.

And in the past, that had been all right. If the argument was truly upsetting to Iseult, she had her ways of cooling down, cooling her mother down. Her tools always came in handy when she needed a respite, even though she knew it would be temporary.

At the moment, she knew, retaliation of any sort would anger her mother further, and her cheek and jaw hurt too badly to contemplate such a thing. She heard a faint knocking over Beatrice's monologue, and the knocking sound began to grow louder. Iseult wondered whether the sound was coming from inside her head until Mrs. Pennington stepped through the door, sweaty and exasperated.

"Are you going to explain to me what on earth is going on?" she said loudly, looking more annoyed than concerned as she inspected Iseult's rapidly swelling cheek. "All sorts of noises and goings-on and pretending nothing's happening. And there's blood on the wall of the landing and Lord knows how I'll clean that up."

Iseult would have liked to leave her mother and Mrs. Pennington to argue with each other instead of haranguing her.

"I tripped," she lied. She and the housekeeper stared at each other, each willing the other to be the first to concede defeat. Mrs. Pennington shook her head slowly, clearly not believing Iseult for a moment, but lacking the energy to press the issue.

"If that's what you'd like the story to be, I won't argue with you. But come down to the kitchen with me and we'll see if we can't at least make it look less angry. Did you bite your tongue, is that where the blood is from?" Mrs. Pennington had sidled right up and was poking her fingers inside Iseult's mouth. They tasted sweet, and floury.

"Are you making a pie?" Iseult intended to say. It was a little more muddled with fingers in her mouth. Still, she was understood.

"Not just one pie; Sarah and I are making as many as we can." Mrs. Pennington, satisfied that the damage to Iseult's mouth wasn't too severe, wiped her fingers on her apron. "And one started burning right before you walked into the wall."

"But why are you making so many pies?" Iseult let herself be led out of her room and down the stairs. Beatrice was still prattling on, but she wasn't saying anything worth paying attention to. Iseult could almost have pretended that someone was humming, if her head hadn't still throbbed with her mother's efforts at punctuation.

Iseult could see (even though her vision was not to be trusted at the moment) that Mrs. Pennington looked cagey, and had something to tell her that she definitely did not want to tell her. And although what Iseult felt for the housekeeper was most likely as close to love as she was ever going to get, sometimes it angered her that she was so often treated as someone who couldn't be trusted with the basic facts of her own life.

"There's to be a bit of an evening tomorrow." Mrs. Pennington was oversolicitous helping Iseult down the stairs.

As much as her head hurt, as shaky as she felt, as constantly as Beatrice was droning on, Iseult felt something inside of her strengthen. "Am I always to be treated like a child who can't be given the slightest bit of information?"

Mrs. Pennington drew breath. "Your father has invited your aunt's family for dinner and he instructed me not to tell you in case you tried to excuse yourself."

Iseult opened her mouth, ready for a retort about her father, but Mrs. Pennington wasn't finished. "And Mr. Vinke and his family will also be in attendance."

Iseult's mouth opened and shut and opened again, like a guppy's.

"But I saw him today," she said more plaintively than she was sure she meant, "and he didn't say a thing to me about it."

They had reached the still-smoking kitchen and Iseult was plonked down in a chair. "Well now, Miss, you leave me out of that part. I'll not come between the bride and groom—don't you roll your eyes at me!"

Iseult knew that Mrs. Pennington was not entirely to blame for the fact that she was always treated like a child. It was more comfortable to be treated like a child, so in many ways she accepted, and often even relished it. It was just that sometimes she hated herself for that acceptance.

"Now, let's see about cleaning you up, because we can't have you looking like this tomorrow night," Mrs. Pennington said, huffing herself down in front of Iseult with several towels and a bowl of cold water. She scrutinized Iseult's cheek and began dabbing away, then set to work on a complicated arrangement of cold wet towels that she tied over the top of Iseult's head, "to get that swelling down."

Mrs. Pennington sat down and put a small plate of raw pie dough, Iseult's favorite, in front of her. She reached out a hand and took a small nibble, smiling. The muscles felt tight with disuse.

"Now then." Mrs. Pennington crossed her arms and fixed her eyes on Iseult. "What do you want to know?"

"About what? The dinner party tomorrow?"

Mrs. Pennington's nose wrinkled. "No, dear, not about the dinner party, although you'll be pleased to know that I've only put things that you like on the menu, even though it annoyed your father. No dear, don't you have any questions about marriage? Without your mother here, I thought maybe you would have some questions, and I know that you aren't particularly close to your aunt, or even your cousin for that matter, and I thought, well, if you had anything to ask, you could ask me."

Iseult put more dough in her mouth, feeling her face grow hot and red. She put a hand up to her cheek and was surprised to feel the slightly raised areas still suffering from the poorly applied rouge. Had that really only been last night?

what does she know the great cow she's trying to usurp us again
     i don't think you're using that word quite right, mother.
     nonsense i still know what i'm about she thinks she can replace me in your affections what could she tell you about marriage that i can't tell you myself i'll tell you anything you need to know don't listen to her what if she's doing your father's bidding the cow the great bloody cow

"What was your husband like?"

"'Was'? *Is*," Mrs. Pennington corrected. "Mr. Pennington has not yet gone to his reward, not that I'm aware. Mind you, it's hard to tell."

It was very difficult to know sometimes if Mrs. Pennington was speaking in metaphor or hard truths. But if you were content to let her keep talking, she explained herself in the end. She continued. "I felt more sure of him in the days when he would run off for a week or two every six months or so. Every time he came back, he was all flowers and apologies, and in the month before he was off again he was a blur, couldn't sit still or stop talking. But that broken leg never healed right, you know, and that slows a man down in all sorts of ways. Oh, he'll still drag his sorry bones down to the local once or twice a week, to keep some semblance of routine, but usually he just sits in that chair and grumbles at the papers."

Iseult felt ashamed. She couldn't remember having heard a thing about a broken leg, to say nothing of what sounded like serial philandering. (She thought that was what was being implied, although she was by no means sure.)

"Do you . . . like him?" Iseult's fingers crawled over for more dough. She wondered why she had such a hard time deciphering other people's feelings. She needed them to come right out and say, *I am happy. I am sad.* She wondered whether she was stupid or whether hers was the normal behavior of the motherless child.

Mrs. Pennington leaned back in her chair, arms folded, eyes distant. "Like him? I wouldn't say that exactly. I'm used to him, that's all."

There was a crumb of dough with flour still sticking to the side, and Iseult blotted it up with her tongue, enjoying its empty taste. "Did you ever like him?"

There was a pause, and Mrs. Pennington sighed. "Of course I

did. When we were young, and he was handsome, at least a little bit. Before we were married, he was charming. Rough around the edges, mind you, but so was I."

rough around the edges indeed when she first came to the house she was uncouth as a beggar child in the street i had to teach her all sorts of manners didn't know how to walk to talk to be polite or silent or do a lady's hair or use a buttonhook

Iseult thought about Jacob. She thought she probably liked him. He was handsome enough, if silver. There was no getting around that inconvenience. He could be bold, and Iseult felt certain he would only get bolder, but he was not half so rough as her father, whom she had never liked at all. She thought boldness was likely preferable to her father's veneer of politeness. It was a very well-constructed façade that most people were unable to see through. But Iseult could always hear the undercurrents. He sneered at everyone. She could not imagine Jacob sneering at anyone who didn't deserve it, and maybe not even at them. Would he sneer at her father? For her sake, perhaps?

"Is that why you married him? Because he was handsome?" Iseult knew that Mrs. Pennington knew that Jacob was silver, but they had not spoken of it. She wanted to know whether it was the gradual waning of handsomeness that made Mr. Pennington intolerable, but she didn't know how to phrase the question. Because maybe Jacob's handsomeness would fade, leaving her with the novelty of his skin color, and she could see how that might get on one's nerves after a time. She had never been one for novelty.

"Well, of course that had something to do with it," Mrs. Pennington said. "But mostly I married him because he made me happy. Well, that and no one else seemed likely to ask me."

"Did he stop making you happy, then? Did it happen right away?"

"Oh, not right away, no," she said. "It was fine for a while, but once the children were born he stayed out later and later, and then he started not coming home at all, weeks at a time." She glanced at Iseult's face and tried to change tack. "I mean, we still had our good times, still do, every now and then—but don't you worry yourself, love. He was always a scoundrel, not at all like your Mr. Vinke."

Iseult stiffened and tried to look haughty, which is impossible when you have a puffy face swaddled in towels. "He is not *my* Mr. Vinke."

Mrs. Pennington just smiled and patted Iseult's knee before rising with one of her customary groans and making her way back to the pies. Iseult felt a sharp stab of pain somewhere indefinable as she thought of what life would be like without the constant companion she almost always took entirely for granted. She tried to keep the panic out of her voice. "You will be coming with me, won't you?"

"Coming where, love?"

"Coming to—to where I go. When I marry." Iseult regretted that she'd eaten all of the dough, because if the answer was to be no, she was going to want a lot of it.

Mrs. Pennington didn't even turn around. "Well, of course I will; why wouldn't I? Silly girl, what would your father want with me about the house all day? I've got a cousin who'll be taking my place here. You wouldn't have met her, though. Next week I'll start showing her what she needs to know, and as soon as Mr. Vinke has sorted out your living arrangements I'll be there."

Iseult smiled even though her face hurt, and another bowl of pie dough appeared on the table before her. She wondered whether she ought to say something to express her appreciation, but thought better of it. Anyway, Beatrice was continuing to grumble, and the nicer a thing Iseult said, the worse the punishment she would get.

Mrs. Pennington came over and unwrapped Iseult's makeshift hat, inspecting the damage. She sniffed. "Could be worse, I suppose. We'll put cool cloths on it for the rest of the evening and hope for the best in the morning. Upstairs with you now, you've a new dress arrived that needs seeing to, you're supposed to be wearing it tomorrow."

Iseult allowed herself to be pulled up from the chair. She hoped that even when she was an old, old woman and Mrs. Pennington much older still, she would still pull her out of her chair like a small child. "What's your daughter like?" She fumbled in a dim corner of her memory replete with cobwebs. "Elizabeth. What's Elizabeth like?"

"Awfully curious today, aren't we?" Iseult didn't even think about picking up the bowl of dough to take with her; she knew that Mrs. Pennington would.

she treats you like an idiot like a child born without a brain in your head maybe she's right because she's coddled you for all these years never having to do a single thing lift a finger say the word know your mind you aren't prepared for the world it would eat you alive

"I can't remember exactly how old Elizabeth is." Iseult hoped that sounded convincing, but she doubted it. As they walked up the stairs, she could see that the rain was slowing, and with that and a belly full of raw dough, she felt about as good as she ever did.

it's because you don't care that's why you don't remember you don't care for anyone but yourself i could just leave again and it wouldn't bother you at all would it you care for no one you are a selfish little witch

where do you go?

i go where you go tied around you you tied around me you are the millstone round my neck and i will never be free of you so you will not be free of me

but i mean when you are not with me, when you are quiet. when i can't find you there inside. where do you go?

i won't tell you not with her here

Beatrice was talking faster, shriller, and Iseult missed the chance to find out much about Elizabeth. From the snippets that made it through Beatrice's irritated pronouncements, Iseult gleaned that Elizabeth was one year younger than herself, and was married, perhaps with children, but she couldn't have sworn to that detail.

Mrs. Pennington asked Iseult to wait in her room while she got the new dress; when she returned, Iseult just stared. What could she say? Gingerly she reached out to touch the fabric, trying not to display her pleasure. Mrs. Pennington held out the dress, awaiting a response.

"It's pink," Iseult finally said softly. Beatrice stayed quiet, but Iseult could feel her beginning to writhe inside, like a cat stretching after a nap.

"Deep rose, the dressmaker called it." Mrs. Pennington laid the dress on the bed with satisfaction and turned her attention to undoing Iseult's things. "Your father was against it, but I said it was high time you were out of those drab colors after all these years, about to be a bride and all. Never have worn a girlish color in your life; I might worry you'd faint dead away when you finally see yourself in your wedding dress, from the sheer shock."

Iseult nodded weakly and let herself be undressed. She'd always told herself she didn't mind dark colors, but suddenly, seeing those yards of gauzy pink fanned out on her bed, she wondered whether that had just been what Beatrice had told her. Mrs. Pennington arranged the skirt and helped her step in and pull it up, the fabric making a whispery *shhhh* as it was pulled over her petticoat and to her waist. The housekeeper paused a moment to tut over Iseult's scarred shoulder, and Iseult felt a twinge of shame, knowing that Mrs. Pennington was pleased not to see any fresh cuts, all the while unaware of the now festering wound on her thigh incurred with the hatpin. More worryingly, she could hear Beatrice, but so low she couldn't make out the words. Mrs. Pennington slid the sleeves over Iseult's arms and began on the buttons in the back, chatting about how the dress would look better over a corset, but there was no need for that right now; this was just to show her how lovely she was going to look in pink. She pushed Iseult over to the mirror.

The first thing that was apparent to Iseult as she looked at her reflection was that no, she did not look lovely. She knew that Mrs. Pennington meant it, and possibly even believed it, but that was because Mrs. Pennington loved her. Mr. Wince would not think her lovely, nor would Elspeth (although she would say she did, too effusively to be believed). Jacob . . . Iseult wasn't going to think about what he would think at this precise moment.

Her jaw looked . . . well, it looked as if it had collided with a wall. She was no beauty and she never would be. The pink made her pale skin appear paler, and the red lumps on her cheeks had an unhealthy yellow undertone. The shadows under her eyes were as purple as ever.

But. But.

She didn't look like a little girl anymore. The neckline of the dress was ingeniously cut, something Iseult would not have thought the dressmaker capable of. The base of her neck was just visible, but her scars were still hidden. Her face might still have been painfully pale, but her long neck appeared almost ivory in color against the rose. Her ribs strained against the fabric, but she could see that Mrs. Pennington was right, and that her figure would look much more attractive with a corset.

She turned this way and that. She could hear the hum of Beatrice's voice gathering momentum, volume, but it seemed far away, like the sound of the seaside before you can see it. Mrs. Pennington was smiling at her in the mirror, and Iseult smiled back, then covered her mouth with her hand to hide her pointy teeth, upper lip sticking momentarily to that offensive incisor. But even with her hand over her mouth, she thought that maybe her eyes looked . . . pretty. Not lovely, not beautiful, not captivating or enchanting or anything that would be recalled half an hour afterward, but pretty. They could qualify as pretty.

22.

In the hours leading up to the dinner party, Mrs. Pennington instructed Iseult to stay inside and rest. She was to keep quiet and not get excited about things. Various peculiar herbal mixtures were applied to the bruise on her cheek, which subsided somewhat. There was to be a very long, very perfumed bath.

Mrs. Pennington and Sarah were rushing around with preparations and instructions and last-minute errands which of course were of no real importance whatsoever, at least to Iseult's mind. She had asked if she could help, but Mrs. Pennington just slathered Iseult's hands in lotion, shoved them into white cotton gloves, and shooed her back to her room. This was helpful, as it's nearly impossible to wring one's hands while wearing cotton gloves. Instead, Iseult paced her room from corner to corner and back again, sliding along the walls, clambering over furniture that stood in the way, and nearly breaking her neck trying to move her dresser, on the odd chance that she would be able to hear her mother there. She moved slowly, she moved quickly. She would catch a word or two, but always when she was in motion.

cruel . . . and . . . what . . .
* how . . . it . . . i . . . you . . .*

She tried communicating with her mother, thinking her questions as she usually did, then whispering, before graduating to
her regular speaking voice. But it was like talking aloud to a wall,
and it made Iseult feel foolish, which in turn made her feel angry,
because who was Beatrice to purposefully make her feel foolish?
Iseult even tried hiking up her skirt and picking at the hatpin
injury to her leg, pressing on the raw wound with her thumb, dig-
ging in with a fingernail until black stars hovered around her field
of vision like dark lace, but Beatrice's drone continued unabated
at the same unintelligible pace and volume.

When the hour of the very perfumed bath arrived (which would
not have usually been so thrilling to Iseult, but Mrs. Pennington told
her she could have her tea while she bathed, which felt delightfully
frivolous, not to mention crumby), Iseult was glad to at least have
a distraction. Her stomach felt jumpy, and she couldn't work out
the main cause: certainly Beatrice, Jacob, and the expectation that
she would behave as she ought to at dinner were the key com-
ponents, but she wished that she knew what bothered her most.
She often felt such warring anxieties. Knowing precisely what the
trouble was didn't exactly solve the problem but could at least
make it a touch easier to attack.

Steam was pouring from the bathroom door by the time the
bath was ready. Sarah carried in a stool and then the tea tray. Iseult
was pleased to see her favorite dainty tea cakes, but worried that
the steam would have an adverse effect on their daintiness. Mrs.
Pennington very much took her time getting Iseult undressed,
inspecting her bare skin closely for wounds. She started breathing
very loudly through compressed lips and flaring nostrils when
she saw the sprinkling of bloodstains on Iseult's petticoat. Iseult

screwed up her own mouth and twisted in her hands the gloves she had finally been allowed to remove. She felt ashamed, but what could be done? It could always be worse, after all.

"What is Mr. Vinke going to say?" Mrs. Pennington's voice went high and shrill, and her face was red, not merely from the steam.

Iseult's stomach lurched. "About . . . He's not going to see it! Is he?"

Mrs. Pennington looked as if she had something to say, but had no idea how to say it. Iseult could feel panic contorting her face, and Mrs. Pennington backed off, instead helping her out of the last of her clothes and into the bath. They both winced as the hot water sloshed over the hatpin wound, but no one spoke.

Once Iseult was fully submerged, Mrs. Pennington began to brush her hair in long, soothing strokes, at least as soothing as could be achieved with the number of snarls that Iseult's hair generally harbored. Mrs. Pennington went over the menu for the evening aloud, but Iseult's brain was crowded with those women, those girls from her father's study. She had looked at more of them than she had pretended to recall. All in their various states of undress. Surely that wasn't something a decent woman would do, let herself be seen in such a state, even by her husband? Surely?

Iseult crammed two tea cakes into her mouth, which was only big enough for one, and found to her displeasure that, as she had feared, the steam had given a leaden quality to the usually airy confections.

Had Mrs. Pennington's dreadful husband seen her naked? Iseult laughed, then choked. Mrs. Pennington had to whack her on the back several times, and she ended up just spitting the whole soggy mess into a napkin. Mrs. Pennington took the disgusting bundle, a lecture about the virtues of small bites and deliberate chewing barely veiled in her eyes, and left the bathroom.

Iseult took an enormous breath and sank completely under the water. The buzzing was no clearer. But Iseult shut her eyes and said anyway—

are you there?

She opened her eyes, blew a few bubbles out of her nose, and said—

are you?

Breath run out, she burst up through the surface, a bedraggled, gasping mermaid. She rubbed her eyes hard, as she'd been told never to do. The water from her hair streamed messily down her face. The buzzing was gone. It was eerily quiet, but not the quiet that signified Beatrice's absence. Iseult ventured a silent

mother?
  yes

mother will you help me?

A very long pause.

of course my darling if i lived you know it would be for you and no one else there can be no one else you belong to me and i with you not even death could change that

Iseult thought about the fact that her parents had kept separate bedrooms. Did she dare ask?

never never your father was a gentleman

As a response to an unasked question, it was spectacularly unhelpful. Iseult reached from the bath for a sip of tea, which seemed tepid when compared with the bath. She screwed up her courage.

mother i feel there is some important knowledge that i am lacking and there is no one that i can ask but you
what is it that you wish to know

Iseult ground her molars. Beatrice knew her every thought. She was obviously still angry, and punishing her through humiliation.

what happens . . . what happens when we are alone, he and i? what will i be expected to do?

Beatrice sighed, which always felt like a draft blowing through from one of Iseult's ears to the other. There was also a little water still in Iseult's right ear and she tipped her head to drain it out. Beatrice sighed again.

didn't your mother tell you anything before you married? or is every woman consigned to the terror of finding out for herself?
it is the way that it is if i told you i couldn't i can't i don't know the words to explain they don't tell them to women i am sorry my love i would tell you if i could the only thing that you must know is that you must do as you should as he says as he will and remember that it will be over soon

Iseult made herself think of him. Was she frightened of him as a whole, or of his component parts? Of course his silverness made her uneasy, but it wasn't out of the ordinary to be put off by that. Everyone was put off by it. His eyes were warm and friendly but not intrusive. You just had to be sure not to look at them too long, or you would notice the silvered white. His size wasn't alarming, exactly, although the closer he got the more alarming it became. He was a very medium-sized man. Perhaps it was his hands that made her most uneasy. Hands that looked normal (barring their color, of course) were still hands that could push and pull a girl to places she had no interest in going.

His voice was pleasant enough, if . . . hollow, somehow. She wondered whether he could hear its echo in his head. It was a weary voice in comparison to Iseult's own, which was too crammed with nervous energy.

Maybe it was the plain fact of Jacob being a man that frightened her. All men frightened her. It was a pity that, if one absolutely must marry, one couldn't marry a like-minded, similarly frightened, and solitary woman. Wouldn't that be glorious, she thought, taking a swig of tepid tea and swirling her fingers slowly in the still-hot bathwater. Especially if the house were large, then she and her introverted wife would never even have to meet.

you are a silly and wicked girl you mustn't think such thoughts
but it wouldn't be any different than how you and i are, mother. we exist together and we need no one else.
how would you live without a man to attend to everything to bring money and food and comforts and shelter who would buy your dresses and your roof and your spoons

Once Iseult was soaped and rinsed and soaped and rinsed again, Mrs. Pennington left her alone to dry herself with a towel. Iseult preferred being wet in her dressing gown to being intimately alone with her towel. So she and her soaking hair and damp body were soon back in her room, not meeting Mrs. Pennington's eye while kneeling damply on her bed, giving access to the hair that was now going to be combed within an inch of its life.

Iseult could tell that Mrs. Pennington was thinking about the evening ahead, silently yanking the comb through her hair. She didn't talk much when she was worrying about details, and Iseult was not talented at jollying her out of that worry. Still, she could try.

"It smells as if dinner is going to be good," Iseult ventured, voice going up an octave on "good" as Mrs. Pennington gave the comb a mighty tug, and Iseult had to grab wildly for the bedpost to avoid toppling onto the floor. There was a noncommittal sound from Mrs. Pennington, signifying that although Iseult's comment was acknowledged, nothing further was going to be said on the matter. Or any other. Iseult's nerves jumped. Something was wrong. A secret of some sort perched next to Iseult on the bed, as real as Beatrice perched beneath her skin. Iseult regretted not drying herself, as the temperature of the dampened fabric had dropped several degrees, and more chilled droplets were being flung from the ends of her hair with each new snap of the comb. She tried again. Maybe something lighthearted?

"Won't Elspeth be surprised to see me in pink?" Iseult was pleased that she was able to make the shiver in her voice come out like a laugh. But Mrs. Pennington made the same noise as before and Iseult's hands turned even clammier as they fumbled for the bedpost. Beatrice began to hum a tuneless something, and Iseult felt half mad. She would have put her clammy hands over her ears, but they would have gotten combed with vigor.

Her mind raced trying to think what could be wrong, but it was going too fast to alight upon anything, a hummingbird with nowhere to land. Something was looming, something worse than the obvious. Iseult felt the need to shudder, but it wouldn't come, it was stuck somewhere between her shoulder blades, and she tried to wriggle them subtly to get it out of her.

Mrs. Pennington was having none of that. "Straighten up,

girl, and stop fidgeting. We need you ready quickly so I can get back to the kitchen. Sarah is getting in everyone's way."

Goodness, there were so many plaits to be done. That was a good way to gauge how important an evening event was. By Iseult's count, there were already eight throbbing spots pulled taut, and Mrs. Pennington was still busily and tightly plaiting away. Iseult turned her mind reluctantly to the number of social pitfalls she was going to have to avoid all at once this evening. It was better than worrying about whatever might be worrying Mrs. Pennington.

23.

It took a lot of time, a lot of Mrs. Pennington wrestling with Iseult's hair, and a lot of Sarah wrestling with Iseult's corset, but ten minutes before the expected arrival of the dinner guests, Iseult was considered presentable enough to descend the stairs. She had caught only glimpses of herself in the mirror as the two women fussed over the placement of every hair and the drape of every inch of fabric, but she did not feel displeased with the results.

She had tried not to sigh with pleasure as the cool fabric slid over her skin. She thought the dress had made the shushing sound, but it was hard to be sure. Her hand nervously went to her throat at the thought, to make sure that her neck was covered appropriately, and Mrs. Pennington gently batted it down.

"Try not to worry," Mrs. Pennington said as soon as Sarah had left the room. "Everything looks as it should. Your hair will stay in place, your dress doesn't show a thing, and you look quite the proper lady."

Iseult felt more grateful than she had words for. Without meeting Mrs. Pennington's eye, she slipped in low and hugged her, quickly and awkwardly, ignoring the firm pinch at her neck.

Mrs. Pennington didn't have time to hug her back, and Iseult hurried into her chair so she wouldn't have a chance. After an expectant pause, Mrs. Pennington said, "I'll leave you until it's time then, shall I."

Iseult had always loved the way that many of Mrs. Pennington's questions weren't questions at all, but assurances that everything was going to be all right.

Alone with Beatrice, Iseult knew that something must be said, but what?

mother i need to ask you a favor please do you think you can do me a favor?

of course of course child i am here at your beck and your call if i lived it would be to please you to serve you whatever you ask just go ahead and i won't expect the smallest shred of gratitude because you never give it do you

Iseult swallowed hard and tasted bile, which she assumed must be the taste of her pride.

please mother can you be on my side tonight?

nonsense child there are no sides here we are one how could i be anything other to you

i mean . . . i mean . . . please don't try to confuse me. you shake my thoughts about in my brain until i can't remember what my own are anymore.

but that's because my darling that's because you have no thoughts that are your own nothing that you have is truly your own everything is mine too mine and me and ours all one-sided if you have a thought it is as much yours as it is mine mine mine you can rely on your mother's thoughts to guide you

Iseult curled her hand into a fist, felt her nails nibbling at the skin of her palm. There was no point in arguing, but she didn't know if she could emerge from this evening unscathed unless her mother agreed to be more cooperative than usual.

if you could please if you could if you please could try not to confuse me not to twist me up inside until i don't know who i am anymore and what i am supposed to do or say

if you think my girl that i am deliberately confusing you then you are both sillier and more vicious than i thought and although it doesn't surprise me well perhaps it does

see? see? just there. you say a thing and its very reverse in the same sentence how am i ever to know your true thoughts and then extricate them from my own?

Iseult didn't realize how angrily she thought that last sentiment, and wasn't prepared for the response, which felt as if something was being ripped inside of her head. And Beatrice's voice, which she felt in roughly the same place, was icy and slow.

extricate yourself you think you can extricate yourself do you know how many times i have wished to be free of you rid of you i kick and i scream and i scratch and i bite but i cannot get out from inside oh why weren't you the one to die instead of me

"Oh, Iseult, what have you done now?" Iseult was jolted out of argument with Beatrice to find Mrs. Pennington at her side, peering at Iseult's hand in alarm and disgust. She plucked the hand up from where it lay in Iseult's lap. "What have you done now? There's blood on your dress you wicked girl!"

Confused, Iseult looked from her hand to the two round spots

of blood on her dress. She didn't like how much Mrs. Pennington's words sounded like Beatrice's, and although she saw the tear
in an old wound in her palm that seemed the clear source of the
blood, she couldn't remember having reopened it herself. And it
didn't hurt— Wait. Like a child who does not weep until his
mother expresses alarm at his grazed knee, Iseult screwed up her
mouth in pain.

Mrs. Pennington's alarm had drained out of her, leaving only
the disgust. "We must hurry, and don't you dare say a word. If
you so much as mention your mother, I think I will lose my mind.
I'll not have you sabotage every chance you have to escape your
father. If I don't get you out of this house, one of you will kill the
other, and if you don't, then I'll kill you both myself to put everyone out of their misery because that's what this house has been
since the day your mother died nothing but misery and gloom
and hatred and the only way you'll escape marrying Mr. Vinke is
if I kill you first."

Cold horror rushed through Iseult and she felt herself sway.
Those were Mrs. Pennington's brown button eyes and warm comfortable body, but that was Beatrice's bile spilling from Mrs. Pennington's familiar mouth. Yet she could still feel Beatrice inside
her, where she always was. How was she doing it? Iseult felt like
a ventriloquist's doll whose owner had bought a new one without
telling her.

"Well, at least that's come out," Mrs. Pennington said, blot-
ting the damp layer of fabric with a towel. "Now, let's take a look
at that hand, and you must promise to keep your hands apart
from each other this evening, because that's how it starts—you
begin to fidget and then those naughty fingers get their naughty
ideas. Sometimes I think they have a mind of their own."

The horror whooshed back out of Iseult, but left a taste of
burnt hair in her mouth. "I shall be careful, I promise," she said,

or rather, someone said. She didn't think it was her. "You are right. I must keep a closer hold on myself, I will behave this evening."

Mrs. Pennington looked at her curiously, but with relief. "It's dry enough. And the bleeding has stopped, but you keep an eye on it during dinner. If it happens to start up again you must signal me somehow. Drop your fork, maybe."

Iseult nodded mutely and let herself be led toward the door of her bedroom. The doorbell rang below and Iseult's stomach lurched, but she kept walking. Mrs. Pennington was crooning comforting things as they walked down the stairs arm in arm, things like "That's the girl, that's the sweet girl, that's the good girl I know." There was no trace of the fury that had filled her voice moments previously. Iseult could scan her body quickly and know that Beatrice hadn't gone anywhere, but the foul burnt taste was still at the back of her throat. Iseult vowed that she would keep an eye on that hand, but she privately vowed to keep an eye on Mrs. Pennington as well.

24.

For better or for worse, all the guests arrived at once: her aunt and uncle, Elspeth and her husband, Jacob and his parents. Mrs. Pennington disappeared with coats and accoutrements, and Mr. Wince appeared in her place. Iseult politely greeted her future husband and in-laws, and suffered kisses from her aunt and uncle, and one of Elspeth's smothering perfumed embraces. Iseult and Elspeth's husband had long since tacitly agreed that they need never speak; they merely nodded at each other. Every once in a while, Iseult thought what a sensible man Elspeth's husband must be, and wished for a spouse as silent. Those prayers, like all her others, seemed to go not just unanswered but patently contradicted. Jacob took her arm as they entered the dining room, and he said in a low voice, "You look lovely in that color, but you seem not yourself. Is everything all right?"

What could possibly be all right in the current situation? Her saliva suddenly tasted burnt and she was tempted to spit. She shoved the urge down and, peering sideways at pretty rosy blond Elspeth, smiling away for no reason, did instead what her cousin would do. She turned her face up to Jacob's, trying to imitate a flower turning toward the sun, and said, "Just nervous, my dear.

It is the first time we are with our families as an engaged couple, and I am anxious that all should go well."

She was laying it on a little thick, but better thick than thin, she supposed. Jacob's hand brushed across her sleeve as he sat next to her, and she felt a frisson of . . . something. She was surprised to find that it was not unpleasant, whatever it was.

Dinner proceeded with an almost unsettling smoothness, which should have served as a warning to everyone present, who were all aware that whatever qualities a dinner at the Wince household might have, smoothness was not one of them. The aperitifs and the soup course passed without incident. Iseult made no strange proclamations about her mother, and not only did Mr. Wince not once insult his daughter, he even told her that he was pleased to see her looking so well and out of her mourning, for they were at least ushering in an era of great joy for their family, brought about by the upcoming union with the Vinkes. To their great credit, if anyone else was surprised by this outpouring of positivity from Mr. Wince, they had the good grace not to show it. Iseult knew that she had a smile of sorts plastered across her face, though its provenance was suspect. The burnt taste was largely gone, but that could be due to the aperitif, which Iseult had followed with several large gulps of red wine, a thing which Mr. Wince would usually comment on, but he was deep in an animated conversation with Jacob's father about the construction of trestle bridges. Jacob was talking to Elspeth's husband about some novel, and three of the ladies (not Iseult, of course) were discussing wedding veil styles as if they were a matter of national importance.

Iseult surveyed the scene around her, marveling at its normality; it was like a dinner party in a book. And whenever she caught someone's eye, they smiled generously. That was very unlike the pitying smiles she usually got. She daintily took another enormous swallow

of wine, and was pleased to note that the last of the scorched taste
went down with it, dissolving into warmth. Sarah came around to
take the soup dishes and nothing was even spilled. Iseult risked a
sidelong glance at her fiancé; it could have been the wine (it almost
certainly was), but she could tell he was handsome if one could
accustom oneself to the silver, and if she were always to see him by
candlelight, she thought she could certainly accustom herself to it.
He sat back slightly to allow Sarah to refill his glass, and gave Iseult
a look that felt more like a touch. She felt flushed and itchy and
as if she had done something secretive and shameful, but she also
felt happy, with the sort of heart-pounding pleasure she had after
traipsing up a high hill to survey how tiny things at the bottom
looked from the top.

And then she felt something else. An unmistakable something else. At that moment, it was worse than any vile thing
that Beatrice could have whispered to shake her confidence. It
was the thing. And it was too late, far too late, she could tell.
Too late to excuse herself upstairs briefly, too late to pretend she
felt faint and be escorted from the room. A shudder ran through
her, and her hand knocked into her water glass but no one took
notice. As long as no one was paying attention, Iseult tried to
wriggle unobtrusively in her seat to discover whether she was
completely past hope. She edged herself slowly into the corner
of her chair, and, if anyone had been watching, they would have
seen her obviously pick up her fork and drop it on the floor. But
no one saw.

Iseult swooped her head under the table to retrieve the fork,
lifting aside a small handful of the fabric of her skirt as she did
so. It was dark in the dining room, even darker underneath the
table, but Iseult could see well enough to know that she was in the
midst of a disaster. There was already blood on the striped ticking

of the seat. Iseult cursed Beatrice, who had chosen the daintily col-
ored fabric of cream and pale blue. There was no response. Even
Beatrice had nothing to say to this.

"Are you feeling well, Miss Wince?" Iseult was surprised by
Jacob's voice so near her ear and she banged her head loudly on
the underside of the table. She hastily pulled herself upright, rearranging her skirts. She found all eyes on her upon her return.

"Ha ha!" She knew full well that the laugh sounded as if she
had read it from a script. "I dropped my fork, and when I found it
under the table, I realized that it was soiled, so I decided to leave
it and come back up here for a new one."

Iseult was grateful for the polite, well-intended chuckles from
Jacob and several others, although she didn't care for the tinge of
unkindness in her cousin's tinkly laugh. Iseult looked at Jacob,
wondering if he cared for it. But Jacob was busy with the lamb
chop that had just arrived. Iseult looked at her own lamb chop,
thinking that she wasn't very hungry, and wouldn't it be so much
nicer if she could have a tray in her room.

*iseult iseult there is no time this is no time for your mind to wan-
der you must get yourself out of this room.*

Iseult felt mildly startled that she had forgotten even momentarily
that she was in the throes of an emergency. She felt as if she was
moving within a cloud or a fog; that was not unusual while she
endured this time of the month, but she seemed to be under the
spell of some added stupidity. And that was when it occurred to
her that she was drunk. She took another tremendous swallow
of wine and looked at her lamb chop. Her eyes felt big. She kept
them turned down so no one could see. A vicious twist of a muscle
near her shoulder blade snapped her back to attention.

*if you do not find yourself a way out of this room so help me god i
will drag you out by the roots of your hair*

how do you expect me to do that, mother? i am as stuck here
as if the blood had already dried. and even if i do manage to get
out of the room . . . it's all over, isn't it? jacob and his parents
will break off the engagement, and father will either shut me
up in my room forever or kill me at last. there is no way i can
escape without their seeing. it's on the chair, mother, it's already
on the chair.

"What's on the chair?"

Iseult whipped her head toward Jacob and discovered one of
the less pleasant effects of drunkenness when her brain swiveled
an instant after the rest of her head. She wasn't sure how much of
her conversation with Beatrice she had hissed aloud, but she shook
her head sharply to try and get the thought out of her head and
concentrate on the task at hand. She then learned how a drunk-
ard's head and stomach are intimately connected, as the movement made her feel distinctly seasick.

"Nothing," she said, attempting to sound light and cheery.
"Sometimes I chatter to myself. Nothing important, in fact when
I'm asked to describe it a moment later I find it has run right out
of my head!"

Jacob looked convinced, although Iseult made a note that her
judgment of his expression might also be clouded. Everything
seemed to be taking too long. They had been at dinner for hours;
why were they all still here? Couldn't this all just end?

At that moment, salvation arrived, in the blessed form of Mrs.
Pennington. Perhaps she had heard the kerfuffle about the fork,
perhaps she had noticed that Iseult looked peaked, perhaps—it
didn't matter. It was like seeing an angel arrive on gilt wings from
heaven, and Iseult wanted to stand up and clap. Fortunately, the

moment she shifted her weight she remembered why she couldn't. She waited patiently while Mrs. Pennington inquired whether anyone needed anything and one by one they all said no, thank you. Iseult stared at the housekeeper with a bright smile so she would know instantly that something was amiss. Mrs. Pennington had the wisdom to position herself at the space next to Iseult that was not next to Jacob.

"Do you need something?" Mrs. Pennington said quietly. Iseult glanced around the table to be sure that no one was paying attention. She thanked whatever God there might be that her father was deep in some business conversation with his brother-in-law.

"My fork," she said softly. "I dropped it."

Mrs. Pennington opened her mouth and then shut it again. With a little hesitation and creaking of her hips, she lowered herself next to Iseult's chair and stuck out a hand to try and find the fork. Iseult looked pointedly at her seat and tugged a little of her skirt aside. She couldn't look at the chair: the nausea was beginning to come in waves.

Iseult had never seen this particular look on Mrs. Pennington's face before. She was accustomed to seeing disgust, and disappointment, and horror, and trepidation, but always in flashes, as Mrs. Pennington was a master at composing herself quickly. But now a look came across that face, and then it stayed there. There was compassion, and worry, and kindness, but most of all there was fear.

The nausea swelled, and Iseult wondered whether she was going to have another problem on top of the first one.

And then a third problem! Mr. Wince had paused in his conversation at the other end of the table and had turned his attention to the panicky tableau on Iseult's side. Jacob, bless him, was pointedly not interfering, but continued to speak with Elspeth's husband. Iseult felt somehow bolstered and reassured by this. She gave what she hoped was a similarly comforting smile to the still crouched Mrs. Pennington. Through clenched teeth she whispered, "Drop my napkin on the seat when I stand."

In that moment, Iseult felt a remarkable sense of calm, so foreign to her that she did not immediately recognize it. Everything would come right. She would exit the dining room gracefully, with Mrs. Pennington's help, and no one would be the wiser. The wedding would go off beautifully, and her father would see that he had misjudged her all these years. Jacob would love her very much, and they would have children who made them proud, neither strange nor silver. She would be contented, and at last feel like just another person in the world.

She rose swiftly, with purpose and determination and positivity, and in the next moment she realized how very drunk she was and how erroneous were all of her preceding thoughts. Swaying as if on a small boat running into a large swell, she grabbed wildly at the table, upsetting her wineglass, her water glass, and much of the other tableware with a crash. Jacob leapt to her aid and took her arm, but unfortunately, so did Mrs. Pennington on the other side, so there was no one to set the napkin in place. The blood on the chair caught Jacob's eye, and as the color left his face (not the silver but the underlying flesh tones) Iseult suddenly remembered a day when their cook (the one subsequently murdered by her beau) had showed her how to blanch vegetables.

Mrs. Pennington saw Jacob's face too, and was not at all subtle in belatedly carrying out her duty of placing the napkin on the chair. Iseult glanced up to see her father's face turning colors as well. His cheeks went the shade of purple Iseult knew well from holding her breath while staring at her reflection. His lips went white, and even though she saw him through drunken eyes and he seemed to be rocking back and forth, she could tell that the clumsily executed ruse had not fooled him.

But a small miracle interceded at that point, not enough to remedy the situation by any means, but enough to keep Iseult moving. Jacob grasped her arm even more firmly, and said in a lovely, kind voice, "Miss Wince is unwell, and I will help escort her to her room." It was a voice that brooked no argument, and Mr. Wince was left speechless, still fuming, nodding his agreement. The sympathetic murmurs around the table sounded to Iseult as if they came from an audience and she herself was onstage. She had forgotten her lines and the other actors were forced to improvise her exit. She felt herself maneuvered gently away from the table, with Mrs. Pennington standing too close behind her. The three of them shuffled slowly out of the room. Iseult cast a thought back to the chair and the napkin, but decided that they weren't worth another. The damage was done and would have to be faced at some point. For now, all she wanted was to be unconscious. She hoped dimly that Beatrice was as drunk as she was, because she did not want to see her in her dreams.

They had reached the staircase when Iseult said very loudly, "I am very sorry the dress has been ruined." She felt a tremor of embarrassment run through Jacob's body at her side, and maybe it was because she was drunk, maybe it was because she was so humiliated, but it made her very angry.

"You'll have to get used to the sight of ruined dresses if you throw your lot in with mine, Mr. Vinke. I rip them and I tear them and then I bleed on them."

"Hush now, my dear, don't make things worse," Mrs. Pennington murmured.

Iseult laughed and Jacob cringed. "Can things get worse?"

They mounted the stairs in silence until Iseult continued: "I suppose things can always get worse."

Her knees buckled; she thought it would be a very good idea to sit down just where she was on the stairs, but found her plan hampered by her escorts, who locked their arms around her elbows. Iseult muttered to herself, "Angry angry angry they're always angry with me for no reason why not give them a real something to be angry about for a change?"

She forced her swimming eyes to focus on Jacob's face, which was as dark red as she assumed the back of her poor dress to be. He wasn't looking at her; he was looking at the stairs as if his life depended on it. Iseult didn't blame him. A great wave of shame washed over her, and she wondered whether one's feelings changed faster when one was drunk. As she was half escorted, half dragged over the threshold to her bedroom, she began to giggle.

"This is highly inappropriate, even if we are engaged, Mr. Vinke," she said. She was still clear enough in her mind to be thankful that her room was at least tidy. She could hear Mrs. Pennington and Jacob discussing her, but Beatrice had taken up scolding her again, so she could not make out what they were saying. She tried to hush her mother and heard herself make a grunting noise that turned into a growl. Her wave of shame receded into oblivion. She shook her head, attempting to shake the noise out, but that made her more nauseated, and she crashed sideways into Mrs. Pennington. Maybe she should go ahead and get sick, right here in front of Jacob. She wanted the humiliation to be complete. Anyway, she doubted that she would ever see Jacob again after this. And Beatrice was gaining in volume and in venom.

you have humiliated your father for the last time little bitch little changeling you are no daughter of mine no daughter of his it's clear someone swapped you maybe the nurse who let your toe fall off the real parents didn't want you they brought you back they insisted they leave with an entire child and because because your father poor father had no wife to know her own child in his grief

*he accepted this poor substitute into his family his home and this
is how you betray him*

"Can't you leave me alone for even a moment?" Iseult shouted,
enough in control of herself to brace her muscles against any backlash from Beatrice. But although she felt something like a burn in
the scars on her neck, it paled in comparison to the way that Jacob
dropped her arm as if it were on fire.

Iseult had never known her emotions to change quite so
quickly. She felt like a boat in more ways than one, tossed into
each new feeling at random, and seasick, oh so seasick. She didn't
want to explain, she didn't want to apologize, she didn't even want
to die, she just wanted to be dead.

She sank slowly down onto her bed, and into that idea. The
bed was soft yet stable; would death be like that? A quiet yet
comfortable nothing? There was a wrench in her neck and she
closed her eyes, wondering how the room could still be spinning
if her eyes were closed. She considered whether there was a point
in apologizing to Jacob, and decided that no, there probably was
not. From her face-down position on the bed, she waved her hand
dismissively at him.

"You couldn't have helped me, even this once?" she shouted
at Beatrice as Mrs. Pennington attempted to shush her and cover
her shame with a blanket at the same time. Beatrice raged back in
decidedly unladylike language. With great difficulty, Iseult turned
her head so she could see Jacob, standing like a tin soldier, but
like the one in every set who couldn't stand up quite right and
always toppled at the very moment when all the others were ready.
They looked at each other as Mrs. Pennington fussed around, and
if Iseult had been sober she would have been impressed that he
maintained eye contact with her.

She lifted her head from the mattress for a moment, but then decided to put it back down and say what she had to say from there. "I release you," she said, very clearly for someone who had consumed as much alcohol as she had. "You need no longer con . . . consider yourself affianced to my disgraced personage. You are free to marry another, should you so choose." Feeling quite magnanimous, she smiled at him, entirely heedless of whether her pointy teeth were showing.

He merely looked at her gravely and said, "I will marry you exactly as planned."

Even Mrs. Pennington was shocked into stillness. There was a charged silence, and then Iseult lurched from the bed, moaning, "I'm going to be sick," and stumbled to the washroom with Mrs. Pennington fast on her heels.

As to what happened after that, Iseult, luckily, retained no clear memories. Needless to say, it was a very long night. Jacob saw himself out, and Mrs. Pennington was akin to a saint. This was because she loved Iseult as much as she loved her own daughter—perhaps more, if she thought about it, because her daughter had a mother and a father and a brother to love her at the very least, and Iseult had no one. She held Iseult's shoulders as they heaved, and stroked her sweaty forehead, and told her over and over that everything would be all right, because she knew something that Iseult didn't, and she was afraid to tell her, and she knew that it would prevent everything from being all right.

25.

Iseult woke the next morning with a monstrous headache. The first thought that came to her shrieking brain was that this must be how Zeus had felt when Athena started banging away on her silver helmet from inside his head. Iseult would have been grateful to hear banging on a helmet; Beatrice might have been using words, but Iseult couldn't make any of them out apart from the frequent obscenities. She very slowly raised herself up on one elbow, surveying the wreckage of her room. The pink dress, so imbued with hope the day before, was now a crumple of fabric on the floor, and through her haze Iseult could see that the bloodstains, now dried to rust, were even worse than she had feared. Her legs were tangled in a clammy swirl of nightgown and bedsheets and damp rags that had been wrung out and put on her forehead. There was a porcelain bowl with a towel draped over it, mercifully concealing the contents.

And over there, in Beatrice's blue chair, was Mrs. Pennington, asleep, which was at least part of why Beatrice had been cursing. Incrementally, Iseult raised herself to a sitting position and edged first one foot and then the other to the floor. Once the room stilled, she stood, holding onto the nightstand for support.

Concentrating hard on uprightness, she shuffled over to Mrs. Pennington, who was snoring softly in a patch of sunlight. Iseult was surprised that Mrs. Pennington snored. Indeed, she was surprised that Mrs. Pennington slept at all. She had a room near the kitchen, but Iseult had never so much as glimpsed its interior. Mrs. Pennington sighed and turned her head from one wing of the chair to the other. A crease ran down one cheek, and Iseult wanted to cry. Instead, she patted Mrs. Pennington's hand softly where it lay on the armrest. And patted and patted until she woke up. Mrs. Pennington looked confused, but then smiled.

"Shall I always wake you like this from now on?" Iseult said, feeling a little better already. Mrs. Pennington's smile did a curious thing, disappearing and then reappearing in less than genuine form, and Iseult thought that the night in the chair probably had not been very good for her. Gritting her teeth, she reached down and helped Mrs. Pennington up. "I do feel surprisingly hungry, is that normal?"

Mrs. Pennington grimaced and stretched and rubbed a spot on her back. "If my husband's any indication, yes. And it's not surprising, you can't have a thing left in your stomach after last night. Let's go downstairs and have Sarah fix us something. I do hope your father has left the house already."

Iseult leaned down to pick up her robe, which had also landed on the floor, noting that any change in elevation made her head feel squeezed. "Oh, this mess!" Mrs. Pennington said, helping Iseult into the robe. She shook her head. "Later, after we've had some breakfast and the dust has settled."

Sarah scuttled about like a frightened mouse in the kitchen, but she managed to make some porridge and scrounged up some bread rolls left from the disastrous dinner party. It seemed that appetites had been lost after her abrupt departure. Sarah scurried from the room once Mrs. Pennington had given her a little nod. Iseult bent over the bowl of porridge; the steam felt nice on her face. She closed her eyes and nibbled on the inside of her lip to be sure that her hunger really was greater than her nausea. Her saliva tasted bitter, but she opened her eyes and hazarded a tiny spoonful. As luck would have it, Sarah could not, untutored, cook a single thing that ended up having any flavor, so it went down smoothly. Iseult stared at the pleasing, comforting gray blandness.

"Will Father still force me to marry him, do you think?"

She knew that Mrs. Pennington was going to sigh a lot during this conversation. "If Mr. Vinke's family doesn't withdraw the offer, then yes, I believe he will. And judging by that young man's gallant behavior last night, I would say he's all for continuing. I didn't expect he'd have so much backbone." The two women exchanged a glance, each ashamed that she was wondering whether his backbone was silver too.

"It was a catastrophe," Iseult said through a larger mouthful of porridge. "However could he be determined to marry *that*?"

Mrs. Pennington crossed her arms and leaned wearily back in her chair. "Well, you certainly made a spectacle of yourself. So I would think it has to be that he's fond of you."

Iseult wasn't up to chewing, so she let the porridge dissolve slowly in her mouth. Beatrice wasn't screaming any longer, but Iseult could hear her fuming; she wondered whether her mother was gathering strength for a renewed attack. How were they all going to adjust to married life? At that thought, Iseult's neck grew hot and itchy, but she resisted the urge to scratch at it. She'd put Mrs. Pennington through enough. She would try to be a good girl. But the evening's debacle had muddled her mind, and there was a detail she could not recall. Feeling stupid, she stuttered, "C-could you remind me, Mrs. Pennington, j-just when is the wedding?"

Mrs. Pennington gave her the smile you give a well-loved puppy or a toddler who's made a bit of a mess. "Enjoy your porridge, dear, you've another month and more."

In the next moment there was a great crash from the pantry, and Mrs. Pennington leapt up to see what was the matter. Sharp muffled words were spoken, but then there was a murmured conversation, with Sarah's voice rising in something like panic. Suddenly Mrs. Pennington rushed through the kitchen at a much greater speed than she was usually capable of, all the time avoiding a look at Iseult. Sarah remained in the pantry. The clatter had shocked Beatrice into silence, but it was a sinister silence, as if she knew something that Iseult didn't, although of course that was impossible.

mother . . . mother . . . can you tell me what is the matter? i am afraid something is very much the matter.

—

please mother i am frightened if you know what the matter is please tell me.

your future is coming sooner than you thought

what? what does that mean can you tell me? you are only making me more afraid making things difficult, please mother, I am sorry for last night, please don't keep secrets from me.

Iseult sat in her chair and shivered. She tapped at the porridge with the bottom of her spoon; it had congealed already. It was a shame that people didn't have that talent, to gradually form a second skin over themselves, a sturdier protective barrier that built up resistance over time, that eventually couldn't be breached. She felt she had been working on such a barrier for years, a thickening of scar tissue that would keep people out. And it generally worked that way, but Beatrice kept ripping holes from the inside that made her vulnerable, unstable.

She hadn't noticed Mrs. Pennington reentering the room until the older woman was crouched down next to her.

"You mustn't; your knees will ache later." Iseult limply pulled at Mrs. Pennington's sleeve, but she would not be budged, and Iseult was frightened by the watery look in her button eyes.

"My dear, I don't want you to worry about a thing. It seems that after last night events are to move a little more swiftly than we'd anticipated," she said, and Iseult was aware of feeling very far away, even as she continued to pluck uselessly at those familiar sleeves. "It's the wedding. Your father has moved it up."

"The wedding?" Iseult managed to squeak. "Mine? To—to when? How soon? I don't think I'm ready—"

"Darling, hush and take a breath." There was a decidedly uncomforting catch in Mrs. Pennington's voice as she patted Iseult's arms. "I doubt you'd ever feel truly ready, so why don't we just go and get it over with, eh?"

"How soon?" Iseult said, feeling the panic rise like the tide.

Mrs. Pennington wouldn't even meet her eye, and Iseult saw a fat tear drip down her cheek that she hurriedly brushed away. "A week."

The world stopped, and Iseult left herself, or maybe it was more that there was a thick shell surrounding her. She smiled, wondering if having a shell made her a snail. Mrs. Pennington was still talking, but Iseult wasn't listening. The matter of Mrs. Pennington's knees was no longer of concern, and Iseult rose and left her there on the floor. Iseult left the kitchen and walked calmly up to her room and locked the door.

She went directly to her mother's chair and sat. Where else would she go? She looked around the room at the things that had always surrounded her. Would they be going with her? She'd no idea. What about her clothes? Was she to be allowed out of mourning for good?

Usually such a thought would have spun Beatrice into a fit, but she sounded happy.

my darling it is for the best you will be very happy and very good and your father will see what a good and happy girl you become and he will change his mind and perhaps one day soon we four can all live together in peace

mother if you are trying to make me laugh i don't know if this is the time. you don't seem to understand what father is doing. he may as well be banishing me. i would be surprised if he can bring himself to speak to me again at all.

But Beatrice was not to be argued with today; she was too excited about the wedding. Iseult was still at a remove from herself, not caring anymore what Beatrice really wanted for her, for them. There were thoughts in her head that she should probably be engaging with, but when she stretched out her hand, they would slither out of reach and drift away. She tried to think of Jacob, about what he might feel about this news of a hastened wedding to a woman he had last seen drunk and bloody, but the thought of Jacob made her stomach flip-flop, so she stopped. She thought she had better resign herself to its flipping for the foreseeable future. Until the wedding, at least. The wedding night? The morning after? Forever? She rubbed her stomach uneasily, almost sure she could feel a large fish slapping its tail against the inside of her ribcage. Would she have to get used to this?

oh darling you are going to feel much much better very soon everything will fall into place and we will all be a family again

This was too much to take, for a variety of reasons. A source of frustration in arguing with Beatrice was that one couldn't turn to face her, only turn inward psychologically. But Iseult was angry now, so she acted impulsively: before she could think of a reason to stop herself, she took hold of the left side of her neck and gave the skin a vicious twist through the collar of her dress.

It was a mistake.

Something like pain, fierce as lightning, shot from the base of Iseult's spine and up and out and through the hand that twisted the skin. Beatrice repeated what she had said, and although Iseult tried to search her voice for a hint of iciness or irony or . . . *something*, she heard only the same good cheer, amplified.

oh darling you are going to feel much much better very soon everything will fall into place and we will all be a family again

And then she said it again. And again. And again. Iseult dropped her hand into her lap as Beatrice sang on and on.

26.

Days passed in a frantic blur, and Iseult would have been affronted to be moved about like a piece of furniture had she not been entirely, ceaselessly distracted by Beatrice, who droned on, repeating the same sentence with no sign of even the slightest pause. Not for the first time in her life, Iseult gnashed her teeth at a mother who never went away, who was never tired, who could outlast her in any argument, no matter how fevered the pitch.

It was the day before the day before her wedding. No one seemed to need anything from Iseult other than that she stay out of the way. Mrs. Pennington said that her dress, Lord willing, would arrive in the morning, which hopefully would be enough time, and that all she needed from Iseult was for her to stay calm and out of mischief. At least Mrs. Pennington was speaking to her. Sarah was her usual timid self, scampering out of Iseult's way whenever she saw her. Iseult passed Mr. Wince in the hall several times, but he pretended not to see her at all. Whenever this occurred, Beatrice grew louder, which made Iseult's head ache so badly that she had to lie down three times before tea. A few times, all too briefly, she drifted into uncomfortable slumber, but Beatrice found her even there, waking her. Instead she wandered about the house, wondering whether she needed to memorize it, and whether, after the wedding, she would simply never see it again.

She wanted to be alone in her room, in Beatrice's chair, because she thought that was the best place to talk to her. She would periodically hover in the doorway, but every surface was still thick with clothing to be packed, and the air was thick with tension as Mrs. Pennington hurled orders at Sarah and a maid borrowed from Aunt Catherine for the occasion. Mrs. Pennington had already tried several times to settle Iseult down to a task, but to no avail. First she was charged with looking through her jewelry box to see if her tastes had outgrown anything, but Mrs. Pennington had always chosen her jewels, and if it had been up to Iseult she would have just thrown out the lot, or whatever one did with jewels one did not care for. The suggestion that Iseult should choose some of the Winces' everyday china was met with blank stares. China, silver, jewels: none of these things held allure for Iseult, none of them would feel like a tangible reminder of anything other than her father's desire that their life look as it should from the outside, no matter the wreck they knew it was.

Finally, since Iseult was haunting the corners of her room, running her hands over the walls and edges, Mrs. Pennington placed her bodily in Beatrice's chair with a very large cup of tea at her side and a ladies' magazine in her lap, with instructions that she find a (simple) hairstyle that might be appropriate for the day after tomorrow.

And all the while, *oh darling you are going to feel much much better very soon everything will fall into place and we will all be a family again*

"Shall I have flowers?" Iseult said, loudly, to be heard over Mrs. Pennington berating Sarah for the way she had placed a skirt in a trunk. Mrs. Pennington sighed in exasperation.

"Of course you will, dear; what kind of a wedding would it be without flowers? I've got someone seeing to it. Now hush like a good girl and let me think."

Iseult held the cup of tea in both hands like a bowl, letting the steam dampen her chin, and tried to tuck her feet up under her in the chair without spilling. It was very comfortable to be remonstrated with by Mrs. Pennington as usual, as if nothing about the day or the situation was out of the ordinary. Her thoughts drifted to Jacob again, and the fish swam lazily around her stomach, quieter but still noticeably present.

There was a sharp pinch in Iseult's spine, and she sloshed tea into her lap as Beatrice finally dropped her repetition.

she would leave you in a heartbeat if it suited her like a baby in a basket and she your whore of a mother you can rely on no one but me me me and your father she is **not** *a part of the family*

rely on him? when he's getting rid of me as quickly as possible? he is the one leaving me on the doorstep like a bastard child, not her. she is going with me wherever i go.

and am i not doing the same and yet you show no gratitude for my sacrifices

Iseult suppressed a snort and felt the unpleasant sensation of a small amount of tea going up her nose. She was able to place the teacup on the table before the coughing fit made her spill all of it. No one in the room took any notice.

you didn't sacrifice, you escaped! you escaped and you left me here to fend for myself!

Even as this thought fled from the part of Iseult that was Iseult to the part of Iseult that was Beatrice, Iseult didn't try to stop it, although she knew that Beatrice would pull no punches. She shrank into herself slightly, and wished she were a tortoise, so there was somewhere to hide. She was prepared for a hurricane. But she didn't get one.

She got chilly calm; she got Beatrice warmed over. Which was more frightening than the hurricane, because it meant that she was losing her ability to predict Beatrice's behavior.

you've no idea my girl what i have what i gave what i could have had had had i not decided to stay here with you as i did as i always knew i would before you were born i knew i would go to extraordinary lengths cross chasms leap gorges for you and for your father i could be happy now i could be at peace but all i wanted was you and your father and me all three together and by god i won't give up now just because you have

Iseult sat motionless in her mother's chair, thinking of Beatrice's wedding portrait and of how a person who looked so bland and malleable could be so steely. Had she really ever expected that when she married she would leave Beatrice behind? She thought maybe she had, in some far corner of her mind that she'd believed Beatrice couldn't reach. But that was ridiculous, of course: Beatrice was everywhere that Iseult was, and also in places that Iseult wasn't. That was the part that didn't seem fair. Beatrice had somewhere to retreat, to be alone. Iseult had nowhere to hide.

Time was doing strange things and her head was empty, drafty, even though she could still feel Beatrice stalking around like a predatory animal, circling, observing. Mrs. Pennington and Sarah drifted from the room in service to other tasks. Finally Iseult managed to creep slowly over to her bed. It was still half buried under clothing, so she curled herself into a corner as if into a nest, and pulled part of a skirt over her head to muffle what she could still hear of Mrs. Pennington fussing with the help. She laid her head down on the pillow, feeling leaden. She wanted very much to go to sleep. And stay asleep. If they couldn't wake her up, they couldn't marry her off.

She had always loved sleeping and couldn't understand people who didn't. It was all of the best things about being dead, but without its permanence. She especially loved the moments immediately before sleep, when she was still vaguely aware of her situation in the world but didn't care about it. And there was always the possibility, minimal though it might be, that when she woke up, her world would have changed for the better. Waking up was almost always the worst part of Iseult's day, and since she was prone to napping, she usually had at least two worst parts in every day. Waking was like swimming up out of a bog. And worse, swimming up out of a bog to find your mother waiting to talk to you. Wherever she was when she wasn't with Iseult, it was clear that Beatrice lacked other conversational partners.

Iseult fell into a convoluted, uneasy sleep, with dreams full of Beatrice, and awoke sweaty and perturbed. Beatrice shouldn't be allowed to invade her dreams as well as all of her waking life. Iseult thought about telling her so, but she was babbling excitedly about the wedding and showed no signs of stopping.

A sound made Iseult realize she was not alone in the room. With a start, she sat up—too quickly: black spiders, dark moss crept in around the edges of her vision and retreated. Mrs. Pennington was sitting in Beatrice's chair, dabbing at her eyes with the corner of her apron, just as, Iseult thought, a housekeeper in a sentimental novel would do. Iseult didn't know what time it was, but she hoped that Mrs. Pennington wasn't crying because they were late for dinner. The clothes that had surrounded her on the bed were all gone, so packing must have continued while she slept. Iseult's mouth was sticky and sour with sleep and she had to cough before she could speak, which roused Mrs. Pennington from whatever gloomy reverie she was lost in. She looked as startled and uncomfortable as Iseult felt.

"Oh, my dear, I must have fallen asleep as well. Hurry and let's get you ready for dinner," Mrs. Pennington said, plastering a cheerful and not at all believable smile across her blotchy face and running over to retrieve a brush.

"Are we late?" Iseult asked in a thick, clotted voice, pushing the last stray spider legs from her eyes, unsure whether she was merely seeing her eyelashes.

"We have ten minutes to get you ready for dinner," Mrs. Pennington said, tidying Iseult's hair.

Iseult breathed a sigh of relief. She hadn't seen Mr. Wince since the drunken dinner debacle, and didn't want to be wrong-footed immediately by appearing late. Would Jacob insist on strict punctuality? She thought not. The fish in her stomach swished its tail and a measure of displaced bile rose up into her throat.

Ten minutes later, Iseult was in the empty dining room. Her heart skittered when she heard the click-clack of shoes coming down the hallway, but she knew at once that they were not her father's: they were not loud enough. Mr. Wince thought the mark of both a good floor and a good shoe was the noise they made upon coming into contact with each other.

A discreet cough came from over Iseult's shoulder. She turned to find her father's lawyer, a rangy elderly man whose name she could never remember, grinning away at her and holding a large sheaf of papers.

"Miss Wince," he said through his droopy yellow-white mustache, "I have been instructed to inform you that you will be deprived of the pleasure of your father's company at dinner this evening. I hope you will be able to make do with my company instead, poor substitute though it may be."

He was very kind, but seemed terribly dim for a lawyer, Iseult thought. He put the papers down next to her on the table and laboriously folded his long limbs into Mr. Wince's seat, bones creaking audibly as he did. Iseult knew from experience that his hearing was not exemplary and that trying to ask questions was more trouble than it was worth.

"Now then," he said, laying a large, liver-spotted hand on the pile of papers and smiling vaguely at Sarah, who was nervously serving salad, "your father has a number of papers that require your delicate signature."

Iseult opened her mouth to ask the question that he had anticipated. "Now, now, there is no reason for you to trouble your pretty head about the contents; these are merely some silly papers that transfer some silly things back and forth so you won't have to worry about a thing." He winked, or rather, Iseult thought that he did. He did suffer from a slight tremor, and the same leaf of lettuce kept hopping from his fork before he could bring it to meet his sagging mustache. "Young miss, would you please fetch us pen and ink? I neglected to bring them myself."

A look of panic rose in Sarah's eyes, so Iseult tried to smile encouragingly, saying, "Ask Mrs. Pennington, she'll find them for you." Sarah fled the room gratefully. The lawyer finally got a forkful of salad to his mouth and looked about triumphantly, perhaps expecting applause for his endeavors. Iseult wondered whether her father was lurking about in the shadows, enjoying himself watching her discomfort.

"Excited about the wedding, then?" He said it so loudly that Iseult jumped in her seat. Again, she opened her mouth to speak, and again, there was no need. "Nonsense, of course you would be, wouldn't you. My daughters were all in a fuss for months before they married. I've five of them. No, four. Five? Five daughters."

Iseult ate her salad, unsure whether the lawyer's vision was as bad as his hearing, and whether she needed to pretend interest in the conversation. She would be just as happy not to. Sarah scurried back in with a pen and inkwell, placing them gingerly at Iseult's side and then departing as she had come in: as quickly as possible.

"Many thanks, young lady," the lawyer exclaimed, bits of salad flying from his lips to the table. He patted the stack of papers again, leaving a smear of tomato, which did make Iseult smile genuinely because it would very much displease her father. "Now, Miss Wince. My eyesight is not what it once was, so you leaf through those papers and sign anywhere that you see a blank line; that should do us quite nicely. I do apologize for the, er, informality of this meeting, but your father had some urgent business to attend to and I thought, well, why not combine my business with the pleasure of dining with you?"

Iseult stared at the lawyer, which, given his poor eyesight, she felt she could do quite safely. He was really very kind, even though he had no special reason to be. He could certainly have left the papers for her to sign alone. Or did her father not want her to be at liberty to peruse these papers? No. If he truly was trying to hide something, he wouldn't have left her alone with only a near-blind chaperone to oversee her work. These must be very dull papers indeed. Sarah entered and left the room several times while Iseult contemplated the tomato smear.

The lawyer began talking about his family, his four, no five daughters, and three, no, two? Two sons? Beatrice decided she'd done enough listening.

be a good girl now good girl and give your father what he's asked for you want to be a good girl these last days sweet girl so you can still see your father and we three can be happy together again as we should have been all this time mother i daresay that less than two days is not enough time to undo twenty-eight years of damage. we have never all been happy together, so we cannot be thought to achieve happiness again. i do wish you could realize that he hates me. it is not the most pleasant truth, but once one accepts it, it isn't so bad. i don't even mind, i don't see why it should upset you so much. he's never hated you, after all, only me.

but you are a part of me and i am a part of you so if he hates you he hates me too but he doesn't hate you i know i know i know that he can't see you rightly you must put it right if it's the last thing you do you were the last thing i gave him so you will put this right you will you will

". . . changed the will, but that's of no consequence to you now. I was once called—"

"Pardon me." The lawyer's words abruptly cut through Beatrice's pleading. Iseult looked at the meat and potatoes that she had been neglecting to eat, and asked him to repeat himself, please.

"We decided, he and I," said the lawyer, mopping his mustache with a napkin already heavy with gravy, "that since you are to marry into such a well-off family, there was really no need for him to settle any inheritance on you. Why not sink it into the business? we said. Well, he said, and I suppose . . . well, I suppose I agreed."

He had a cloudy, far-off look in his eyes that would have made him look very wise but for the gravy all over his mustache. "Yes, I do suppose that I agreed with him."

"He has disinherited me?" Iseult said in as steady a voice as she could manage. The lawyer had gone back to munching on a piece of bread and did not respond. Again, more loudly, she asked, "He has disinherited me?" The lawyer looked up and smiled, tipping the top of his ear toward her with buttery fingers, as if that was where the deficiency lay. And Iseult shouted, no longer making it a question: "He has disinherited me!"

The lawyer had clearly understood her this time, and looked pleasantly befuddled: not at the content of what she was saying, but at the anger that apparently accompanied it. He made a motion as if to pat her hand instead of the papers this time, but he was put off either by the distance or by the fact that Iseult had whipped her hand off the table. "My dear," he said calmly, "it is purely a matter of business. It would be foolishness to settle more money on you when he shall see no return on it, as he will with the steelworks."

It wasn't that Iseult had expected better of her father, because she did not. But just because an event isn't surprising doesn't mean it doesn't hurt. Iseult didn't give a fig about the money. She felt her humiliation crystallize into something hard and opaque. He was selling her for a bargain. Had he paid Jacob's parents outright to take her off his hands? Or had they taken her for nothing? She couldn't imagine that to be the case.

"Now stop this sulking and sign those papers and I will bother you no longer." He shook his head and returned his attention to his meal.

Iseult had lost any appetite she might have had. It wasn't that she had expected better; it was merely that this would be a very public slap in the face—if not now, then whenever her father passed away. There would be scandal and whispering, which he hated, so his motive here was puzzling. Would he risk the news coming out while he was still alive? Surely to disown his one and only child and his heir would ruin his carefully crafted reputation. Between the sounds of the lawyer noisily masticating and Beatrice rattling around in her head, Iseult was finding it hard to concentrate. Was there any point in confronting her father? Mostly likely he would end up humiliating her further, calling her greedy. After all, her new husband's family was quite wealthy, whyever should she need more money? She knew that Beatrice would keep rumbling until she spoke to him about it, but that might be preferable to any confrontation.

She poked at her beef with a fork, and the skin of gravy that had congealed across the top swayed slightly, small shiny ovals of grease sliding back and forth in the light. She didn't know if any action (or indeed, inaction) of hers had even the remotest effect on the outcome of anything. She supposed that if she really felt like it she could crawl under the dining table and lie there until she starved to death. What could her father do? He couldn't drag her bodily to the wedding. Not that he would hesitate out of deference to her, but he wouldn't subject himself to the disgrace.

Her stomach felt curdled, the fish swimming slow in the stagnant mess. Had she actually believed up until this point that there was still a means of escape? She liked to think she was more realistic than that, but she felt a finality in this moment that she had not felt before. Her father had pushed her and Beatrice out into the cold, slamming and locking the door behind them. There was no point in continuing to struggle. There was to be no respite. She was nothing more than a pawn in whatever game this was. She knew that she should stop fighting, but resisting her father had been her natural instinct for as long as she could remember; she had no idea how to stop. She might as well have tried to change her eyes to blue, or regrow her lost toe.

First things first. She needed to sign her way through this stack of papers before they were soaked in the gravy still flying from the lawyer's fork and mouth.

She signed and signed and signed, paper after paper, while the

lawyer ate and spat and dozed off in his potatoes. She signed until
her hand was cramped and her fingers stained with black. Her
father wasn't in the house; she wondered whether she would even
see him before the wedding. She wondered whether she should
read over any of the documents she was signing, but that proved
to be an exercise in futility. Although she could understand the
individual words perfectly, each document was written in a legal
vocabulary that was designed to obfuscate. The pen was increasingly loath to cooperate, and the ink either dripped all the way
from the inkwell to the page, or clotted up and refused to flow
onto the paper. Ink puddles were beginning to form and distort
the words.

Worst of all, she had begun to cry. She hardly ever did, and
although she had cried more than usual in these stressful days,
she didn't know why this behavior of her father's was making her
cry. She hastily brushed away tears with the backs of her hands,
hoping that the lawyer wouldn't notice, knowing it was unlikely
that he would, unsure of whom she was trying to hide them from.
Beatrice was talking in a sickly sweet, crooning voice, which only
made the tears leak faster, only made her throat burn with a sob
she kept swallowing. The blurring words were becoming even
blurrier, and she felt ashamed of herself.

Somehow she made it through the mountain of papers without completely dissolving. She didn't trust her voice to let her
politely excuse herself and instead prepared a weak smile, but it
didn't matter, because the lawyer was snoring. She laid the pen,
dripping with ink, on the table next to the papers. Her father
would consider this an unforgivable sin, and Iseult hoped the ink
would stain the table. He could sever all ties with his only child,
but the ink stain would be a permanent reminder that she had
existed.

She left the table and the sleeping lawyer and plodded up to her room, feeling immensely weary. Mrs. Pennington and Sarah were chattering in the kitchen, and she supposed she should go and alert them to the situation in the dining room, but the tears were still running down her cheeks and showed no signs of stopping.

27.

Iseult went to bed in her clothes, having locked Mrs. Pennington out, and refused any further interaction. The tears continued as she lay on her side, racing down to puddle in her ear before her hair was flooded with them. There seemed no reason to stop them; she didn't know how much time alone she would have as a new bride, so it was likely best to drain her body of salt water while she had the chance. Sometimes that worked.

As evening fell, she thought of the hiding places around her room for her sharpest tools and implements, and made a mental note to think about what to do with them tomorrow. Beatrice was still sniffling, and Iseult was too tired to reason out the logistics of transport to her new home at this hour. She wished that she could use her tools now, but propriety stopped her. She couldn't risk bleeding on the wedding dress. Her insides gnawed at her again, and she willed herself to breathe, willed her heart to slow. It paid no attention. She chewed the inside of her mouth until blood added a metallic tang to the salt of her tears, but that made her cry harder, and it was harder to breathe, and mid-sob she choked on phlegm and sputtered and coughed and rubbed at her face, trying to calm down. It didn't work, so she heaved her dampened self off her bed, tripping over her skirts.

Which was when she caught sight of herself in the mirror and began to laugh through her tears, because what else was there to do? Her hair was half up and half down, bedraggled strands clinging wetly to her neck. Her entire face was mottled with smears of black ink, and a red streak of blood shot from the corner of her mouth up across her cheek. She looked utterly mad, especially now that she was laughing as well. Beatrice was not laughing along. Beatrice was silent.

"Mother?" Iseult said aloud. A hair was stuck to her face; she dragged it out of the way, leaving a pale patch on her cheek. She could have sworn that her voice echoed, but surely that was her imagination. "Mother, are you there?"

She was embarrassed at having spoken aloud. She wasn't sure what had compelled her to. She shook her head sharply, trying to get ahold of herself. She marched herself to the washstand and scrubbed at her face until it burned, but the ink and the blood were gone. Well, the ink rimmed her fingernails now, but that was preferable. Certainly she would get an almighty cleansing from Mrs. Pennington before the wedding. Iseult ignored the shudder that ran through her whenever she so much as thought that word. Thinking it, she felt, was akin to Pandora's opening of her mythical box. Iseult had always felt sorry for Pandora. After all, she was only curious: that was her great sin.

Iseult went back to bed, this time under the covers, but still in her clothes. She let her troubled thoughts dart here and there until her eyelids and limbs grew heavy, and her breathing was slow and quiet and she was at last in the wonderful moment when you are still aware of all of your problems, but it simply doesn't matter because you simply don't care.

darling darling are you there don't fall asleep

no. i am not here. not anymore. i am asleep. leave me alone. why must you always wait until the worst moment? can't you wait until morning?

it's important darling i'm important what i have to say i must say now it can't wait and you aren't sleeping you're lying again you lie so much more than you did haven't you learned yet that you can't can't lie to me not me

mother. i must get married in two . . . much less than two days. i sleep here only two more nights, can you not let me rest in peace these nights, these last nights?

no no there's no time you must go and speak to your father, beg his forgiveness beg him not to cast us out

Iseult sat up quickly, slamming her hands down on the bed, hair flying every which way, delicious heavy sleepy feeling entirely gone. She knew what she must tell her mother, and she wished that she didn't have to, but she had to. It most likely meant she wasn't going to get any sleep, but she wouldn't get any sleep if she kept silent, either. She might as well stand up for herself.

i am not going to speak to him, mother. not tonight, not tomorrow, possibly not ever again. you can't force me. i know you shall try, but it's pointless. i am not going to speak to him, and i am certainly not going to beg, for forgiveness or anything else.

Iseult breathed shallowly, hands clenching in the sheets, preparing for Beatrice's inevitable backlash. She felt first a small sharp pinch in her shoulder, and the pressure slowly grew. And when Beatrice began to speak, her voice was menacing and sickly sweet.

*i don't think you are hearing me listening to me understanding
me my dear it is not a subject that is up for discussion you see you
must see you will see you do not get to win. . . . do you understand? do you see you may as well be blind i am ashamed you are
so stupid iseult. . . . you do not get to win. . . . you get to live. . . .
you do not get to do both*

Beatrice continued talking, but the words became meaningless
to Iseult as the pain in her shoulder increased, soon engulfing her
neck, her back, eventually swallowing her from head to toe. She
communicated her feelings to her mother through gritted teeth.

**i said no, mother. i am not going to apologize to him. not only
would it do neither of us any good, you or me, if i did, i am not
sorry for anything that i have done to him. the only reason that
he even notices my existence is that it irks him so. he either
ignores me or uses me as a pawn. i am removing myself, i am
removing *us* from the game. you can pinch me and poke me and
scrape your teeth and nails down the inside of my neck but it's
no good it's no use no good.**

The pain radiating through Iseult was bad, but it was bearable.
But Beatrice was screaming now, and it was the same thing over
and over, Iseult couldn't decipher the words, but each string of
sounds seemed identical to the last. It was a chaotic sound that
she would not be able to sleep through. She wasn't sure she could
listen to it another five minutes. No matter the brave stand she
had just taken, no matter her true intentions, she needed to mol-
lify her mother and she needed to do it fast.

**mother! mother! you're right, you're right. i'm sorry. i'll speak
with him.**

Beatrice's screaming ceased in a whoosh, like a candle being blown out. Iseult's heart was pounding, and she thought she could feel Beatrice's pounding in tandem. She waited for it to subside before proceeding with caution.

mother it's going to be all right, you and me. i'll speak with him.
when when will you when
tomorrow. i'll speak with him tomorrow.
why not tonight get it over and done and tied up and settled i'm afraid you're lying and you're not going to talk to him and i'll have to do something
you mustn't do anything, mother. i'm not lying. you would know if i was lying, wouldn't you? you always know. i'll speak with him tomorrow, i promise. it's too late tonight. i'm tired and so are you. tomorrow is going to be a long day and the day after even longer so i need my sleep don't you think?
you promise you'll do it tomorrow you'll apologize truly for your disobedience and your your your disgraceful attitude as a daughter for every wrong thing you've done to him for holding him responsible for your sadness for all of it?

Iseult knew she couldn't allow herself the luxury of following through on her reaction. She clenched her fists until her fingernails bit at the skin of her palms, and she imagined herself sweeping her true thoughts away where Beatrice couldn't access them.

for everything. i'll be sorry for everything. but tomorrow. tonight you must promise to let me sleep. no waking me up to remind me, no running through my dreams, please mother. i just want to sleep these last two nights like i have died. then i can be prepared for what is ahead of us.

don't wish for a sleep like that you don't know what you're wishing

Iseult released her fists and curled up on her twisted and sweaty sheets. Beatrice almost never talked about what it was like for her. Iseult did not want to know. To know could be worse than to hear that sound again.

Beatrice was mostly quiet, making little murmurs now and then. Iseult breathed shallowly for a while, not wanting to disturb the calm. Eventually she felt certain that it would hold. She closed her eyes and slept.

28.

Beatrice was as good as her word, for once. Iseult fell instantly into a sleep of which she remembered nothing eight hours later when Mrs. Pennington drew back the curtains. Iseult sat blinking in the weak sunshine, trying to remind herself that the room should look exactly as empty as it did. It wasn't that there was dust around spaces that had long been occupied—Mrs. Pennington would never have allowed that—but there were places on the wallpaper that were a slightly different color: places shaped like the bureau and desk and shelves and vanity, which had all been removed. The only things remaining were her bed, and a mirror against the wall, and her mother's chair.

"Aren't these last things going as well?" Iseult said. Mrs. Pennington jumped as she turned, not having realized that Iseult was awake yet.

"Yes, well, some of them." Mrs. Pennington patted at her frazzled hair, to no avail, and came over to bustle Iseult out of bed. "The chair will come with you, of course, but I thought you'd like to have it here right up to the day. The mirror, well, that's an old thing, isn't it? And apparently the new house already has enough mirrors. And there's no need to keep the bed, is there?"

"Isn't there?" Iseult asked, hunting for her robe and not finding it. "Where am I to sleep?"

Mrs. Pennington stopped to plump a pillow, her face splotching red. "They'll have a bed for you, Iseult, there's no need to take another."

Iseult didn't have time to be anxious, because Mrs. Pennington was divesting her hurriedly of her nightgown and shoving her into her clothes.

"Why are we hurrying so?"

Mrs. Pennington stopped dead and stared at Iseult.

"My dear, I know you can be scattered, but surely you haven't forgotten that there is to be a wedding tomorrow. And it is to be your wedding."

Iseult tried to match her withering look for withering look, holding her arms above her head so Mrs. Pennington could yank a chemise over her head. Her first response was muffled and she was obliged to repeat herself.

"I said, of course I know. But that's tomorrow. What could I possibly be needed for today?" In one look, Iseult was completely out-withered. Mrs. Pennington's hands went to her hips.

"First on the list is the dressmaker's, where we very may well be all day." Mrs. Pennington pushed Iseult's hands into her blouse, and yanked the neck more sharply than was strictly necessary. "Then we must make sure that you've got proper shoes, and jewelry, and then it's right back here to give you a bath, and there's your hair to be done. You'll not be out of my sight for a moment today, so don't you go getting any ideas in your head."

"But I must—"

speak to your father iseult tell her you must speak to your father
you promised you know what will happen to us if you don't

"—visit my mother's grave one last time."

Thinking fast was not one of Iseult's talents, but she thought fast enough to try to buy herself a little time alone.

"Why are you blushing?" Mrs. Pennington peered at her suspiciously.

"I'm not," Iseult protested weakly, and looked about for a distraction, finding it blessedly quickly. "Can you do something about this thread?"

Mrs. Pennington pursed her lips at the offending thread trailing from the waist of Iseult's skirt, looking as if she didn't entirely believe in its existence. She reached into a pocket hidden behind her apron and pulled out scissors, batting Iseult's hands away out of habit. Seeing the scissors, Iseult wasn't sure whether they made her feel nothing, or whether all she wanted in the world was to wrap her hand around them and plunge the points into her temple once and for all. In any case, she refrained, and Mrs. Pennington dispatched the thread with a single snip. The scissors disappeared and Iseult raised her eyes to the anticipated skepticism in Mrs. Pennington's.

"You've not been to your mother's grave in ages," she said, circling round Iseult, pinching and tucking and pulling at bits of fabric, whisking away bits of the fuzz and strands of hair that forever clung to Iseult's clothing. "I've been hoping those visits were a thing of the past."

Iseult made a noncommittal sound, not sure where this line of conversation was heading, hoping that Beatrice wasn't jumping to any conclusions. Mrs. Pennington pushed Iseult down to sit on her bed and began work on her hair.

"Oh, it's not that there's anything wrong with visiting the place now and then, but it was maudlin to go so often, to grieve so hard and so long for a woman you never even knew. Your father should have put a stop to it when you were a child, but I was instructed to let you go as often as ever you pleased. Maybe it made him feel you were doing the grieving for him, too; Lord knows *he* never troubled himself with a visit."

The last words turned into a fierce grumble. Iseult was not surprised. She knew that there was no love lost between the housekeeper and her father, she just usually didn't voice such outright criticism. Iseult looked down at her hands in her lap and waited to see what would happen next. Her hair was being tugged sharply, a sure sign that Mrs. Pennington was fired up about something.

"I'll see if I can arrange a time for you to visit today. Mind, it's not that I don't understand the wanting to go, day before your wedding and all. It's natural. But that's how I want it to stay, natural. A young newlywed needn't be mooning about the cemetery at all hours, no matter how it makes her father feel. His guilt is his and he ought to be the one doing penance for it. But no, he's put it on you all these years. I have never approved of it and I never will."

Iseult was alarmed, she could feel Beatrice gathering . . . something. Strength, a voice, something.

"Then you know . . . about the will?" she said, against her better judgment. It was opening a door that would be better kept closed, but maybe it didn't make any difference after all.

"I do. I know about the will, and I know about a lot more besides." Iseult could feel hairs being tugged out at the root with the force of Mrs. Pennington's brushing. At least, that was part of it. Her scalp felt unnaturally tight, as if her mother was pulling in the opposite direction to make it all worse.

"I mean to speak with him about it," Iseult said, for Beatrice's benefit.

"Why on earth would you do that?" Mrs. Pennington was spitting out words now. Iseult could only placate one of them at a time. "Not only will it not change his mind, it will cause an almighty row, and you'll likely be up all night weeping, with eyes red as cherries for your wedding, like your mother."

Iseult would have sworn that she felt cold slender fingers wrap themselves delicately yet purposefully around her throat. She knew better than to ask for an explanation of that statement, no matter how badly she wanted one.

"No, my dear, the sooner you put your father and this house behind you, the better. I don't want you to look back, not once. And that goes for your mother too. Go to the grave today, and then say goodbye to all that. She gave you life, but little else, poor thing. Let all that be part of your old life. Leave it here and don't ever look at it again."

Iseult was having trouble breathing. She put her hand on Mrs. Pennington's, which had rested on her shoulder. They were both silent, but Iseult could hear Beatrice breathing. Mrs. Pennington leaned over and swiftly kissed Iseult's hand, whispering into her ear, "I'll make sure you have a moment today to get away to the churchyard and say your goodbyes to your mother. And after today, you never need go there again."

There was a tremendous crash at the window. Iseult and Mrs. Pennington jumped, and the hairbrush fell to the floor. Iseult was afraid to look at the window, and wondered, just for a flash, if she might see Beatrice there, raging. Mrs. Pennington had more backbone and rushed right over, peering down into the yard below, and heaving a sigh of relief.

"It was a bird crashed right into the pane, poor thing! Look, there's a feather and a bit of blood on the glass. Oh, how terrible."

Iseult walked over to join her at the window. She was right, there was a dirty fluff of feather and a smear of rusty blood. Iseult put her hand against the glass, wondering how hard she'd have to run into the window to be excused from her wedding tomorrow. Mrs. Pennington looked at her sideways, reading her mind as she could sometimes.

"Don't you even think of it as a bad omen, Missy. Your luck's so bad that bad omens are good."

Iseult smiled despite herself. "That doesn't make sense."

Mrs. Pennington stood back and looked Iseult over with a critical eye, then licked a thumb to wet down Iseult's left eyebrow, which tended to stick up in a manner that made her look alarmed. "Look smart, and be downstairs in five minutes. We've to be at the dressmaker's. And I'll be sure to sneak you to the churchyard sometime after that."

Iseult smiled until Mrs. Pennington bustled out of the room, then began to worry her left eyebrow with her fingertips, which was why it tended to stick up so often. When she leaned her forehead against the windowpane, she could see the bird on the ground below. She thought she saw it move, but there was nothing to be done for it now. She felt responsible somehow, living in the house as she did.

She took a breath and looked around for a mirror, but when she remembered that it would be staying when she left, she felt too betrayed to look into it. She fumbled at her eyebrow, then slapped her hand at her skirt to get it out of her system. As she went down the stairs, her hand floated back to her eyebrow.

The appointment with the dressmaker was predictably tedious, doubly so because of Iseult's mounting anxiety over the visit to Beatrice's grave.

The dressmaker, her assistant, Mrs. Pennington, and Aunt Catherine were fussing around her grimly; the atmosphere was very different from that at the previous appointment. Iseult had precious little knowledge of womanly things, but she rightly guessed that no one present thought that moving a wedding date up several months suggested propriety. She was being very much ignored, which provided her with more time to worry. How strange, she thought, to stand in her wedding gown, with the wedding one day hence, and to feel so very absent.

when are you going to speak to your father you promised so you must i know you will but when time runs short
    when i can, mother, i can't very well run down the street like this, can i?
    if you've lied to placate me i'll know it no one knows you as I do no one knows you if you lose me you've no one

"Stop fidgeting, if you please," Mrs. Pennington said sharply into Iseult's ear. She wasn't aware that she'd been fidgeting.
    "Sorry," she murmured, holding her arms out at a gesture from the dressmaker.

don't cross me my darling i've told you what to do and i expect to be obeyed you must speak to your father you must apologize make amends or else

—

    and i hear you asking what you aren't brave enough to ask little coward little shameful thing
    and what's that, mother? what's the question? is it "what follows 'or else'?" by all means continue your thought. i'm listening.
    or else i'll kill you

"I said stop fidgeting!" Mrs. Pennington huffed. "You're getting married whether or not this dress is finished, which I'm sure we'd all prefer that it is."

Iseult ducked her head meekly as the dressmaker stitched around her waist, making barely noticeable clucking sounds.

"I'm not a chicken!" Iseult suddenly said indignantly, and three startled faces turned toward her. She coughed. "Nerves. I'm nervous. Please forgive me."

Aunt Catherine said something weakly humorous about brides, and the women went back to ignoring Iseult.

i said i'll kill you
  believe me i heard you
  you heard me do you believe me
  i don't understand why. if you kill me, what happens to you? wouldn't that defeat . . . whatever your purpose is?
  my purpose is none of your concern

Iseult became aware that she was being stared at.

"Nice of you to return to us, dear; now, would you like to take a walk while some adjustments are made to the dress?" Mrs. Pennington raised her eyebrows and spoke in a voice that most people reserve for very small children.

"Yes, please, if I may." Iseult felt stupid and small. The three women eased her carefully out of the yards and yards of dress, and she was docile and malleable in their hands. She no longer knew whether she had any intention of speaking to her father. Her thoughts had all gotten confused inside her, all jumbled.

Iseult was perturbed to find she would not be allowed to take the dress off in solitude, the lace being considered far too delicate for her clumsy fingers. Once she was down to her petticoats, she was sure the dressmaker and Mrs. Pennington would leave her in peace, and she was already scanning the room for anything even vaguely sharp, peering down at the floor for a stray straight pin. She needed to assuage Beatrice's anger, and any worry about Jacob seeing fresh wounds was swiftly receding. But when the dressmaker finally left, laden down with armfuls of ivory, Mrs. Pennington did not follow, but started shoving Iseult's limbs back into her street dress.

"I can do it myself," Iseult protested. Mrs. Pennington gave her a look she was very familiar with, lips pursed and eyebrows raised.

"Miss Iseult"—that was never a good sign—"if you think you're being left unattended for one single solitary moment before the ceremony, you've another think coming."

Iseult wilted. Even her poorly constructed, second-choice, last-minute plans fell through.

"I'm not going to hover by the grave, but I'm afraid I'm under instruction from your father not to let you out of my sight, and for once, I must say I agree with him. I will stand at a proper remove, but I will accompany you to the churchyard and back home."

Iseult attempted a joke. "Do you not trust that I won't run off?"

The eyebrows went down. "No, Iseult, I don't trust that. I can see it in your eyes, love."

Iseult looked down, as if that would help, although she did catch the glint of a needle caught in the nap of the carpet. Mrs. Pennington tipped Iseult's chin back up. "I can't say as I blame you. You're in a terrible situation, as I see it. But I do believe that it will turn out that you are far happier in your new life with Mr. Vinke than you ever were with your father."

Something like a shudder or a chill ran through Iseult from her head to her toes. She couldn't tell whether it was caused by Beatrice or by Mrs. Pennington's kind words. "And you'll be with me. That's all I really need," Iseult said as Mrs. Pennington finished with the buttons at her gnarled neck.

"Well, now we are all ready to set off," Mrs. Pennington said, far too cheerily to sound normal. But Iseult left well enough alone and followed her silently out of the room, with a twinge of regret for not being able to secrete the pin on the floor somewhere about her person.

29.

The walk to the churchyard was somber, Iseult silent and Mrs. Pennington only pointing out banalities; conversation fizzled when Iseult failed to respond. The weather battled itself, combining chill and humidity, and it was distinctly uncomfortable.

Mrs. Pennington, as promised, left Iseult at the churchyard entrance, settling herself on a stone bench in view of Beatrice's grave. Iseult walked inside, feeling eyes on her.

She sat where she always sat on the ledgerstone, fingers tracing the old familiar letters. But nothing else felt the same. She sat stiffly, awkwardly. She didn't feel the welcome she always had before. Perhaps it was because Beatrice had so recently threatened her life. Perhaps it was that. She didn't know where to begin. It was as if she were sitting with a stranger who relied on her to speak first, but she wasn't even sure what the stranger looked like. And Iseult felt entirely disinclined to begin. But stranger or not, Beatrice was her mother, and Iseult had no choice.

i . . . i do mean to speak to him, mother, i am waiting for the right moment.

—

how can i convince you that my intent is honest?

by doing it

and i shall. this evening, i hope.

i will believe it when you have done it until then pray do not humiliate yourself with your wheedling attempts to placate me

mother can you not see at all the predicament i am in? how this wedding terrifies me? how betrayed i feel that my father has thrown me to the wolves, and cannot wait to turn his back on me forever and for good?

of course i see it iseult i was in the same predicament myself

then how can you be so entirely devoid of sympathy for my plight?

because i was a good girl who did as my father instructed me

but you were so unhappy! do you truly wish the same for me? what if i don't escape by dying in childbirth? what if i must stay with this man i do not know for years and years? what if he is worse than father? must i still continue to thank my father for the nightmare he has cursed me with?

yes

Beatrice's voice dripped with ice and venom, a tone that brooked no discussion. Suddenly Mrs. Pennington was at Iseult's side, brisk and comforting. Iseult rose and leaned into her arm, knowing it was the only place she felt close to safe, by the side of this woman whom she had always taken for granted. She'd no idea how to express her gratitude. Maybe she would think of something by tomorrow morning.

Mrs. Pennington started to go on about everything that had to be done in the now less than twenty-four hours before the grand event. Iseult clenched her fists with all her might, to prevent any more of her dignity from slipping through her fingers. There wasn't much to begin with, and there was even less left now. She gripped Mrs. Pennington's arm tighter. Mrs. Pennington squeezed Iseult's arm in return, but kept talking. If Iseult had been paying attention, she would have heard a slight catch in her voice.

But Iseult was looking across the street at an elderly woman, who walked along slowly with an equally decrepit dog. She wondered whether Jacob might permit her to keep a dog, and the thought cheered her a little, but not very much.

30.

The rest of the day was filled with preparations, some worse than others. Some even verged on the pleasurable, and all that kept Iseult from succumbing to enjoyment were the intermittent pangs of . . . what? Fear, anxiety, outright terror. One moment she was sitting in Beatrice's chair as four women, presumably friends of Mrs. Pennington, crouched round her rubbing fragrant oils and creams into her hands and feet, and then she was being thrust onto a precipice, some ledge on a mountain or a building too tall to consider as real. She looked down and her stomach dropped right out of her, but the next moment she was back in her chair and the women were chatting quietly to themselves, nonsensical as birdsong, and even though Beatrice still buzzed in her ear like a wasp—*your father your father you must when will you there's no time foolish child silly bitch can't you see what's at stake of course you can't little fool little harlot*—she felt her spine press against the back of the chair and she felt her hands and feet rubbed gently as if they were cared for and she felt the scarred stretches of her neck and her back and untold tiny nicks and ridges prick and twitch and tighten in unison as if they wanted something, but what was it that they wanted? To be softened and cosseted and smoothed by kind motherly hands or to receive yet more blows? Might the best thing not be to be covered coated enveloped in scar tissue so thick that no barb could penetrate? Would she need to leave the smallest space soft and free, or was that begging the world to bite her heel?

Never mind. Mrs. Pennington had spirited away her carefully curated collection of tools. Even her fingernails were being filed down. Her tongue traced her sharp teeth, and teeth were reliable, but she couldn't reach her neck with her teeth, now could she.

The gaggle of women (of whom she was growing more fond by the minute) finished with her hands and feet and focused their efforts on her hair and her face. More oils and creams, and brushes much softer than any Mrs. Pennington had ever employed to remove her tangles. They brushed and coiled and braided and pinned and then wrapped her head in a netted cloth so the arrangement would keep until tomorrow. Her face they patted and smoothed and massaged until it felt tired and plump and new.

As it grew dark outside, the gaggle left one by one. They said nothing to her—no goodbye, no wish good luck—and by the time Sarah had left her dinner on a tray and only Iseult and Mrs. Pennington remained, there was no sign that the women had been there at all. Iseult balanced the tray on her knees, nibbling at this and that, and Mrs. Pennington uncapped the jar of salve, the smell of which had always signified rest, and with a scooping wet sound began to caress Iseult's neck and shoulders. Iseult willed herself to block out thoughts of Jacob and Beatrice and her father and tomorrow and life and death, and to rest in the silent comfort of now.

Beatrice was grumbling—*why are you eating in your room you should be eating with talking to your father little liar don't presume that i will let this go let you go you won't you can't get away from me and i will see you reconciled to him see us reconciled*—but Iseult firmly set her mind to, if not enjoying the last moments of this life, then at least to being in them, not losing them to Beatrice.

She continued resisting, and Mrs. Pennington continued with her own quiet task, and the two women sat in silence, doing something un-extraordinary that they had done a hundred times before, connected only by hands running over skin, as if the world were not about to end.

By daybreak, Mrs. Pennington was rushing from one room to the next, in the middle of at least six tasks at all times. Sarah brought a tray with silent swiftness, and Iseult calmly settled down to her breakfast in Beatrice's chair. She thought she was feeling quite serene until she took a bite of a biscuit, at which point all her terror raced back into her body. And then all was panic within and without.

The gaggle was back, inexplicably (Had they slept here? Would they be coming to the wedding or were they to work strictly behind the scenes?); Mrs. Pennington oversaw them, distracted, frequently rushing out to attend to something else, Lord knew what.

The gaggle put Iseult into her clothes, careful of her coiffure but also not too careful, and now and then a pin hit the floor. She was not sure why she was being put into street clothes; at last, she gathered that her bridal attire was patiently waiting in the church vestry for her arrival and subsequent transformation. (Were the gaggle coming there? Were they to follow her about forever?)

i've warned you if you don't speak to him you'll rue the day

but which day, mother? today? tomorrow? the day i was born and you died?

i need you to—

no time no time now no mother they're taking me away

**before the ceremony oh god i promise only leave me alone with
my thoughts for once oh please**

The gaggle whisked her off, without much breakfast, into a waiting carriage; Mrs. Pennington was inside and Sarah following
somewhere behind, and Iseult thought she'd better ask where Mr.
Wince was but then she thought better not better not and the
stones that bumped under the carriage made that biscuit threaten
to come back up.

The ride was longer not as long as it should have been and
thoughts flitted by such as *This is where my mother was married
buried* but what good was it to know that now and here and there
between outside two thoughts she thought Jacob and she thought
silver white whitesilver and then a rush of something wrong and
pink that was a blur like the clock face and her stomach lurched
and something swarmed hot and cruel in her chest and what to
do there was nothing to do they were hurtling Mrs. Pennington
laughing but why and she couldn't grasp her own couldn't stand
in her own thoughts as usual she was swirling into Beatrice she
must talk to her father no—

They were at the church. Iseult was bustled in by the front
walk, and she almost glimpsed Beatrice's grave but not quite and
then they were inside so it must not matter better not. There was
a group of black-clad men waiting for a funeral? No, for her wedding! Or yes for her wedding. As they passed them Iseult tried to
twist her neck to see whether Mr. Wince was among them but she
Beatrice she said better not better not better

What time was the wedding? What time was it? No one
answered Iseult because she hadn't asked. She was being put in
her clothes dressed like a big dumb doll and she thought to say
stop but why? No one was stopping.

At last she was buttoned and laced and tied and the net on her head was replaced with a veil and Iseult wondered how she looked but the vicar was not a vain man and kept no mirror which Iseult thought a shame for such an occasion.

Beatrice was beginning to rattle to clang about and Iseult felt herself sliding into her as if they were both just ooze and then Sarah smiled shyly and gave her a timid hug and left and then that was it.

Iseult wiggled her body to shake herself free of Beatrice's ooze and there she was in a wedding dress veil shoes in front of Mrs. Pennington who had tears that distorted those button eyes and Iseult looked about for that handkerchief brides are supposed to have but found none so she had nothing. Mrs. Pennington hugged her tight and said, "Darling girl, all will be well. Your father would like to speak with you for a moment before."

Iseult felt her two feet solid on the ground and her bones in her skin and her skin in her dress because that's what Mrs. Pennington was. Clarity and solidity and sureness. And at the mention of Mr. Wince even Beatrice shut her mouth.

Iseult smoothed down a wrinkle in her ivory skirt and nodded to Mrs. Pennington, who opened the door. Iseult kept her eyes on the ground and saw her father's shoes walk into the room. They were even more superb than the shoes he wore for everyday. The shoes walked over until they were right under her downturned head, and Iseult couldn't stop herself from leaning down further to see if she could see her reflection in their glossy surface.

"Straighten up, for God's sake," Mr. Wince said, grasping her shoulders roughly and giving her a shake. Beatrice twisted inside Iseult's neck. Mr. Wince put Iseult back at arm's length and cast a critical eye over her. He sighed. "Well, I suppose it could be worse."

Iseult could feel Mrs. Pennington's anger radiating from where she stood by the door, but she knew she wouldn't say a word.

Beatrice pulled at something inside and Iseult knew that this was the moment in which she would either have to do something, or resolve to do nothing. And neither option was very attractive. But if she said nothing, Beatrice would likely rage through the ceremony, and perhaps it was easier to do her best, or at least pretend it was her best.

"Father . . . I'm sorry." The words tasted bad as they came out of her mouth, but at least they were out.

Mr. Wince had a variety of laughs, and at this moment he laughed one of the most unpleasant ones: a vicious, mocking snicker. "And what, exactly, are you sorry for, Iseult? Forgive me, but I can think of more than a few things that I am due apologies for."

Beatrice was still and Iseult knew that her mother wanted her to be still as well, but if she hadn't balled her hands into fists she would have screamed. She willed herself to breathe normally, and to continue. "For disobeying you."

Mr. Wince switched over to the laugh that was more of a shout, a bark. He walked in a circle, clapping with slow delight, and Iseult hated him. He pretended to wipe a tear from his eye and delicately touched the edge of his nasty little mustache. "For any particular disobedience, my dear, or is this a blanket apology that is meant to make up for every insult of the last twenty-eight years?"

"For . . ." Iseult swallowed whatever pride she might have had, hoping that her next words, at last, would suffice. For Beatrice, for Mr. Wince, for *someone* to acknowledge her effort. "For misbehaving so. For whatever it is that I did that made you disown me."

He wasn't laughing anymore. Iseult's eyes darted up to meet his. Neither of them knew it, but their eyes looked very similar at that moment: very large, the whites threaded with angry red webs.

"The narcissism," he said, shaking his head in amazement.

"You still think that it has to do with you. That I care about what you do and who you are. That you can hurt me."

Whatever she had swallowed stuck in her throat, and Iseult found herself, as always, on the back foot, laughably unprepared for a conversation she found herself in the middle of. She wobbled backward and bumped into the vicar's desk, but at least it was a solid thing to hold onto. Mrs. Pennington was in the corner, not looking as if she was going to get involved. Iseult could think of only one other thing to apologize for, and as she had no other options, she plunged in.

"I am sorry that I killed her!" Iseult shouted, for the only way she could get it out of herself was to say it at an impossible volume. In the ensuing silence in the vestry, the organist could be heard beginning to play. Mr. Wince's eyes were wide, wide. He shook his head quickly, shaking something off. He walked up close to her, astonished. Iseult stood her ground, although with the desk behind her, she was trapped anyway.

"Why, you little idiot," he said softly. Iseult could feel his hot breath on her face, but she willed herself not to flinch. There was a hint of brandy about him, but that could have been left over from the night before. "You still don't know. You really still don't know."

At this, Mrs. Pennington rushed over and grabbed Mr. Wince's arm. Iseult felt a pang of fear. "Please don't, she doesn't need to know, surely there's no point!"

He shook her off, eyes still trained on Iseult, and Mrs. Pennington stumbled backward. Iseult tried to reach for her but Mr. Wince blocked the way deftly. Mrs. Pennington started to cry quietly, head held in her little plump hands. Iseult looked at Mr. Wince, defiantly, or with what she hoped was defiance. Really, she was scared. But the only way to the other side of this would be going through. So she did. "What is it that I don't know?

iseult stop stop don't listen to him he's a liar a madman he's not going to tell you the truth

Beatrice's shriek was so loud that Iseult cringed and closed her eyes for a moment. Mr. Wince pinched her arm, hard, twisting the skin at the last moment. Iseult, Mrs. Pennington, and Beatrice all made sounds of protest. Mr. Wince grabbed Iseult by the shoulders and shook her, trying to force her to look him in the eye. "All these years," he sneered, "filled with self-pity because you thought you killed her. Ha! That would at least have made you interesting, to have real guilt on your conscience. And all these years of being told by my sister that the truth would destroy you. What do I care if it destroyed you? It destroyed me. Why should you escape the truth when I can't?"

Beatrice was in free fall inside her, and Iseult felt strong enough to stand taller in her father's grip. She looked him in the eye. And waited, at the edge of a cliff.

"You didn't kill her. She killed herself. And she tried to kill you."

He said it so calmly, in such a banal monotone, that Iseult wasn't sure whether he'd actually said anything at all, and it was only in the ensuing silence that the words began to turn over in her mind.

"Such a perplexed look on that pointy little face." Mr. Wince laughed. "I have to say, I didn't think you were dim enough to swallow that story we fed you about the midwife, but your aunt Catherine and Mrs. Pennington were right. You are dim enough."

Iseult knew she wasn't fully grasping the situation, but she was getting there, and she knew that she could not be looking at Mrs. Pennington when the realization finally hit. Much as she hated to, much as she hated him, she continued to stare into her father's eyes. "Then tell me the truth."

More silence. Mrs. Pennington had even stopped crying. Beatrice was stiller than still. Even Mr. Wince barely breathed. "Tell me the truth!" Iseult screamed, hands in tight, humiliated fists.

He put his face right up in front of hers. She could see every pore in his nose and the bloodshot whites of his eyes, red veins like nameless rivers on a map, but the rest of his face was a blur. The smell of the brandy was now so strong that it made her eyes smart, but she would sooner have died than cry in front of him now, so she merely blinked furiously.

He straightened up, straightened his jacket. There might have been a smile playing beneath his mustache, but she couldn't be sure. "From the start, she could hardly stand the sight of you. Oh no, your birth was not the extraordinary tragedy you have been led to believe; on the contrary, it was quite normal. But from the moment she laid eyes on you in your swaddling clothes, your mother had a distinct aversion to you. Would turn up her nose when you were brought into the room, as if she'd smelled something unpleasant. No one spoke of it, but everyone noticed. 'Give it time,' the doctor said, your aunt said, 'she had such a shock with her father, it's no wonder she's out of sorts. She'll come round,' they said. But she never did."

Iseult had to will her hands not to fidget. A morsel from her breakfast that had been stuck between her teeth suddenly dislodged itself and she chewed on it like a hungry rabbit. She wondered if he'd always planned to do this, moments before her wedding. How ridiculous, she suddenly thought. Here she was in her wedding dress, being told that the one thing she had believed her whole life was a lie. And still, Beatrice was motionless, silent. Not absent, but hunched, wary, ready to pounce. Or to flee.

"For months she didn't leave the house, wouldn't look at you, wouldn't hold you; she shut herself up in her room, in her chair, just as you do." Mr. Wince gestured toward Iseult. He patted at his vest pockets for his pocket watch but put it back immediately after taking it out, without checking the time. He sighed, resigned. "She wouldn't talk to me, but then she hadn't talked to me all that much since her father died. It wasn't that I cared much how she felt about you, but she should have at least tried to keep up appearances. And she didn't. One night I confronted her about it, told her she should try to take a bit of interest in you. 'There's a good girl,' I said. I thought she took it to heart, really listened to me. She looked as if she was listening."

Mr. Wince stopped his circling momentarily, stroking his mustache thoughtfully. He turned to face Iseult again. "The next morning she was her old cheerful self again, the way she'd been before her father died. Kissed me at breakfast, fussed over you in the nursery, gave Mrs. Pennington here the morning off because she wanted to see to you."

Iseult had forgotten Mrs. Pennington was even there, still standing in the corner, a dumb statue. Mr. Wince went on. "I left you with your mother, pleased that I no longer had to worry. I left for work. I had come down the front stairs and was turning into the street when I heard a sound from the roof."

He had, surely he had planned this all along, for twenty-eight years, this one moment of revenge. But was his vengeance against her? Or was it against Beatrice? Had everything been Beatrice's fault, all along?

He studied Iseult for a long time. "I looked up and there she was. There you both were. She was standing on the edge of the roof, with you dressed and rosy in her arms. She looked down at me. She smiled. And she jumped."

Mr. Wince came up close and leaned in, his mouth to her ear, his mustache tickling her cheek. "That's how your collarbone was broken: when you both landed on the pavement."

Iseult felt hollow, a husk of something. Beatrice crouched in a corner, afraid. Mrs. Pennington started to whimper. "Oh, don't you start," Mr. Wince said. "It wasn't your fault. She would have found a way to do it even if you'd still been there."

Mr. Wince cleared his throat. "Well. I'll give you a few minutes to collect yourself." And he let himself out of the room as if . . . as if all he was doing was leaving a room. As if nothing had happened.

Iseult found that, after all, she was still breathing, still standing. She unclenched her fists, saw the angry red half-moons running along her palms. She took a deep breath and then another, and saw that at least her body was still functioning correctly.

"Oh, Mrs. Pennington, if you weren't going with me I know I should die," she said, and she knew she had never said a truer thing.

Mrs. Pennington looked at the floor. And Iseult realized that she had been lied to all along in every way.

"You're not coming." Iseult didn't think she had said it, but the words came from her mouth. "He won't let you."

Mrs. Pennington was weeping now and shaking her head and her shoulders, wringing her hands, and Iseult knew she had nothing left. She didn't ask why, for all of that was quite clear. She rose up, her spine straight, even though she could feel Iseult no Beatrice Beatrice hammering clamoring and Iseult knew, for once, what was supposed to come next.

"Would you please, would you wait outside for a moment?" Mrs. Pennington shook more and cried harder; Iseult would have liked to comfort her, but what good would that do now?

Mrs. Pennington left the room and closed the door, and Iseult waited a moment before quietly turning the key in the lock. She looked around the room as Beatrice began to bray.

why have you locked us in wicked child

i'm not a child and i haven't locked us in i've locked him out so they can't stop me

*stop you from what what horrible thing are you planning
i am sorry iseult i am sorry but i don't deserve whatever you are
planning to do you must just act as if nothing has happened we
must go on and get you married there is no other way now there
is no other way*

there is one other way

Iseult pulled open desk drawer after desk drawer until she found
what she sought. She said a tiny prayer of thanks that the vicar
was a well-organized man, a tiny prayer of thanks that she had
been handed the chain of events she needed to escape at last. She
said no prayer for Mrs. Pennington, who had a real family she
could love; no prayer for Sarah, who was too stupid to know her
own unhappiness; no prayer for Jacob, who had survived his silver humiliation thus far with wisdom and good cheer and would
surely weather this as well; and certainly no prayer for her father,
who deserved what his vengeance brought him. No prayer for
Beatrice. No prayer for Iseult.

*stop iseult and think i'm sorry i pushed you i'll be kinder we'll
behave together we'll figure out a way to speak to him to fix things
later just think what you're doing this solves nothing listen to me
you had better listen i am sorry but you cried so as a baby you cried
and cried and i never asked for a baby i never asked to marry i
didn't want any of it but no one asked me there was no other way
out i thought to save us both please iseult listen please please—*

Iseult said a tiny prayer that the seamstress wouldn't find out
about the dress, and she wrapped her fingers around the knife she
had found and then said the last and tiniest prayer: that the vicar
would not be blamed for keeping so sharp a knife (for bread and
cheese? for envelopes?) and then she held it as high as she could

reach, for bravery, and then she plunged the knife into the scarred place where her neck and her shoulder met.

It was hot and cold silver whitesilver and Beatrice jerked like a fish on a hook that believes it still has a chance. Iseult pulled the knife back out with effort and knew that she wouldn't be forgiven after all, because the blood was flooding the ivory lace, which she had in truth been fond of despite the circumstances. The knife skittered from her hand and clattered to the floor and now the skirt had a splotchy trail of red.

there is still time to stop this call someone edward this mustn't can't we've time darling i'm sorry you'll see you don't have to marry we'll figure out a way i can make it up to you somehow to us please

Heat and cold suffused her whole body, reaching out to the tips of her fingers and toes like hot oil or frost and she tried to sit down for she was suddenly tired but her knees were funny and she slipped in the blood that was now puddling on the floor and she fell to her knees but she was going to finish this.

Why did Beatrice keep talking?

Iseult grabbed at the soaked fabric by her shoulder and ripped it so she could get at the wound. Her hand was slick with blood and she forgave herself for wiping it off on the vicar's vestments that lay neatly folded on the bench next to her. She took a deep breath and counted to three counted to four counted and forced her fingers her hand inside her neck.

She could feel her there and Iseult's eyes popped wide in surprise. Oh! *Oh!* She could feel skin, feel Beatrice squirming wildly from her grasp like a naughty child. Iseult grinned because she knew who would win this time. Fingers in, up to the hilt now so to speak, she grabbed, missed, grabbed again and caught . . .

something. One hand groped for the fallen knife while the other held fast to the small fishy thing. And Beatrice shrieked words that Iseult couldn't hear even though she was louder than a hundred birds crashing into glass and Iseult held on to Beatrice with one hand and with the other brought the knife down again and again and again until that was all and Mrs. Pennington had been right that all was well and it was done.

31.

Nothing appeared in the papers. The wedding had been announced in the tersest fashion, and so few people knew, and those people were told quietly with as few details as possible.

Jacob was married to someone else, an invalid (a wealthy one), within the year. It was true that he thought of Iseult from time to time, but how much can you really think of someone you only met four times, even if that someone was your fiancée? Mr. Wince married within six months—a childless widow—and pretended to forget that Iseult and Beatrice had ever existed, save in monthly nightmares that he refused to explain to his bride. Mrs. Pennington handed in her notice the day Iseult died. She left her husband and went to live with her son and his wife.

So it was a very tidy ending, except for the mess in the vestry. The vicar had to transfer to a new parish, the carpeting was replaced, and the new vicar was never told what had occurred. Criminally speaking, the case was a suicide, and was closed without further ado.

The only thing that could never be explained to anyone's satisfaction was the finger. When the police were summoned and the door broken down, Iseult was dead, her wedding dress and veil drenched in blood from the self-inflicted mutilating wounds to her neck. In fact, she had been so vicious, so savage in her attack on herself, that she had completely severed two of her fingers, which lay in a pool of blood by her head.

No one could ever say for certain where the third finger that lay next to them came from. It seemed to belong to no one.

Acknowledgments

Ever so many thanks to my mom, Jill, Wendy, and Tim, for letting me check out all the library books, and for always letting me finish a chapter before setting the table. To my dad, who would find this book extremely strange, but would read it and be proud of me anyway. To my best friends, Emily and Ruth, who kept me going, no matter how much was required in terms of snacks and happy hours. To every friend who volunteered to read a book about a woman whose mother lives in her neck. To my agent Kate McKean, who kept me calm and didn't let me sell myself short. To my editor Caroline Zancan, who knew exactly what I meant and how I meant to write it.

About the Author

Molly Pohlig is the associate editor for *Vogue Knitting* magazine, and has written humorous pieces and personal essays for *Slate*, *The Toast*, and *The Hairpin*. Originally from Virginia, she currently lives in Brooklyn.

About the Author